NEVER ENOUGH!

A Novel

Cali Canberra

Published by:

NewChi Publishing
11110 Surrey Park Trail
Duluth, GA 30097

This novel is a work of fiction. Any references to real people, living or dead; and real events, businesses, organizations, and locales are intended only to give the fiction a sense of reality and authenticity. All names, characters, places, and incidents either are the product of the author's imagination or are used fictitiously, and their resemlance, if any, to real-life counterparts is entirely coincidental.

ISBN: 0-9705004-1-6
Limited Edition

ISBN: 0-9705004-2-4
First Edition

First Edition

Printed in the United States of America

I want to thank everyone who assisted me by providing accurate information for this book:

- Ken Lapine, Attorney at Law, for legal advice and great editing;
- Mike at the Department of Justice, Office of Internal Affairs;
- Robert at the Department of Justice, Asset Forfeiture and Money Laundering Section;
- Marcus - former assistant, U.S. Attorney's office;
- Luis A. Monserrate Jr. - former FBI agent;
- Terry Cooper, GBI Crime Scene Investigator;
- Tennent Neville, reference librarian, Buckhead Branch, Fulton County Library - for editing assistance.

Thanks to my husband and daughter for their support and encouragement, and to "Slaw," for her insightfulness in catching a gigantic error in the first 'final draft' of this novel.

I would also like to thank everyone who helped me promote my first novel, *Trading Paper* - making the production of *Never Enough!* possible. There are too many people to name - you know who you are.

I do want to offer a very special thank you to Bill Pennington, President (International Arabian Horse Association). It took particularly strong character to endorse my writing - something you believe in - most especially when you knew there were people in the Arabian horse business that opposed what I write about, regardless of the fact that I write fiction. Bill, thanks for your support and going out on a political limb for me.

Cali Canberra novels are fictional.

For true and accurate information about Arabian horses and ownership of Arabian horses, contact:

International Arabian Horse Association

10805 E. Bethany Drive - Aurora, Colorado 80014-2605

(303) 696-4500 www.iaha.com

Arabian Horse America

12000 Zuni Street - Westminster, Colorado 80234

1-877-551-2722 www.arabianhorseamerica.com

www.calicanberra.com

for extensive links to resources about Arabian horses

Prologue

Intense rays of afternoon sunshine pierced through the tinted plate glass windows and skylights, warming the enormous penthouse-loft of Soaring Enterprises. Grace Ashley switched on the antique brass ceiling fans, then knotted her wavy deep auburn hair on the top of her head. Mentally preparing herself, she tapped her delicate fingers on the displaced acrylic painted hollow plywood door.

"Come on in!"

"Hi, Ryan. Are we still on for dinner tonight?"

"Of course. Shawna's anxious to see you before our trip."

"I'm bringing my famous cappuccino cheesecake that you love. I made it at two in the morning... I couldn't sleep."

You'd never know she hadn't had a full night's rest by looking at her - she radiated health and spiritual well-being. Grace Ashely was comfortable in her own skin, possessing a casual elegance that few women could pull off.

Ryan Sanders patted his slightly bulging midsection.

"Don't bring cheesecake! I won't be able to resist it. I promised Shawna that I would start eating healthy and getting regular exercise. She started back at jogging, which is a signal to me that I need to drop a few pounds."

"How many times have I heard this?"

"Only a few!"

"A few?" her eyes glistened as she suppressed a grin. Luckily, she couldn't relate to needing to watch calories. Even at almost six feet tall, her size ten frame was uniquely athletic and feminine.

"Okay. Okay. A few times a year!" he wasn't as embarrassed as he tried to sound.

"That's more like it… a few times a year for at least the past decade!" she accused him.

"This time I'm serious," he said with the conviction of a has-been actor on an overacted sitcom.

"You know what would be good exercise for you?"

"What?"

"Replace your office door! Yourself. Do all of the work yourself! Even carry the new lumber and hardware. Hammer every nail yourself."

"No way! I'm never getting rid of this door."

"Why in the world are you attached to an old warped door? The rest of the loft is done tastefully, then you've got this tacky door!"

"Don't you get tired of nagging me about it? It's my door! What do you care?" Ryan said, part kidding, part serious.

At twenty years old, when the simple beauty of Grace Ashley's face required only a single stroke of mascara and lightly tinted lip-gloss, she landed an intern position at Soaring Enterprises, a privately-held company specializing in the entertainment industry. Ryan still hadn't told her about his door. Other than his business partner, his wife Shawna was really the only one who knew the story.

Ryan Sanders founded the company and operated the business on a shoestring for several years. When he finally moved to this prestigious Manhattan location, he brought along the door from his humble beginnings so he would forever be reminded of his roots. The general public knows his company for producing and directing Broadway plays and films for the silver screen. Insiders in the entertainment world utilize Soaring Enterprises for procuring and reselling stage plays and screenplays to other production companies. Thanks to Grace Ashley, as of a few years ago, the company also works with top literary agents, buying novels to make into movies.

"Your door is none of my business. I couldn't care less!" she said, attempting to goad him.

She was still astounded by the visual contrast in his office. An ancient door with peeling paint right next to original works of art, including an oil painting of Ryan's Arabian stallion.

"Good. We'll forget about the door and get back to what you should bring for dinner!" Ryan insisted.

"Fine with me! What should I bring?"

"How about that Chinese vegetable and tofu dish you made in Aspen? That was great!"

"The dish I made on the trip that you broke your leg skiing?" she asked.

It was an inside joke. She took advantage of every opportunity she could to remind him of how poor of a skier he was. Normally, she wouldn't act that way, but before the accident, regardless of the fact that he was a relatively inexperienced skier, he was always giving unsolicited advice to everyone about ski maneuvers. It was annoying. The accident finally put him in his place and he left giving advice to their ski instructors from that trip on.

"Sure. But I'll need to leave work early to grocery shop…"

"Like you punch a time clock?"

"I put in long hours! For eighteen years I've worked my ass off for you!"

Ryan knew she was right; he hoped she wasn't getting upset. He couldn't tell what she was really thinking. This was nothing new - he couldn't tell what most women were thinking.

He took a deep breath, conscious of balancing their working relationship and their friendship.

"I appreciate all the hours you work and your talent. I just meant that you know you have the freedom to leave when you want. You're not on a time clock."

"Not now that I'm *'Vice President of Acquisitions'*... no, I don't punch a time clock anymore! That's because I don't have one at home, where I do a lot of my work," she said.

A faint smile crossed her face. Actually, she loves her position in the company - very few people get paid to read at their leisure. It suits her personality to be free to work at home without interruptions from her staff of thirteen editors. She supervises nine assistant editors and four senior editors who read, then recommend or reject submissions. If a stage play, screenplay or novel is recommended by her staff, they prepare a summary along with a formal recommendation as to who they think might be interested in acquiring and/or producing the work. If she concurs with the senior editors, she writes her own report for another department, who in turn attempts to sell the work to another production company. On rare occasions, there is a body of work she feels would be suitable for Soaring Enterprises to produce. At that point, she meets with Ryan. If he's interested, he reads it and takes over.

"Are you complaining? I pay you quite handsomely," Ryan said.

She fidgeted for a moment. "I'm not complaining! You just need reminding sometimes. I don't want to be taken for granted just because of our friendship outside of work, and, by coincidence, Shawna's my closest friend. I don't know what I'd do without her support right now."

"Support?"

"Well, yes. Since my break up with Evan."

Ryan couldn't comprehend women who had it all. Women like his wife, and Grace Ashley, who was brilliant in business, breathtakingly beautiful and enjoyable to be around.

"You're still dwelling on him? It's been almost a year!" he said, hoping he had used the right tone. Tone is very important to women.

"I know. But I really thought he'd leave his wife. We were together for five years. He promised me."

"Let's talk about it tonight," he said softly.

"Sure," she said with a hint of sadness, regretting bringing it up at work.

Ryan put his feet on the solitary empty corner of his desk next to a bronze sculpture of an Arabian mare and foal. Clasping his hands behind his head, he leaned back in his leather swivel chair and stretched. His eyes sparkled with pride as he thought about his wife.

"I can't believe that Shawna won't let me throw a party for her… she deserves it."

"At least she's celebrating. Do you remember the last time she was genuinely excited about her career advancing?" She didn't give him time to answer. "How many people can go from being on the local news in a small town to being named the most influential female news journalist on television? On top of that, she has no ego about it!"

"Maybe that's part of what I love about her, but I'd still love to give her a party."

"I can't stand how humble that woman can be! No matter what she achieves, it's never enough!"

"I know." He rolled his eyes. "I was surprised she was willing to go out for a quiet celebration dinner when she got the contract as head anchor." He picked some lint off of his navy slacks. "Now that she's got *Eye On The World with Shawna Sanders* and fifty grand a segment, you'd think she'd finally think that was worthy of a real party!"

"You'd think so," Grace said as she shook her head and sat down at the opposite side of the desk, as if she had all the time in the world.

Ryan took a sip of the mocha coffee that had been on his desk since late morning. It was his daily routine: ask for coffee, drink half a cup, then hours later hope the same cup would magically still taste fresh and be hot. Of course, this day, like all days, the coffee was now cold and bitter. The involuntary pucker of his own mouth reminded him of how Shawna's face looks when she eats lemons, rinds and all.

"Even if she won't let you give a celebration party, we're going to have a great time tonight and let her know how proud we are, right?" Grace Ashley confirmed.

"That's the least we can do!"

Taylor, Ryan's personal assistant, poked her head into the office and asked if they wanted anything from the deli; they declined.

That was Grace Ashley's cue. "I guess Taylor told you I have a couple of things I thought you'd want to look at when you get back from your trip."

"Oh, yeah. This morning she mentioned that you were excited about one story in particular. Tell me about that one first," he said, reaching for the brochure about the Bora Bora Lagoon Resort.

Ryan and Shawna planned to leave for the resort early the next morning if their pilot recovered from the flu. He wouldn't consider allowing anyone else to fly their new Gulf Stream.

"Okay. The one I thought you'd be most interested in is a romantic comedy. The story is simple. It would be great for a Christmas opening. It's about a woman who meets a man at an art gallery…"

Ryan cut her off. "Is it by that new writer, Benjamin Christian?"

"Yes."

"How long have we had this?"

She referred to the report. "About eight months."

"Spellbinders has it under contract. They were bragging about it last weekend at that charity dinner. What else have you got?"

Regardless of the fact she had no control over how long the company's system took to get a potential project even to this point, she felt personally responsible that the company missed something that looked like it would be a blockbuster hit. Her enthusiasm diminished slightly.

"I'm not exactly sure that you would want to produce this one. It's not a style or a story line you've ever done before, but I wanted to throw it out at you while I was here."

"Go ahead."

"It's just a manuscript, an unpublished novel at this point."

He glanced up and nodded his head, indicating he was in fact listening. His mind wandered as he was engrossed in the brochure's photographs of Bora Bora, a breathtaking island in the South Pacific. The photo that most fascinated him was of French Polynesia's 115 Technicolor Islands, 150 miles northwest of Tahiti. The aerial views showed the islands being surrounded almost entirely by a barrier reef and small offshore moto islets, creating something reminiscent of a medieval castle surrounded by a moat. The Bora Bora Lagoon Resort is the only developed property on Motu Toopu, one of Bora Bora's uninhabited offshore motus's.

As she continued, her voice level raised a notch, gaining his attention again. "One consideration is that it would be expensive and time consuming to produce. Actually, maybe it would be more suited for a television mini-series. I don't know," she said, sounding unsure of why she was even presenting it.

"Sounds like a waste of time!" he said, although he hadn't even paid attention to half of what she was telling him.

He selected another brochure to thumb through.

"You're right. I'm sorry. It's just that I thought you might be interested..." her voice trailed off.

"Hmm."

"I'm wasting your time," she said as she stood up.

"You're not wasting my time. These things happen."

He took his feet off of his desk.

"Well, I better go grocery shopping for veggies and tofu. See you tonight!" she reminded him as she stood to leave.

Ryan looked up from the brochure. "Do you have the manuscript with you?"

She gave him a questioning look. "Sure. Right here."

"Since you liked it so much, maybe I'll read it on my trip, just for the hell of it. Shawna's always got a book to read when we go away."

Grace Ashley handed him the thick notebook. "Tell Shawna to call me if she needs me to pick up anything on my way over."

Part One

Chapter One

August, 1983

Pick up the damn phone, she thought.

She paced her red clay tile floor, tightly gripping the receiver. The hollow desperate feeling in the pit of her stomach was becoming way too familiar. If she could only take it all back - undo the chain of events - but no, it was too late now.

Greed had set it all in motion. It wasn't her game. All she wanted was out. Now, her fierce brown eyes closed, holding back a rush of tears.

His answering machine picked up on the eighth ring. She drew in a deep breath, preparing to sound as calm as possible.

"Jared, I got your message. I can't believe you would leave me a message like that. If the police ever heard what you said! *Please,* I'm asking you to just give me a month or two! We discussed this yesterday. And last week. What do you expect me to do? I need more time."

She resisted slamming the receiver back into its cradle.

The bile rose in her throat, then slowly drained back down, making the burning sensation in her chest so intense she thought she might explode. She grabbed the bottle of antacids she kept handy on the kitchen counter. Her hands trembled as she opened the container and poured who knows how many tablets directly into her mouth. After chewing the chalky substance, she guzzled an ice cold Fresca, washing down the residue that coated her mouth and tongue.

She caught her reflection in the kitchen window. *I'm disgusting,* she thought. Even the reflection couldn't hide the defeated expression on her face. Was her groan all in her head, or had she made the noise out loud?

Get your act together, she told herself. She used cold water to moisten a paper towel, folding it into a small square, then patted her face and neck.

In the presence of her current circumstances, she swallowed hard, corrected her posture, and faked a smile as she dialed the phone again.

"Mira Randolph?"

"Yes, this is she."

"Hi. This is Rene Killian. You called and left a message on my machine."

"What was it in reference to?"

"You didn't say. I'm a consultant and a broker in the Arabian horse industry. Could you have been inquiring about my services?"

"Oh. Yes, that is why I was calling. My husband saw your ad in Barron's."

In the August 1983 issue, the financial publication featured a special section with multiple articles about equine investments. A staff writer for Barron's called Rene, saying she needed more information for one of the articles that was to feature various people involved in the marketing and sales of upper echelon horses. Of course, Rene was happy to give a phone interview. Within the hour, the advertising department called.

Relying on meeting people at social events wasn't bringing her enough business lately. The advertising sales rep convinced her that an ad placed, even if for only one day, would be worthwhile. She risked two thousand dollars for an eighth of a page.

"I appreciate your calling me. What part of the country do you live in?"

"We live in the Tahoe Keys. Are you familiar with the area?"

"Lake Tahoe area I presume?"

"Yes."

"What a coincidence! Have you heard about the Arabian Horse Fair in Reno? I'm flying up for it in the morning."

"No. We haven't read anything about it. You're the first call that we've made. My husband and I always talked about buying horses, but our children were never interested. Now, the last one is off to college, and I'm afraid that I've got empty nest syndrome!"

"Have you ever been around horses?"

"Casually. Wherever we see horses we stop and visit... at Sea World we love the Clydesdales, and when we go to the racetrack we walk around wherever they let us. When we were in Lexington we went to that fabulous Kentucky Horse Park!"

"So, you've never ridden, taken lessons or anything?"

"Not lessons, but when we vacationed in places that had rental trail horses, my husband and I rode when we could convince the kids. When they were younger, that is."

"Do you want to ride or to breed?"

"We hadn't thought that far. The Barron's article intrigued my husband, and he said I should call you. That's as far as we've thought... I don't know that we're a very good prospect."

"Don't worry about it. I'm sure you just need to learn more about Arabians and the tax advantages of owning top quality horses. I certainly wouldn't expect you to commit to buying horses until you've had a chance to understand the industry."

"Good. I appreciate that. By the way, where are you located? I only have your phone number."

"I live in Scottsdale Arizona."

"We love Scottsdale! In fact, last winter we bought a condo at McCormick Ranch."

"I live right off Pima Road! When do you plan on visiting here again?"

"Not during the summer, I can guarantee you that!"

"Well, as I said, I'll be in Reno tomorrow. Can you and your husband meet for dinner? I can tell you about my experience and my services, and answer any questions for you."

"I'm afraid we have plans tomorrow evening. Perhaps we could get together over the weekend."

"Would you and your husband have time to come to Reno? We could meet at the MGM Grand, where I'm staying, and get to know each other a little, then go to the Fair together."

"I suppose," she said hesitantly, not knowing if they wanted to spend that much time.

"It would be an ideal way for you to see first hand what the show horse aspect of the industry is like, how nice the people are, and see some of the most gorgeous Arabians on the West Coast."

"What exactly is this Fair?"

"People from all over the West gather together for this prestigious show and exhibition. I'm not sure what you expect, since it's horses, but let me prepare you…it's not a jeans and tee-shirt crowd…its designer sportswear and fine jewelry!"

"Sounds like our yacht club," she said, now getting enthusiastic at the prospect.

"Good. Then you know how to dress. I'll take you around and give you an education most people can't get right off the bat when they're considering buying investment quality horses. The coliseum exhibit hall has a huge area they call Stallion Row - they should have about 100 stallions."

"Sounds overwhelming!"

"It won't be if you're with me! You'll love it. The horses are living works of art that reproduce themselves. You'll see mares, stallions, yearlings… basically all ages and bloodlines. There's nothing like it!" Rene sounded sincere, knowing the canned pitch would get their attention if they really had money.

"How exciting! I can't wait to tell my husband," she said, not letting on that she didn't know the terminology.

"I think you'll learn quite a bit. The farms display their stallions and their breeding programs as if they were Tiffany's displaying their fine jewels."

"I'm sure we can arrange to meet you."

` ` ` ` ` ` ` ` ` `

As Rene packed her Louis Vitton bags for Reno, she prayed that Jared wouldn't call again before she left town. How many times did she have to assure him that she would sell his horses for the profits she projected? Was his threat real? A million emotions whirled through her body. Nauseous from apprehension, she second guessed the choices she had made.

Having a prospect for making a sale was somewhat of a relief, but it didn't diminish her anxiety. It was unlikely she would make enough profit in one transaction to bail her out of her predicament. Wasn't this how she drifted into this nightmare in the first place? Thanks to Jared, she felt like there was a time bomb ready to go off, but she didn't know the precise day it was set to detonate. If she couldn't dig her way out of the tunnel she inadvertently dug, she'd walk away from everything she had built up - if she even survived.

Given the market conditions, it was challenging for her to reconcile her conflicting feelings about being a broker of elite Arabian horses. The more money horses sold for, the more she made, which was good business. On the other hand, she was content to make a decent living. Okay, an exceptionally good living. What was wrong with making money by sharing her passion and love of Arabians?

She assembled a packet of marketing materials comprised of magazine and newspaper articles about the Arabian industry, and copies of recent auction results and private treaty sales prices. Mira would want substantiation about the strong market. As she thought about how high the prices had become, a knot formed in the pit of her stomach. Was she desperate to make a sale, or was it a guilty conscience? Either way, she hated the feeling. Now, it could be life or death.

Chapter Two

Somehow, what was once a hobby evolved into a business where, with enough money and the right advice, anyone can create the illusion of success and superiority. These new farm owners weren't necessarily genuinely knowledgeable about what horses they owned or bred, what they were buying, or what they were selling. This game was taken seriously, yet most of them didn't really have a clue.

The turmoil of her conflicting emotions got the best of her. Ironically, she both loved and loathed events like the Arabian Horse Fair. Without these ostentatious events, she couldn't be in the business. In fact, there probably wouldn't be an actual 'industry' without events like the Fair. The whole concept of owning, showing and breeding incredible Arabian horses turned from a labor of love into a commodity business. A traded commodity rather than animals who were breathing, feeling, caring creatures deserving to be treated with respect and devotion.

Now, Rene was playing in the big leagues, and no one was telling her the rules. Her game strategy wasn't working, and Jared was making her life a living hell.

` ` ` ` ` ` ` ` ` ` `

Checking into the Reno MGM Grand, Rene spotted at least a dozen top trainers and several of their clients in the lobby. Not one person acknowledged her. Maybe everyone was avoiding her - she wouldn't be surprised.

She resented these people. At the same time, she envied them. It punctuated the fact she knew she was an outsider - a fraud wearing a mask, trying to fit in with the elite crowd of financially successful people. Most of the farm owners were wealthy business people brought into the Arabian industry by slick trainers. The trainers gained their trust, easily convincing the deep pocketed naïve people that with enough funding, they could be players in the Arab business. The checkbooks and credit cards of the wealthy were the meal tickets for the trainers. ^^

\` \` \` \` \` \` \` \` \` \`

At least the suite was beautiful - it should have been for $250 a night. She turned on the shower letting the bathroom fill with steam as she unpacked her cosmetics and disrobed. Once she stepped into the marble and etched glass enclosure, the hot water caressed her twenty-eight year old body, temporarily melting her tension. It was as if she were cleansing herself in advance of the sins she would undoubtedly commit.

Eventually, seeing the wrinkles on her fingertips snapped her back to reality. She reluctantly shut the water off. She sat on the commode wrapped in the oversized thick terry towel, lost in her thoughts, trying to convince herself she wasn't doing anything she should feel guilty about. Selling horses was her profession.

Once the steam disappeared, she patted her body dry and smoothed lotion everywhere she could reach. Loneliness swept over her as she wished someone else was there to spread lotion on her back. Someone she cared about - someone to confide in - someone to talk sense into her.

Not wanting to face the urgency of desperately needing to sell Jared's horses or take the chance he wasn't bullshitting her with his threats, she took her time, carefully applying fresh makeup and arranging her hair into a long elegant braid.

If it were up to her, she'd be in faded denim jeans and a soft cotton tank top – but that wasn't the costume that helped sell horses. Instead, to accent her suntan she slipped on her ivory colored Ann Taylor silk jumpsuit. She carefully attached a new fourteen-carat gold Arabian horse head belt buckle to the soft leather that fit comfortably around her thin waist. Next, she pulled on her custom boots from Rodeo Drive. She couldn't help but remember - the boots were the same price she had paid for her first pleasure horse, a Quarter Horse with Three Bars breeding. Now, the final accouterments: her twenty-four carat gold and diamond matching necklace, earrings and bracelet. She lightly dabbed Poison perfume on her collarbones and wrists.

It didn't quite feel like reality as she struggled to recognize herself in the full-length mirror. The costume that was required to conduct business was on. It was time to do the acting.

She felt ridiculous being dressed up like this. Was she just kidding herself, thinking she portrayed the picture of success? She had to at least dress like the people she was trying to impress - otherwise, they would never buy horses through her. They only do business with their own.

Rene always saw everything as a scene. If things weren't perfect, things weren't right. In the beginning, when she ventured out on her own as a young adult in Scottsdale, all she cared about was making a lot of money. She couldn't be a bartender forever. That wasn't what she was meant to do.

But this? She only fell into this profession. Sometimes it felt so natural, but at a gut level, Rene knew that brokering Arabians wasn't her ultimate destiny. In the interim, until she figured out what she really wanted, she decided she might as well keep selling expensive horses. Other people were doing it. Why shouldn't she? She wasn't trying to take advantage of anyone. She was just capitalizing on what the so-called market leaders were doing. It shouldn't matter that she thought the prices were ludicrous. She didn't create the market - she only fed off of it.

So why was her gut wrenching only minutes before she was meeting Mira and Preston Randolph?

Trying to justify how she spent her time, she told herself that eventually she would use the experience and do something that made her proud of herself and hopefully make her feel as if she were actually contributing something to society.

Until now, once she made a certain amount of money, an amount she could live comfortably on, the money didn't really matter. It was just a way of keeping score. If she made large sales with large profits for herself, she felt successful. When she didn't make a sale, or at the very least meet a serious potential buyer, she felt like a miserable failure and that life just wasn't worth living.

Once she took care of her immediate crisis with Jared, her next goal was to make one of the biggest sales in the industry. If she could do that, she would get the seal of approval from these people who were strutting around all full of themselves. Wouldn't she?

` ` ` ` ` ` ` ` ` ` `

As the glass elevator descended to the lobby, butterflies took flight in her chest. The door opened into the opulent hotel lobby buzzing with the background noise of the slot machines. Approaching the entrance of the restaurant, she saw a couple dressed in designer sportswear, the woman toting a very expensive leather purse. She hoped they were Mira and Preston Randolph.

Sure enough, they were.

Once the pleasantries were over and their meal served, it was time for Rene to give her Emmy winning performance.

"I've always loved horses ever since I was a kid. I just sort of fell into the Arabian business. I bought a wonderful jet black Quarter Horse and moved him to a boarding stable where there happened to be quite a few Arabs. The next thing I knew, I sold my Quarter Horse and bought an Arabian. Of course, it didn't take long for me to discover that there was an actual industry developing in Scottsdale, only a few miles from where my horse was boarded. To make a long story short, I immersed myself in learning about Polish Arabians, and grew to love them."

"Sounds like this is your life," Preston Randolph said as he buttered his rye toast.

"It is. I'm not academically inclined, so I didn't go to college. Instead, I learned everything I could about Polish Arabians...the genetics, the breed and strain standards, conformational traits and how different bloodlines cross with each other. My hobby became my expertise. It didn't take long before people began asking me to help select horses for them."

"That's great! You didn't even go to college at all?" Mira asked. She had married her husband two months after her high school graduation and hadn't attended college either.

"No. I'm not the disciplined or academic type. I've got a good mind for business - hopefully enough common sense, and I know a superior quality Arab when I see one."

"Not every field requires a college degree! But don't tell that to our kids… all three are in college now. Two in undergraduate programs, and one in medical school," Preston said.

"That's why we're looking into horses as a new hobby that we can do together, now that the kids are gone. Anyway, tell us more about you."

"Well, as I was getting ingrained in the Arabian horse scene, within a few short years, the ownership of quality Arabians went from a hobby to a profitable investment."

Preston chimed in. "It sure did! What piqued our interest about Arabians in particular was the Barron's article touting the unbelievable tax benefits and unique lifestyle. We really admire how the farms in the article aren't in it for the money…that they just happen to be making a lot of money from horses they love."

Rene knew the shtick that rolled off everyone's tongue: the money is irrelevant, they are preserving the breed and appreciating the animal itself. *Yeah, sure, the money doesn't matter!* They *claim* they don't care about making money from their horses. The owners that weren't trainers bragged about making plenty of money from their primary profession.

"Tell me, what makes the horses appreciate so much in value? The article didn't explain that," Preston inquired.

"I suppose it's a matter of supply and demand. The market leaders get more and more people interested in buying high quality animals, and then the prices continually escalate. Everyone keeps buying more horses because they're profiting from the ones that they have. I just go with what the head honchos are doing. In fact, you could say that my success comes from riding on their coattails."

Preston wasn't satisfied with Rene's answer, but he didn't press her further. "What year did you get involved?"

"When I got my first Arabian gelding, who was only a few thousand dollars - since he was just a gelding, - other people were paying about $15,000 for high quality broodmares… that was in 1978."

"How did that happen?"

"Good marketing, I guess. I'm not sure. But I can provide you with auction results, sales lists and magazine articles to show you the prices." *But, the big farms aren't in it for the money. They let their clients make the profits. Oh, how generous…*

"I still don't understand why there's so much appreciation," Preston said.

"If people make money, they're willing to spend money. Everyone is happy and they enjoy the horses!"

"The Barron's article says that if someone buys a yearling for $30,000, in a couple of years, that horse will be worth $45,000 and that she will have a foal that they could sell for $40,000 and that could happen every year for twenty years. Is that how you see it?"

"Sure. It happens all the time when you buy quality Arabs. With this kind of profit, the horses naturally go up in value. It's a great market, and it's only getting better! The values have never gone down."

People were buying and selling like crazy. They were crazy. Of course, they didn't think so, but anyone with a working brain could see it. Even Rene, but she couldn't tell a prospect or a client what she thought.

"What did you mean earlier when you said Polish Arabians?" Mira asked, intentionally guiding the conversation to be about the horses rather than the investment.

"All Arabians originally came from the desert. Various countries took horses from the desert to their own country, began their own breeding programs, and devised and maintained their own studbooks. The Arabians were then referred to as specific strains, such as Polish Arabians, Russian Arabians, Egyptian Arabians, Spanish Arabians, and so on. With a trained eye, you can see that the breeding programs from the various countries produce a unique product. Although each program retains some of the basic characteristics of the original Arabian, they also infused specific characteristics."

"In the few pictures I've seen, they all look alike - except for their color," Mira said, not at all concerned about her lack of knowledge.

"When you learn more, they won't! I'll teach you."

Mira leaned forward, as if she would understand the concepts by being closer to her new mentor. Her facial contortions showed definite signs of wanting to learn more.

Rene continued on. "As an example, Egyptian Arabians tend to be very fine boned, smaller in size, and generally are not all that athletic, but to their credit, they can have beautiful exotic heads and picturesque bodies. Egyptian Arabians can be great investments also, but I don't deal in them. Polish Arabians tend to have larger and stronger bone density giving them more power and athletic ability. Generally, they're taller, and usually don't have as beautiful of a head as that of the Egyptian Arabian. The Polish Arabian is more predictable in its breeding capabilities and has a longer life span than most other strains."

"So, do you sell all strains of Arabians except the Egyptians?" Preston asked.

"No. Only Pure Polish and Polish cross Arabians. In my opinion, they're the best, and they usually sell for the most money. From what I've experienced, the most athletic, smartest and the kindest horses descend from Poland. Polish Arabians have always been very strictly bred; the Poles cull out any horses that don't meet the needs of their breeding program."

Rene prided herself as being an ambassador of the Polish Arabian. She burned inside with a duty to educate potential horse buyers about them - while earning a lot of money.

"So, honestly, do you consider yourself an expert in the business?" Preston asked, wanting to get down to business.

"Yes, I do. And I don't have a vested interest in selling you a particular horse like the independent trainers or the farms do. I make money no matter what horses you buy through me. If you go to anyone else, they'll sell you whatever they want to sell at the time. It's really not in your best interest."

"What would you say makes you an expert?"

"I don't mean to brag, but I know pedigrees better than just about anyone that hasn't worked at the stud farms in Poland. I've got a keen eye for type...the genuine characteristics that an Arabian horse should possess. I know all of the details about equine conformation...the bone structure and any faults a horse may have. I can tell you which faults are genetic and which aren't. Basically, I've got an eye for a superior horse. An athlete versus a halter horse, even if the horse is standing still in a relaxed posture."

The couple nodded with interest. Rene continued.

"You may go to a seller and fall in love with a horse you think is beautiful. Trust me, too many horses only appear of quality to a non-expert because of the external reasons, like they are in great condition. Extensive physical conditioning, a deep cleansing bath, hot oil treatment and detailed clipping hide what the horse looks like naturally. Nature is what makes a great horse, not all of the things that humans can do to alter nature's creation."

"Well, you certainly sound impressive," Mira said enthusiastically.

"Besides knowing about the horses, I have relationships with people in the industry. It takes years to cultivate all of the right contacts in this business. I don't want to speak negatively about the industry, but I see through the marketing. I know the right questions to ask and to avoid. I research the truth about claims made by sellers of horses and by stallion owners."

"This certainly is intriguing," Preston said.

Mira nodded her head again and her eyes glistened as bright as her diamonds.

Buying signs!

\` \` \` \` \` \` \` \` \` \` \`

Rene took Mira and Preston to see the English Pleasure competition in the show ring and then on a tour of the exhibit halls. She introduced them to a lot of people so they could see how friendly everyone was, careful to not let them get too friendly.

Late in the afternoon, they parted company after having agreed they would talk early the following week.

Still, Rene wasn't off stage. Every minute at the Fair was an opportunity to be productive, even if the task was only to be seen.

Dean King, the owner of a farm in Central California, had expected to meet with her during the Fair. When she approached his booth, he was talking to a group of people speaking with a Danish accent. He motioned for her to watch his new farm video and have a drink...always complimentary from the farm's wet bar.

Dean was unmarried, and he won bonus points for owning over 250 Taco King fast food restaurants in California. He had money to burn and a small farm filled with above average horses, although he could easily afford the best. She had once visited his farm. To his credit, it was very functional and not at all ostentatious. He personally showed her each and every horse. It was obvious he thought he had the best. He actually cared about each individual animal, which was rare with most wealthy owners. He wasn't putting on airs of being a big and important breeder trying to impress other people. It was clear his horses were a big part of who he was. Rene was hoping to sell him his first high quality horse.

Just before the farm video ended, Grady Reed approached her, giving an acknowledging pat on the shoulder. He clearly didn't want to interrupt her viewing of the video. As he lowered himself into the sofa, Grady subtly pulled at the creases in his slacks to make sure they didn't wrinkle at the top as he was sitting. He crossed his legs in the way only confident men can, without appearing effeminate.

Grady, a lawyer from Beverly Hills, specialized in both equine law and in the entertainment field.

"Hi Grady. How are you?" Rene asked when the video production credits appeared on the screen.

Was this luck or what? She didn't have to seek him out!

"Not too bad. And yourself?"

"I'm doing well. I'm sorry to hear about your wife though."

"Yeah. Life can sure throw some real curve balls."

"I know, but you didn't deserve..."

Dean unintentionally interrupted her. "Sorry to keep you. Thanks for waiting," he said to Rene.

"Sure. Do you have time to visit about Alishia?"

"I'll try, but you know how it is here. You never know when someone will drop over...that's what I'm here for."

"I understand," Rene said, hoping she didn't sound like an outsider. After all, she never had an exhibit at a show, and certainly Dean and Grady were aware of that.

"Thanks for the sales tape you sent. I really love how Alishia moves. She's got plenty of action!"

Alishia was a mare she bought for Jared.

"I know. She's a great mare. I brought the still pictures of her that I took myself. The proofs aren't back from Spartonski yet," she said, referring to one of the best equine photographers in the world.

Grady tried to interject himself in the conversation about the mare. Rene casually turned toward Dean and resumed her conversation, hoping Grady would politely excuse himself for a few minutes.

Dean brought Grady, his lawyer, in on the conversation, wanting his legal advice in regards to his potential purchase. Legally, his company owned some of his horses, he owned some personally, and then there were others that were owned by a Trust.

Before she had an opportunity to try to close the sale, a man approached Dean about buying some horses. Dean politely excused himself, leaving Grady and Rene to continue their conversation.

Grady was usually a little too confident, but today he looked down, and a bit vulnerable. He brushed his hand across her thigh as he reached for his drink on the coffee table. A shock of electricity shot through her body. *Keep your cool. Remain professional.*

"It looks like Dean might be awhile. I think I'll grab dinner at the steakhouse across the street. Would you tell him I'll catch him later?"

Grady's response was slow in coming, then, he finally said, "Do you mind if I join you? I could use some time out of this place myself."

"Sure. I wouldn't mind the company."

Her plan was working without even putting any effort into it.

Chapter Three

Following the hostess to their booth, Grady took the liberty to gently guide Rene by having his hand at the small of her back as they walked through the restaurant.

"How about a bottle of Merlot?" he asked.

"Would you share it with me? I'm not a lush!"

"Of course we'll share it," he told Rene. "We'll have a bottle of your best Merlot," he said to the waiter, trusting his judgment.

"Are you trying to impress me, Grady Reed?"

"No. And I didn't mean to imply that you drink too much."

"I know. I'm just trying to lighten your mood. You seem really down."

"More like distracted."

"By anyone I know?"

He gave her a blank stare.

"I'm sorry. That wasn't appropriate. I didn't mean to be insensitive."

"Everyone thinks they have to watch every word they say around me now, as if I'm going to jump off a tall building if they say or do the wrong thing."

"That must be uncomfortable. I'll try not to make you feel that way."

"I'd appreciate it."

Rene didn't know what to say. Most conversations would lead to each person asking the other what's new, or what have you been doing lately, or something to that effect, but she didn't want to put Grady in the position to come up with an answer.

"I think I'll have a filet tonight. I'm craving red meat," she said.

"Did you know that it affects your serotonin levels? They say it makes you more relaxed. For me, it just makes me tired."

"I need to relax. I better have the larger cut!"

"Been working too much?"

"Not really. In fact, it's sort of the opposite. I'm frustrated because I really need to sell some horses right now and I don't have many prospects," she said, trying not to sound desperate. "The only prospects I have are Dean and the people I was with today."

"Who were you with?"

"I had breakfast with some prospective buyers, then we spent from about ten-thirty until five-thirty watching the show and going around the exhibit hall and the barns."

"Why so long?"

"It was a good way for them to get a taste of 'the life' and learn a little bit about different types of Arabs."

"The life! That's a great way to put it… I like that."

"Yeah, I coined the phrase, can you copyright it for me?"

"It'll cost you."

"How much?"

"How much you got?"

"Now you sound like a trainer!"

"No kidding. But I shouldn't say a word. If it weren't for trainers I probably wouldn't have half my clients."

"Are the trainers your clients or are the clients of the trainers your clients… did that come out right? Maybe I've had too much wine already!"

"You've only had one glass."

"I had a few drinks at the exhibit hall."

"Those don't count. Don't worry about it."

"That's my theory! But I already feel this wine."

"Good… maybe I have a chance of taking advantage of you! This was good timing," he said.

His own glass of wine was apparently loosening him up.

"It would be the other way around. I'm looking to take advantage of you," she said, knowing she meant she wanted some free legal advice. She knew he took it as a flirtation - which come to think of it, she really didn't mind.

He refilled her wineglass as the waiter served their fresh baked crusty bread.

They ordered their Caesar salads, filets, new red potatoes with dill and asparagus topped with béarnaise. To anyone looking in, it appeared they were very comfortable together. In reality, Grady was doing what his shrink suggested… just take the first step now that he moved from the house. Get out of the condo and the office and get on with life. Make new friends. He didn't need to date yet, but a little female companionship wouldn't do him any harm.

"So, are the people you were with today good prospects for buying?"

"I think so. They certainly have the money, and the wife has the time to spend with the horses."

"Time? I thought you only sold to investors."

"They are investors, but I like to get people who'll actually be involved."

"You are drunk, aren't you?"

"A little! But it's got nothing to do with what I'm talking about."

"You teach people? Never heard of such a thing."

Rene couldn't tell if he was being sarcastic or not.

"The more they learn, the less likely that they'll have buyer's remorse...and hopefully, the more horses they'll buy."

"I've gotten my share of phone calls from investors when it was too late for them to rescind their contracts," he admitted. It was always because people made a spontaneous emotional decision to buy, and later realized they didn't know enough to feel comfortable.

"So what do you do? Tell them it's too late and then send them a bill for a couple hundred bucks?"

"None of your business!"

"Guilty as charged. I can tell."

"You barely even know me!"

"Don't need to. I have a sense about these things."

"Well, lawyers may have a lousy reputation, but so do horse traders!"

"I'm not a horse trader! Call me that again and I'll sue you!"

The lively banter ended when the waiter delivered their dinner, which they ate in relative quiet.

By the end of dinner and the second bottle of wine, Grady's confidence level rose.

"Want to call it a night?" he asked.

"Go back to the show?"

"No, I mean, back to your hotel."

"Oh," she said after a hesitation. Rene blushed and looked down at her lap.

Her plan was working without even trying.

\ \ \ \ \ \ \ \ \ \ \ \

The next morning Rene woke to the telephone ringing. It was Grady, calling to invite her to breakfast and to apologize for coming on to her the night before. She accepted his apology and his invitation.

The waitress took their breakfast orders.

"Do you know much about the Ivy brothers?" she asked, hoping to get an honest answer.

"Like what?"

"Anything about their reputation?"

"As far as honesty to their clients, or what?"

"I guess. But mostly, I'm concerned they'll try to steal my clients."

"Which clients?"

"The couple I was with yesterday. I told you about them at dinner."

"Aahh. You're trying to protect your commissions."

"I'm concerned. I've brought new clients to their farm to show them horses for sale, and the next thing I knew, they dumped me and then did business directly with the Ivys."

"Did you ask them to at least pay you a referral fee?"

"No. I should have."

Grady immediately dismissed the idea of advising her that she could actually sue the Ivys for tortious interference with a business relationship, disparagement, and a host of other causes of action. It wasn't a guarantee she would win, but any counsel for the Ivys would recommend they make a nuisance settlement because there was no way a judge would grant a motion to dismiss. Any litigation would be time consuming and costly.

"You didn't want any conflicts. You wanted to be the professional. Now, you've learned to look out for yourself. Good plan."

"Right. So how do I protect myself? I'm tired of spending so much time and money getting people interested in the business, educating them, and then just losing them to a big time farm or a trainer with a wall lined in trophies and ribbons. You don't know how many times this has happened to me. Not just with the Ivys, but with other operations too! I'm sick of it."

"I'm sure you are."

"Can I hire you to sue them if they do it to me again?"

"There's really nothing you can do about it. It's just business," he said, feeling a tinge of guilt.

Rene would have been a small-time client. He'd rather wait until the Ivys called him. He was confident they would need to retain him eventually. It was common knowledge they weren't too happy with their lawyer in San Francisco.

"This business…"

"Why deal with the them again if you're already concerned about them?"

"Preston took a liking to Leslie. I could barely drag him out of their booth yesterday. Leslie has that charisma people are drawn to. And their booth is first class… they would have known something fishy was going on if I tried to avoid going to their booth."

"Must be frustrating."

"It is. Mira even asked for their business card in front of me. I guess it doesn't matter. They have all the contact information on the farm brochure and the syndicate marketing materials. I hate this part of the game. Who wins the client game… the winner gets the money, the loser gets a kick in the teeth."

"Well, I guess you know it's unlikely a prospective or new buyer will sign an agreement that guarantees they will do business with you, even if you are the one who got them interested in the first place."

"I know. I wouldn't even ask."

"And, of course, no matter what document a trainer or a farm signs which says you'll get your commission, if they don't want to pay you, they'll find a way out. Your biggest problem is you really shouldn't be taking people around or teaching them too much. You need to make them think they need you."

"They do need me. And I try to emphasize to them why they should use me, but I can't make the business look so greedy or crooked. There's a fine line as to what's appropriate to say."

"Kind of like dating."

"Right. You can't show all of your cards at once, or you risk them walking out on you before they really understand," she answered as she placed his hand high on her thigh.

She was reeling him in ahead of schedule.

Chapter Four

A few weeks later...September 1, 1983
Santa Barbara, California

For the third time since Reno, Rene drove from Scottsdale to Malibu to stay with Grady in his new beach front condo, and to do some horse business on her own. During her previous visits, they went to a farm in Thousand Oaks and several farms south of Los Angeles.

Today, she needed time alone. The picturesque drive north up the coast on Highway 101 to Santa Barbara should have been relaxing, but thanks to her usual apprehension about how she would be able to portray herself, she was on edge.

Ivy Farms was open to the public for a formal preview of the horses being offered in their private auction later in the month. Traditionally, the annual sale established higher prices and values for some of the most expensive Polish horses in the world. The prices obtained in Southern California weren't as high as in Scottsdale - still, no one could really complain.

Once again, she would see the stallions Freedom and Aston and the resulting generations from them. Although she looked forward to seeing the horses, she was more focused on meeting Dominick Castinitas, the famous film director/producer, and a client of Chandler and Leslie Ivy. She hoped he would be there today. Dominick was actually the breeder of Freedom. He owned several syndicate shares in the stallion, and he owned mares consigned to the auction.

Thanks to Grady's influence, she sold Jared's mare, Alishia, to Dean King for double what he paid only a few months before. Still, his threat loomed over her; she was quite desperate to meet some of the heavy spenders who would be at the farm's open house and preview. After all, Ivy Farms lured clients away from her. In fact, when she followed up on the Randolphs, they said they were going to the Ivy Farms auction before deciding to buy. They wanted a better feel for the business, and Leslie Ivy convinced them to come to his auction.

Today she planned to try to meet at least one potential client. To her credit, she had a knack for determining if a person was a live prospect. If they weren't, she had no use for them. Making friends never crossed her mind when she really needed to make sales. These were people she could profit from or not. Nothing more. Nothing less. ^^

` ` ` ` ` ` ` ` ` ` `

Ivy Farms was a beautiful showplace, but nothing compared to CSC, Dominick's farm which was only ten miles away. Chandler and Leslie Ivy purchased Freedom from Dominick when the colt was only 3 months old. Eventually, they syndicated him for a record price of $15 million.

Rene was curious about the fact she hadn't heard of the majority of people who owned shares in *The Freedom Alliance*, the unique name they gave to the syndication. Usually people who purchased stallion syndication shares bred mares to the stallion and advertised it. When the stallion was the quality of Freedom, generally, well-known breeders owned shares.

Other than Dominick and a handful of other farms in *The Freedom Alliance*, you never heard about syndicate members except when Freedom himself was advertised. As a general rule of thumb, ads promoting syndicated stallions, including Freedom, listed each syndicate member, their city and state, and the share numbers they owned. Doing this in the ads made the syndication appear credible and made the breeding rights appear to be in high demand. With Freedom, the entire syndication sold out quickly, with shares subsequently being resold for a substantial profit.

` ` ` ` ` ` ` ` ` ` `

A large crowd began to mingle in the reception area of the show barn at Ivy Farms. Rene wanted to speak with Rhonda, the marketing director, before she was too busy with other people.

"How many mares did Freedom breed this year?" Rene casually asked Rhonda.

"One hundred and fifteen mares, with ninety-eight conceiving. Fifteen of the mares belong to the farm."

The answer was too rehearsed.

"Don't you think that's over breeding him?"

"No. We don't think so."

"Breeding that many mares a year is going to dilute the value of his babies," Rene said with authority.

Rhonda's upper lip tightened as she set her jaw, but she didn't reply.

"What about Aston, you're not breeding him to that many mares are you?"

Aston was a stallion imported from Poland. He had been a Polish National Champion and a reasonably successful race horse. He descended from an entire line of Polish Champions: a rare treasure.

Rhonda looked out toward the Olympic sized arena, concentrating on something much more important than Rene's questions.

Two can play this game.

"I understand that the Ivys want to keep him more exclusive," Rene continued.

"The farm bred Aston to thirty-five of our own mares, and we sold twenty-five outside breedings for $10,000 each. We've already pre-sold all of his outside breedings for next year for $12,500 each."

"I didn't know that..."

"Excuse me, but I need to meet with a client who just arrived from New Jersey," the marketing director said, abruptly excusing herself.

Insulted, Rene slipped out of the lobby and wandered to the closest of the four back barns.

"Hi. You're sure lucky to work around such beautiful horses!" Rene said innocently to a man cleaning an empty stall.

"Yes. This wonderful to work," he answered with a heavy Hispanic accent.

"Do you take care of all of the horses?" Rene inquired, sounding naïve.

"Not all. This is visiting mare barn. During season all stalls are full with mares wanting to breed. I take care of all horses in this barn," he said with pride.

This barn is big, but it doesn't seem big enough to house all of the visiting mares, she thought.

"How many stalls are here?"

"Fifty stalls. Twenty-five mares to pastures. No all owners want mares in stalls," he told her as he closed a stall door behind him. "I need to get tractor. Have a nice day."

Most clients with horses at Ivy Farms boarded them year round since they didn't usually own their own farm. Part of their enjoyment of owning the horses was going to visit at a facility like this. The mare owners who didn't keep their horses boarded out year round at least kept them there for three to five months; the mares could settle in and come into their heat cycle. Once the mare was bred, the farm insisted they wait a month to see if the mare were pregnant. If she was, they still left the mare for 30 to 60 days more to make sure she didn't absorb the fetus and need to be rebred. *Cash flow.*

She didn't need to be Einstein to figure out the marketing director said Freedom alone had bred one hundred client owned mares, and Aston had bred twenty-five client owned mares. That was a discrepancy of fifty mares! Rene wanted to give the marketing director the benefit of the doubt until she could speak with someone else.

She strolled up and down the barn aisles, stopping at each individual stall with a horse in it, studied each horse and the engraved pedigree sign. She also took mental note of the names of the horses in the empty stalls. Sometimes she saw the names of heavily advertised mares and made a mental note about who they were being bred to. The stall signs also had the owner's names on them, which Rene filed in the back of her mind. Once she looked in all fifty stalls, she went to the preparation area in the center of the barn.

She found a groom studiously working in a wash rack strategically situated in the middle aisle of the barn. The young woman was softly singing to the radio as she applied oil to a mare's eyes and cheekbones.

"Hi. What a beautiful mare."

The groom looked up and smiled, then used her forearm to wipe the sweat from her cheeks.

"She sure is…and she's quite the athlete," she politely responded as she artfully finished applying oil along the contour of the mare's shoulder blade.

"How long have you worked here?"

"This is my 5th year," the groom answered as she bent down to open the can of glossy black hoof polish. "I love it. I'm the head groom, and during the breeding season I prepare all of the client's mares for breeding… and I help with the actual breeding," she boasted with great pride and enthusiasm.

"Wow."

"You look familiar. Have you been here before? I'm usually better at recognizing horses than people, but you look really familiar."

"You do the breeding? How many client mares were bred this year?" Rene asked nonchalantly, ignoring the question.

"A total of 75 mares between the five stallions."

"Five stallions? I only received brochures on two. Freedom and Aston."

She finished coating the front feet with black polish before she answered.

"Oh, yeah, that's because the other three stallions are owned by clients who don't have farms or they don't have qualified personnel to do breeding. They pay us to breed them. Those stallion owners all have at least a dozen mares each, so we breed their stallions to their mares, and a few outside breedings to their stallions, but not many. Those three stallions are young and unproven, and not promoted yet. We treat them with all the same care and consideration though."

The young woman obviously loved the horses and had pride in her work.

"So, how many mares did Freedom breed this year?"

"About 40." She finished the last hoof, stood up, and stretched her back.

"What about Aston, how many did he breed?"

"Only 5 before we discovered he was sterile."

"Aston?"

The blood rushed to her face.

"Actually, I shouldn't have even said anything. Please don't tell anyone I told you. I'll be in big trouble," she pleaded as the color now drained from her face. "Besides, the vet says he's fine now, but it's too late for this year since breeding season's over."

"What made him sterile?"

"They think he contracted a virus from a newly imported horse," she said nervously.

Rene assured her she wouldn't tell anyone.

The groom sprayed silver hair glitter in the mare's forelock, mane, and tail as a finishing touch. They told each other to have a nice day and went their separate ways.

By then, it was quite obvious that Rhonda, the marketing director, was dishonest.

Next, Rene talked to Luke Remmacs, the head trainer. He was the typical semi-friendly, semi-aloof trainer, tops in the field. Chandler Ivy still trained some of the horses, but because he was an owner of the farm, they gave Luke the title of head trainer. Leslie Ivy no longer had time for training now that the business had grown. He dealt in the business, marketing and sales aspects, and he still showed the horses in the Regional shows, at Scottsdale and at the U.S. and Canadian Nationals. Other than that, he rarely touched a horse anymore.

"Luke. Hi! I haven't seen you since Nationals last year!" Rene enthusiastically said with a familiarity that didn't really exist.

Rene always sounded that way if there were other people within earshot. *What did they know?*

"I'm great. Just really busy getting ready for the auction. To be honest, I'm exhausted from breeding season. We had so many mares to cover we were still breeding in July!" he said with far too much self -importance.

"Are you personally involved in the breeding? I thought you only do the training."

"Most of the time I handle the stallions during breeding if it's a live cover. I don't usually handle them for artificial insemination though. I can control the live covers better than a lot of the staff, and keep them less excitable for when I ride them. Besides, I've always loved the breeding and foaling out the mares when I have the time and energy."

"How many mares did Freedom and Aston each breed this year?" she inquired.

Luke's answer was the same as Rhonda. Rene felt a rush. She had them on something substantial. Now, she had to figure out how to prove it and how best to use it. ^^

Ivy Farms had deep pockets, and she caught them in some serious fraud. The more she thought about it, she remembered that the next issue of *Arabian Horse International,* a thick glossy monthly trade magazine, was due to be delivered to her house within days.

Ivy Farms bought the front cover, and, of course, the cover story to promote the auction at the end of the month.

Most people in the industry didn't even know magazine covers and feature stories were paid for, and often were written by the farm or their own PR agency. Rene hoped the information submitted to the magazine would claim in writing the same figures Luke and Rhonda grossly overstated. She would wait until she received the magazine. That would give her time to decide how to handle what she knew. ^^

Chapter Five

Today, the bleachers at the preview ring were packed with people reeking of wealth, admiring the horses being offered for sale. They were great prey for Rene. That's one of the reasons why she was there without Grady.

She scoped out an affluent looking couple and scooted down the bleachers.

"Excuse me. Do you mind if I sit here? You've got the best seats… mid-level and center!" Rene asked politely.

The leathery skinned man looked up and blocked the sun from his eyes.

"I don't own the place. Sit where you want."

"Rod!" the woman said as her perfect pearly whites glistened, making her smile look like it belonged in a toothpaste commercial.

She was probably around thirty years old, and the four carats on her ring finger are not the kind horses love - they were the carats older men buy to impress the ladies, Rene thought.

"All I'm saying is, she doesn't need my permission! Hell, I don't even know what we're doing here!" he said.

"We're looking at horses!"

Rene took off her linen jacket and placed it at her side as she nodded at them.

The man wore Perry Ellis jeans and a Ralph Lauren polo shirt; his clothing didn't seem to fit his age or mannerisms. The younger woman surely selected his wardrobe.

He turned to Rene, and in an attempt to amuse his partner he asked, "Tell me, what are all of these people doing getting liquored up just to see some horses? Where I come from, you go out to the pasture and drag an old nag from the field, saddle up and go out on the range."

The woman clasped his forearm and started laughing.

"Rod...Stop it! She's going to think you're serious."

"He's not serious?" Rene asked, playing along.

"No! He's trying to make you think he's some good old boy cowboy. Today is the closest he's ever gotten to a horse in his life! And I had to drag him here. Didn't I, honey?"

"Well, I did promise you a horse for an engagement present," he said.

Rene tried to conceal her optimism.

"You're getting married? Congratulations!"

"Well, not quite yet," the woman said with a tinge of disappointment.

"But you are engaged?"

"Yes. But, he still has to tell his wife... get the divorce... clear up those complications," she said.

"Carol...now you stop it! She's going to take you seriously."

"We're getting married next month!"

"That's wonderful. An Arabian horse is the best engagement gift I can imagine. When I get married, that's what I'll hope to get."

"Do you have horses?" Carol asked Rene.

"Yes, and I'm a bloodstock agent."

"A bloodstock agent?" Rod asked.

"I find horses for buyers."

"I used to be a real estate agent," Carol said.

"You'll never work another day in your life now, honey," Rod told her as he squeezed her hand.

"What do you do?"

"I'm in the aerospace industry."

The live band started playing Chariots of Fire as handlers and horses could be seen lining up outside of the show barn in the distance. Within a few minutes, the bleachers filled to capacity, people three and four deep surrounding the oval preview ring.

The music lowered, allowing the crisp clear sound system to amplify Henry Coppers impassioned voice.

"Ladies and gentleman, now, what you've been waiting for! The superstar horses of Ivy Farms! The best of the best! I now present to you the world-class stallion you've come as far away as Canada, New York and Florida to see. It's Freeeeedommmm!"

In a flash, the exuberant bay stallion hit a lick at a full extended trot, making his bold entrance into the preview ring with Luke Remmacs on the end of the lead line. The pounding of the horse's hooves kicked up emerald green pine shavings.

Henry Copper, the professional announcer, fell silent, knowing he could not be heard over the whistling and applauding of the crowd - which was Freedom's cue: as a natural response to the attention he knew was just for him, he lifted his tail, pranced and popped his ears forward as he snorted through his enormous masculine nostrils.

Seasoned Arabian lovers in the audience whistled and stood to cheer the stallion on as if he were Elvis in concert. The enthusiasm was contagious. Newcomers followed along, surprised at their own reaction to the charismatic animal. Luke deftly removed the thin gold filigree and patent leather halter, swung it in the air and turned a thousand pounds of testosterone loose in the ring to strut his stuff.

"What is everyone so excited about?" Ron practically screamed to Rene.

"The horse! Isn't he spectacular?" Carol answered before Rene responded.

"Yes! This is exciting. It's how the farm gets you all pumped up and wanting to buy at the auction!" Rene said.

Freedom seemed to be living for his audience, showing-off his unbelievable cadence, then, every once in a while he reared high into the air and followed up with a buck. When the crowd cheered, he took several strides at a canter. Just to make sure people were still paying attention, he abruptly stopped, stood perfectly squared facing the bleachers, then promptly swung his head high in the air and whinnied, announcing that he was the King. Every rock hard muscle in his body was flexed in excitement: the snort from his oiled air passages sent the crowd into wild excitement as the band played Chariots of Fire.

Rod wasn't impressed, which disappointed Carol.

"I saw that horse earlier standing in his fancy stall. He's just a horse. What's the big deal? And what's with these people?"

"It's just meant to be fun and make the event exciting," Rene explained.

"I think this crowd is ridiculous if you ask me! It's just a horse! And that stall of his… the woodwork is as nice as what I have in my den…and the custom wrought iron stall grates…and engraved silver name plates…come on!"

"Well just keep quiet and let me have fun, honey!" Carol told him.

"Fine. This is your day. I'm going to get a drink. You ladies have a good time."

"We will. Bring us some wine!" Carol said as she winked at him.

Rene hoped he wouldn't walk back by the preparation barn. He was obviously a sharp man, and would pick up on all the artificial things they were doing to make the horses look better than usual. Applying oils as makeup highlighters, putting ginger in the rectum of the horse so they would keep their tails high, spraying a light coat of glitter on the hair, and everything else they do to make horses look fantasy-like.

When Carol and Rene looked back out toward the preview ring, Freedom was rearing up and playfully striking out while on his way back to the stallion barn. Aston was next, acting just like Freedom, and the crowd remained just as enthusiastic.

Without delay, a silvery-gray mare was turned loose in the ring. Carol was observant and asked why there were four men in with the mare. Rene explained that they were controlling the movement of the horse as much as possible by shaking small plastic containers with tiny rocks in the bottom; the sound imitates a rattle snake. She told her how the response of the horse is to move away from the sound. If the men didn't urge the mare, she may just stand around sniffing the colored shavings - certainly not the best way to show off a beautiful horse.

Rod did not come back with wine, which was just fine since champagne was being served in the stands and around the ring.

"These horses look so much better than the ones in the pastures," Carol observed.

"These horses are all conditioned, and about a week ago, the horses had all of their hair shaved off..."

"That must take forever! I know how long it takes me just to shave my own legs!"

"It takes about 3 hours. Then, they rub mayonnaise into the skin to prevent it from getting dry. By today, the hair has grown back just enough to show the color. Probably starting at about five this morning, the horses were bathed with expensive shampoos and deep conditioning treatments, then they were sponged down with a very light coating of a mixture of Shapley's Oil and warm water, then allowed to dry again. That's how you're able to see so much of their muscling."

"Wow. What a production. And look at their manicures!"

Rene laughed! "I guess that's what you could call it! They lightly sand the hooves using three different grains of sandpaper, then black or neutral shoe polish, then they buff the hoof before they paint it with a clear glossy sealant."

"Sounds like the pedicures I get at the salon. Now that Rod and I are together I go in for the whole treatment. They do my hair and make-up and everything!"

Rene acted as if she was amused by Carol's attitude. "Same with these horses. An artful groom applies special highlighting oil around the horse's eyes, on the muzzle, on the cheek bones and inside their ears. It's like a make-up effect on women. The oil either highlights the good features of the horse, or the groom can distort what the horse actually looks like if they needed to. If the horse's shoulder doesn't have enough angle to it, they put oil near the shoulder line of the horse to make it look like that is the real angle of the shoulder, when it really isn't. There are lots of other tricks too. Like letting feet grow longer than they should, especially the toe, and then putting weighted front shoes on. The weighted shoes make the horse trot higher than what is natural."

"How did you find all of this out? It's amazing."

"Experience. And time in the business. Being an insider. New people don't have a clue. That's why they use me to help them buy their horses."

Rene and Carol talked through the entire presentation of another thirty-two horses.

After the preview, across the expansive lawn, the buffet tables were covered with fabulous gourmet food; portable bars were close at hand, no matter where you were.

"Let's find Rod and get a table to eat at," Carol suggested to Rene.

"Sure. Will you need to ask him if you can do business with me, or can you just buy through who you want?"

"I'll just tell him that I'm going to let you find me a horse. He won't care, especially after I tell him how much you taught me. I had no idea there was so much to knowing a great horse and identifying what you like about a particular horse," Carol confessed.

"Most people don't know what they don't know! That's why I can be of such an important service to you. The main thing right now is that you'll need to decide if you want to be able to ride the horse you buy, or if you'll just pay to have a trainer ride and show... or if you'll want to buy a broodmare, and of course, you'll have to decide how much money you can spend."

Carol bit her lip. "The amount of money doesn't really matter. A couple of months ago he sold a division of his company for just under a half billion dollars! I think I'll tell him I want a broodmare *and* get a show horse that will stay with a trainer. It would be fun to have a foal and watch it grow up, and it would be exciting to watch my horse be shown."

I've got a live one!

"That's a good idea...plus, while your show horse is being trained, you can take riding lessons, and eventually get good enough to ride your own horse!"

"Oh my God! I'd never be good enough to ride a horse that costs that much money! I'd be afraid I would do something wrong."

"Don't worry. Take lessons from a top notch instructor, and she'll talk to your trainer and let you know when she thinks you're ready. The trainer will be there with you to coach you on how your horse is cued. No one will let you do anything harmful."

"I don't know! Lets take one step at a time. This place is so breathtaking, isn't it?"

"I can't say that I'd mind owning a place like this!" Rene said, hoping to plant a seed in Carol's mind.

If he has that much money, maybe I can get them to buy a big farm and start a long term breeding program. They could be a gold mine. All those commissions and markups!

Blooming potted flowers were scattered throughout the lawn and a small fountain sat in the center with a life-size bronze statue of a mare and foal. The tables were far enough apart from each other that people could have private conversations without having to whisper or lower their voices. A nice touch.

Most prospective buyers were with spouses or business partners and need to talk confidentially.

Carol spotted Rod sitting at one of the many sets of imported patio furniture with hand painted canvas umbrellas.

"Rene, there's Rod! It looks like he's already got a table for us," Carol said, glad they didn't have to wander throughout the sprawling grounds looking for him.

Rene looked in the direction her new client was pointing. Rod was sitting with Leslie Ivy.

In an instant she felt as if she were swimming against a swift river current that was pulling her into a riptide.

She followed Carol's lead to the table as she swallowed hard and held back the tears that wanted to gush from her eyes. Suddenly, she was sick to her stomach. If only she could just collapse and wake up to find out that her being in this industry was just all a horrible nightmare. At this point, she would happily go back to being a carefree bartender with a Quarter Horse gelding to ride just for fun and companionship.

Leslie stood and faced the women.

"Rene. It's good to see you. I see you've met Rod and Carol," he said as he gave her a snide look with his snake eyes.

"Yes..."

Looking her directly in the eye, he acted as if she hadn't started speaking.

"Have a seat. I need to have my secretary draw up a contract for Rod to sign," he made a point of saying as if he were jabbing her in the side.

Carol and Rene were speechless as Leslie turned on his heels and briskly walked to the farm's administrative offices.

"You're turning red," Rod told his trophy girlfriend.

"Am I?"

"What's wrong? You said you wanted a horse, so I bought you a horse. You'll own it within an hour!"

"Thank you dear, but I thought we were just here to learn and observe. I thought I was going to be able to pick out my own horse."

Rene remained silent in her exasperation. It wasn't her place to butt in, but she had plenty to say, if only it were appropriate.

"Leslie Ivy assured me he has the perfect horse for you. Someone else is coming later today that he's sure was going to make an offer on her. He took a liking to me and was kind enough to give me the opportunity to snatch up the mare right away."

"What does she look like?" Carol said, stunned at what had happened.

"A horse. I don't know. She was really shiny though! Cost me $250,000! That should be good enough for you babe," he said as if it didn't really matter and that he did what he promised - he bought her a horse.

"$250,000? Are you serious?"

"Yeah. She's got some rare bloodlines or something. Leslie said he just decided to offer her for sale and she was so good she wouldn't last 24 hours. That's the kind of horse you deserve sweetie."

"Rod, that's too much for one horse! Rene said she could get me really great horses for $75,000 to $100,000."

"They must not be as good as the horse I just bought you... like I said, the bloodlines are really rare. Only the best for you honey."

"But Rene's been teaching me so much. I'm just starting to understand what I like and why. She's just spent all this time at the preview teaching me characteristics and asking questions that I never even thought about."

"Well, thanks Rene, but it looks like we're all set here," he said, as if he thought the whole thing was ridiculous, including the entire function today.

"But Rod, I told Rene I'd let her find a couple of horses for me. She was going to give me plenty of options...and an opportunity to understand what I'm really getting... and what I'll even do with the horse."

"Too late now doll. Sorry."

Rene stood up, skeptical of what Leslie Ivy had told Rod. She thought it was absurd for him to pay that much for a horse as a gift without Carol even asking for the horse!

"I'm really not needed here anymore. It was nice to meet you," she told both of them as she tugged on her earlobe. "I wish you the best of luck with your new horse. Welcome to being an Arab owner!"

"I'm sorry Rene. I do have your number. I'll keep in touch," Carol assured her.

I'll never hear from them again. The Ivy's have a goldmine now. Damn it!

Rene did her best to appear unconcerned as she walked away feeling defeated and exasperated. Ivy Farms was going to pay for this! She already planned on using their lies against them, but now she was more determined than ever.

There was nowhere here that she could scream her lungs out and beat on a soft pillow and cry so hard she couldn't breath. Food would be the next best thing for now. ^^

After what happened with Carol and Rod, she deserved all the food and liquor that she wanted. Self-conscious about eating around other people because she always had an enormous appetite, at that moment, she decided to not to worry about what anyone else thought. On her plate, she piled smoked salmon, a mini-quiche, tuna sushi, caviar, a prawn and scallop kabob, a slice of mango, Dolfino and Brie cheese, and lavosh.

She grazed the delicacies on her plate as she was entertained by the dozen or so weanlings romping around running in and out through the huge oak trees. Moments like this pastoral scene were why a small part of her loved what she did for a living.

Enjoying the horses was momentarily calming her down and helping her to put into perspective the idea that she had lost yet another sale to a big farm. The distraction of the horses didn't hold her attention long - it was time to retaliate and to hatch a solid game plan as to how she would escape this business - without having to hide from Jared. ^^

Chapter Six

Leslie hadn't uttered a single word to Rene for the rest of the afternoon, but each time he walked past her or happened to be in her vicinity, she was sure he was ridiculing her. Their relationship seemed to have become a cat and mouse game - she didn't intend to play it any more - or at least she didn't intend to be on the losing end any longer.

The crowd started to thin out. Rene left before it was painfully obvious that she didn't fit in with those that remained. With so few people, soon she would no longer blend into the scenery.

As she drove the winding San Marcos Pass Road, the intense glare of the sun on her windshield nearly blinded her. Luckily, she approached a turnoff at a viewing area near the top of the mountain. She veered her car into the last parking space available. The entire area bustled with people taking pictures, staring out at the spectacular ever-changing colors of the sunset in the canyon.

As soon as the vibrant colors in the sky disappeared Rene reclined her seat and dozed off.

Almost an hour later, she startled awake to find only two other cars in sight. Dim halogen security lights dotted the parking area. When she inserted her key in the ignition, a crazy thought crossed her mind - *would Jared ever go so far as to blow up her car if she didn't come through?* It happened in the movies...

Driving out of the view area toward the road, the welcome breeze from her open sunroof and windows cleared the cobwebs in her head. She inhaled the crisp and invigorating clean night air, yet, she had an eerie feeling. Once she pulled back out onto the pavement, it was the kind of dark that even the sliver of the moon couldn't help.

In spite of her intense concentration on the meandering two lane road with steep cliffs off to her right side, it only took one close call around a tight curve for her to accept the fact that she couldn't rush back to Grady.

Heading down the mountain as carefully as possible, she was shaken by unexpected thunder and a bright bolt of lightening. Without warning, a torrential downpour came from the forbidding charcoal sky. With nowhere to turn off, there was no option except to push herself to drive in the near blinding rain. Her hands ached from grasping the steering wheel so tight.

The rain dissipated into a light drizzle by the time she was in the heart of Santa Barbara. Within a couple of blocks she discovered a quaint cafe to unwind in; it was almost a three hour drive until she could be with Grady. As soon as she finished her first cup of coffee she called him at his condo. There was no answer, so she dialed his office.

He picked up the phone on the first ring.

"Grady Reed."

"Hi...it's me. You sound exhausted!"

"I'll be fine. It's late, where are you?" he asked as he sorted through file folders.

"In Santa Barbara. You're at the office still?"

"I got behind in some work with your being in town."

"Sorry, but you invited me!" she reminded him. She had actually planned on staying in Solvang, but when he invited her to stay with him again, she couldn't refuse.

"I know. I want you here, but I've got work to do."

"You won't believe the day I've had! I can't wait to tell you everything."

"Something exciting?"

It depends on how you look at it. "You could say that."

"Are you up to driving? It's pretty late if you're tired."

"I think I'm up to it. I'm having more coffee, then I'll decide," she said, hoping he would sound as if he missed her.

"Good idea. I think I'll stay at the office and get caught up. Call me when you're back to my place. I gave you a key, didn't I?"

"Yeah. I have the key. If I decide to get a hotel, I'll call you back. Otherwise, I'll call when I get to your place."

"Sounds good."

"Why are you working so late?"

"This is the norm for me lately. I still need to write a brief and review a settlement agreement."

"Can you sleep in?"

"No, but if we don't go out to lunch I can leave the office at about two tomorrow, unless something unexpected comes up."

He missed her gentle touch. She was helping him get over what had happened with his wife.

"I think I'm going to need your legal advice."

"Sounds serious. Hey, did you pick up any clients?"

"No. But almost. I wish you weren't so far away."

"Did you meet Dominick?" he asked, hoping he wouldn't need to introduce them.

"No. I didn't even see him at the farm. Of course, the place is so big, he could have been there without my running into him. Anyway, I'll tell you about everything later. Miss you."

Grady was hopeful for a good roll in the sack, but all Rene wanted to do was tell him about Rod and Carol spending $250,000 like it was meaningless, and, of course to tell him about the lies from both Luke and Rhonda regarding the number of mares the stallions bred this season, and that Aston had been sterile for the season.

She couldn't believe that he didn't seem phased by their deceitfulness.

"You're acting like it's no big deal that they're lying!"

The corners of his lips turned up, not quite into a grin, but definitely exposing the fact that he found her naïveté amusing. He sat cross legged on his bed, and lit up a joint that was waiting on a nightstand. After he exhaled, he answered her as if he were practically bored with the conversation.

"I'm a lawyer for God sakes! Don't you think I hear about these kinds of things all the time?"

She looked deflated, as if she thought she was bringing him some really interesting news.

"I guess I didn't really think about all the reasons your clients use you. I suppose I just thought about the aspects of your drawing up contracts or dealing with people who think they were ripped off by a seller, or whatever."

"That's only part of my business. A lot of it is advising clients on issues like this, and dealing with settlements of disputes over business practices, people discovering outright fraud, securities violations…"

"Securities violations?"

"Yes. Why?"

"Nothing," she said as a lump formed in the pit of her stomach.

"The stories I could tell you…I deal in things you probably never dreamed of," he said as he tried to pass her the joint, which she refused.

"Okay. So to you, this is no big deal. But to me, it's going to be my ticket to freedom! That's why I need your legal advice."

"$250 an hour, and not in my bed."

"We have our clothes on!"

"I'm serious," he said with a devious smile spread across his face.

"Well, I'm a high class hooker. I charge $500 an hour… we'll trade, and you owe me big time!"

"$500 an hour?"

"Yep."

"You're selling yourself short," he said as he winked at her and unbuttoned his shirt.

She was flattered, but ignored the comment.

"This is serious. I need some legal advice."

"To tell you the truth, I can't really give you any."

A blank look swept her tired face.

"I can't just casually give you legal advice, especially since we're in a relationship. It's not ethical and…"

"Come on Grady! Of course, we've got a good thing going now, but the only reason I started seeing you was for free legal advice!" she said as if she were kidding.

They both laughed, then he conceded. "You have to promise you won't hold me to anything I tell you."

"What do you mean?"

"Promise me you won't come after me for malpractice, claiming I advised you on something. In a professional setting, I would be taking notes that would become part of a record. Obviously, we're not doing that here."

"Fine. I have no interest in having a problem with you. Now, can I ask you a few things?"

"Shoot."

"First, how can I legally blackmail Ivy Farms?"

"You can't. That's the point of the word blackmail."

She quickly sat erect in the bed. "You know what I mean. I need to find a way to get them to pay me a shit load of money to not disclose what I know."

"That's blackmail. It's illegal, and I won't be a party to this. I'm going to pretend you never broached the subject."

"What can I do about this?"

"You can expose them if you have proof of the number of mares really bred, and if you have proof of their claims as to the numbers bred. You have to be careful that you aren't slandering them. You can't expose it as gossip… I suppose you'll have to go to one of the major equine magazines or newspapers. Then, they'll confirm your story."

"But how do I get money from it?"

"You can't legally get money from it."

She pounded her fists in frustration. "I need money and I need it fast! This is a way I can get it!"

Grady couldn't believe what he was seeing or hearing. This was not the woman he knew; this was a side of her personality she hadn't exposed before. He had to admit, it was kind of exciting.

"Calm down. You're not being rational."

"I am rational. They can't get away with this! And the clients Leslie stole from me. I'm fed up and I want out of this business," she said. Tears started streaming down her face. She felt defeated; beaten down, like the whole world was against her.

"You are not being rational. If you want out of the business, just walk away. You're smart and ambitious. I'm sure you could do just about anything you set your mind to."

She wiped the tears away, but her eyes stung from the salt.

"You don't understand. I need a lot of money."

"Don't we all!" he said, trying to lighten the mood.

"Grady, this is serious. I can't tell you why, but I need a lot of money. These lies that I caught Ivy Farms in can be my ticket out. Trust me. This is soooo important!" she pleaded.

He peered deep into her eyes and wondered what was haunting her. It was clear this wasn't the time to ask.

"Listen Rene, if you want to expose them, go ahead, but you haven't been damaged, so you have no legal claim against them."

"There's got to be something I can do to make money. I know you can help me… you're a lawyer!" she pleaded.

"Do you have any evidence? Hard evidence?"

"Not yet, but surely they tell everyone the same thing that they told me. And why would the Mexican and the groom lie about how many mares were bred?"

"You aren't damaged by it, so you don't have a legal claim against them."

She ignored what she didn't want to hear. Anyway, suing them wasn't her goal.

"I think I'm going to be able to get proof of the lies. The next issue of *Arabian Horse International* is doing a story on them. I'll bet you anything that they'll be making statements in print about the number of mares bred."

"You're probably right…"

"I could get the Registry to tell me how many mares were reported to them."

"That's a good idea. I think they'll tell you, but I'm not sure. They may give in to pressure from one of the magazines if they won't give you the information. I can check into the Registry rules and regulations about disclosure of information to the public," he said, making her hopeful.

"You know, none of the Arabian publications would ever do a story about this, or even investigate it. The Ivy's are major advertisers! The publications would lose their business, plus, they never do stories about anything negative in the industry."

"Right. But you could go to the major all breed publications - ones sold on every major newsstand."

"Yeah!"

"So, let's go to sleep," he suggested.

"Wait a minute. This doesn't get me any money!"

"I told you, you can't blackmail them."

As they undressed and brushed their teeth her mind searched for solutions. Under the circumstances, blackmail still seemed to be the only option. Perhaps it was a matter of finesse.

She spit her toothpaste into the sink.

"How about this...I gather the evidence, then show them what I have. Then, I offer them one of my own horses for sale...for a ton of money. I don't threaten them or anything," she said with rising excitement in her voice.

He climbed into bed and covered himself to his waist.

"Speaking legally, you can't. It's an implied threat. Legally, it wouldn't matter that you never said a word about it."

She slipped into the bed next to him.

"I don't like your attitude. I think I need to get another attorney!" she said playfully.

"Fine by me!"

"Fine," she chuckled. It had all become so absurd.

He reached for her waist and drew her close to his body, just wanting to make love then go to sleep.

His words hit her like a ton of bricks. "You said 'speaking legally' – are you trying to tell me something without coming out and saying it?"

He looked into her eyes and a smile crossed his face. She was as sharp as he thought.

"You know, it's a criminal attorney you'll need if you do what you're talking about and things go wrong."

That finally silenced her.

Chapter Seven

Three days later, back home in Scottsdale, she still hadn't received her subscription copy of *Arabian Horse International*. The suspense was killing her.

She dialed the long distance number.

"Arabian Horse International. How can I help you?"

"This is Rene Killian. Is Pat Lodam available?" she asked as she stretched the telephone cord so that she would be in line with the cool air flowing from the air conditioning vent in her family room.

"He's just getting ready to leave the office. I'll see if he can take your call. Just a minute."

"Hello Rene. I've gotta run, I'm on my way to Scottsdale."

Pat heard a rumor that Rene was trying to put together an investment group to buy out the magazine from him. He needed to kiss ass, just in case it was true.

Rene had started the rumor, which had no basis.

"So that's what a publisher does on work days?" she asked, knowing that his humor was similar to hers.

"I do what I want! Are you jealous?"

"If I were you, I wouldn't come to Scottsdale today… it's so hot that even with my thermostat set at 66, I can't cool my house. The palm trees aren't known for their ability to shade!"

"I'm going to Bello to see a new filly that was born early this morning. I haven't been able to keep this mare pregnant for four years… she's 28."

Thinking only of herself, she asked, "Is the new issue out?"

"Just off the press. I approved the blue line, but I haven't even looked at a printed copy yet!"

"Great. Bring an extra copy with you and I'll pick you up at the airport. We'll go see your miracle filly together…unless you have other arrangements."

The flight wouldn't take long once Pat was airborne. They arranged to meet at the Scottsdale Regional Airpark. It was only ten minutes to the farm from the airport and five more minutes the opposite direction to her house.

` ` ` ` ` ` ` ` ` ` `

Rene convinced Pat to give her a chance to pack her bags and fly her to Santa Barbara in his private plane. He was returning to Palo Alto in Northern California anyway. The flight was smooth, but under the circumstances, she was on edge, knowing Jared's threat was still looming over her.

She rented a cherry red Porshe 911 and headed back toward the Santa Ynez area. She planned on checking into the Sheraton in Solvang later in the evening. Still, she hadn't come up with a plan as to how to use the information she had against Ivy Farms.

As she drove through the valley, she spontaneously decided to drop in at CSC, named *C* for Castinitas and *SC* for Wilson St. Claire. Wilson was Dominick's trainer and minority business partner in the horse operation. The gates had been closed when she tried to visit on her last trip. Today, she would claim to be looking for mares to buy for two different clients.

The day was a heavenly, pollution free day, the sun shining in the cloudless sky. As she pulled up to the entrance of CSC, the mailbox flag was up. Adrenaline rush! She couldn't resist.

Casually, she stepped out of her car as close to the mailbox as was physically possible. Walking around the car, she acted as if she were checking the tires - she was actually looking to see if anyone was around. All clear. The black metal of the mail box was surprisingly hot even though it was only seventy degrees outside. Quickly, she grabbed the manila envelope addressed to AHRA in Denver. With practiced expedience she placed the envelope in her briefcase, locked it and covered it with a towel.

The suspense of not knowing what was in the envelope made her pulse race. She didn't dare open it until she left the property. Her face tingled with excitement.

After calming herself, she turned into the CSC driveway and slowly drove down the long oak tree lined blacktop drive. The reception area for the main barn and offices was stunning: life-like oil paintings of famous horses from Poland, fabulous bronze sculptures and other artwork tastefully decorated the three story high walls and massive open space of the Spanish architecture. The spacious area had comfortable leather sofas, coffee tables, a large screen television, a video player, and a fully stocked bar.

A beautiful young vibrant woman with short gelled hair greeted her immediately. "Hello. Can I help you?"

"Yes. I was wondering if you have a sales list and if anyone can give me a short tour."

"I'm sorry, but we don't see people without an appointment. Our staff is very busy. I can give you a sales list though."

"Okay. I appreciate it. I assumed because you have horses in the Ivy Farms auction your farm would be prepared for visitors. Sorry to bother you."

"That's all right," she said as she handed Rene a silver metallic embossed folder. "Please, feel free to make an appointment some other time."

"I'll do that."

"Why don't you go to Ivy Farms and see our consignment horses, since you're in the area," she suggested.

"That's a good idea, thanks."

"Actually, It's almost lunch time. You might want to wait a couple of hours."

"Sure. Thanks for your help."

\ \ \ \ \ \ \ \ \ \ \

Rene drove directly to Ivy Farms, hoping people would be out to lunch. Walking down the barn aisle, the crunching of gravel under her shoes alerted the stalled horses who were munching their hay. Horses peered out the open Dutch doors to see who was in their haven. A few horses nickered, hoping for more grain or juicy apples.

The lounge and office was unlocked. She walked right in, as if she were expected. If anyone had been inside, the clicking of her shoes on the tile floor would attract their attention.

She waited a few minutes in silence.

"Hello, anyone here?" she called out so that it didn't appear that she was snooping if anyone walked in.

No answer.

Nonchalantly, she stuck their guest book into her oversized purse, then casually wandered over to the administrative office.

She continued calling while scanning the offices with her darting eyes looking for anything interesting and confidential.

No answer.

She stepped back out into the lounge and called for someone again.

No answer.

Ignoring the whispered friction of her slacks, she entered Luke Remmacs office. At first glance she was surprised that a trainer had such an elaborate office, then she remembered that image is everything in this business.

Again, she called around.

No answer.

She opened each desk drawer. There was a file folder labeled '*The Freedom Alliance.*' Although she knew she was taking a huge risk, she heisted the entire file, sliding it into the front of her slacks, flat against her stomach. In the bottom drawer she spotted a small canvas notebook with a brass lock on it. A moment later, it was in her briefcase.

One more open office, shared by Chandler and Leslie Ivy. She couldn't resist.

Again, she called for someone.

No answer.

An appointment book and a phone book, each made of fine Italian leather sat open on one of the desks. The next thing she knew, she added them to her collection.

She spotted a stack of paper in the trash can next to the same desk. At a glance, it appeared to be a list of clients with addresses, phone numbers and credit information. She didn't have time to look that closely. The papers fit perfectly in her oversized purse. They wouldn't be missed.

Her heart and pulse pounded as she strolled back to her car, trying not to draw any attention to herself. She was a nervous wreck knowing that anyone from the farm could stop her at anytime. Painted in gold with a dark green background, two signs at the farm entrance were placed where they couldn't be ignored – *'Private Property. No Trespassing'* and *'Horses Shown by Appointment Only.'*

A few miles away, she entered the Lake Cachuma campground. Her heart rate was almost normal. What a relief. She could breath easy now. After driving along the scenic road, she pulled into a view sight of the lake. It didn't take long for her adrenaline to start pumping from anticipation.

Rene ripped open the envelope she stole from the mailbox at CSC. She savored the moment and felt a wave of tension melting away.

Wait till Grady sees this! Now I have the proof!

The Stallion Breeding Record for Freedom: an official document required by the Arabian Horse Registry of America. Each stallion has its own official breeding record. Itemized information on the form included each mare's registration number, the specific breeding dates, and a declaration that the specific mares were bred by hand, by artificial insemination or by pasture breeding. The required document by the Registry was a sworn statement of truth that can only be signed by an authorized person. It was public knowledge that Ivy Farms bought Freedom from CSC.

CSC must have the records because Ivy Farms hasn't paid off Freedom yet!

Next. Her fingers tingled as she browsed through the papers from the trash. It appeared to be people whose credit is approved starting at $100,000 credit limit and going up to $10 million. *Why $10 million?* There's something very strange about such an outrageously large credit limit.

This information could be priceless to her. She was thrilled.

Faint sounds from a car stereo playing Jesse Colin Young startled her - someone in a black Mustang convertible had pulled up next to her Porshe. She couldn't chance reading anything else with someone parked next to her.

Don't get caught now.

The rhythmical pounding of her pulse frightened her. She needed to go somewhere else that this couldn't happen again. The suspense was eating away at her, but she knew she would have to wait.

The 40-minute drive to the coast felt like an eternity. At least it was scenic and there was no rain or fog to inhibit her from absorbing the beauty of the area. It took all of the self-control that she could muster to drive the speed limit on 101 South.

At the beach exit she spotted a Mexican restaurant. A frozen Margarita sounded great just about now. She deserved a private celebration.

Declining the valet's offer to park her car, she selected her own parking space. She nonchalantly looked around to see if she were being followed. Paranoid that someone might have clairvoyant powers to know what she had done, she securely grasped her locked ostrich skin briefcase.

At Rene's request, the hostess sat her on the patio with a view of the ocean. A cocktail waitress promptly brought her a twenty ounce frozen raspberry Margarita. The food waiter took her order for a Chili Relleno dinner.

Finally, she pulled out the leather bound 3-ring style appointment book. On the inside pocket the words *Leslie Ivy,* engraved on a gold nameplate. Inserted in a flap, a light gray notepad with haphazard writing: at least twenty pages written utilizing blue, black, red, and green inks, with no colors seeming particularly significant. Random words were circled. Occasional sentences crossed out but still legible. Phrases and words sketched to make them bold. Words and names with arrows, asterisks and stars next to them. At a glance, there was no rhyme or reason to the writings, but the pad must have importance or Leslie wouldn't have saved the pages.

Next, the appointment book. Mixed in with recognizable names were names she had never heard of, which was only odd because adjacent to several of the unfamiliar names, in parenthesis, there were initials. None of those telephone numbers had area codes.

The final mystery in the notebook. Seven pages with a two column list. In the left column, the name of a horse. In the right column, a list of five to fifteen names with dollar amounts written in parenthesis next to each name. Further down on the page, a different horse and different peoples names and dollar amounts.

Are the same horses being sold to several people?

Rene concentrated on not reacting to what she was reading as she skimmed through more papers. It was almost impossible for her to remain expressionless. She really didn't know what to think... she never dreamed of anything like this.

At last, she put the leather notebook away and locked her briefcase, neglecting to look at *The Freedom Alliance* file.

The hot oval cast-iron platter filled with Chili Relleno, rice and beans arrived just as she was ready to order another drink. As she ate, her mind wandered; she couldn't concentrate or completely develop any single thought. Her head felt like a whirlpool full of information. Hopefully Grady would be able to help her decipher the information.

Rene discretely offered the waitress an extra $20 if she would get her a Margarita 'to go.' She paid her bill and returned to her car holding the briefcase for dear life in one hand and her drink in the other.

After locking the briefcase in her trunk, she activated the car alarm and walked a half block away to the beach - then she doubled back to her car to make sure she had really set the alarm.

Her imported boots were undoubtedly getting ruined from walking in the sand and she knew her clothes would get stained too. She was so ecstatic that she didn't care. Not after a day like today. She partially buried her Margarita in the sand so that it wouldn't spill, then sat down and removed her boots and socks.

The sunset was as magnificent as a postcard. Santa Barbara, on the beach with an exiting future ahead of her - if she could decide what she wanted her future to be, now that she truly had options. She inhaled slow deep cleansing breaths and gazed off toward the surf. The sun lowered itself behind the horizon just as she finished her drink.

She desperately wanted to see Grady, but was worried what he would think about her stealing from the farm.

Should she tell him?

She had nowhere else to go. Suddenly, she was reminded how alone in the world she really was.

Chapter Eight

Four days later...

Grady was trying to fondle Rene under the linen covered dinner table. She tried to ignore him, hoping that he would stop. Morton's Steak House in L.A. didn't seem the appropriate place for him to have been doing this.

It was his turf...and if that's what he wanted...and if that was how she could get what she needed from him to accomplish her plan...well then, what the hell!

"How long have you been Dean's attorney?" she asked, ignoring where his hands were.

"Quite a while! What a character..." Grady laughed as he took another swallow of his scotch.

"What?"

It only took him a split second to reply.

"Where shall I begin? He pays for three illegitimate kids from three different women. I drew up the settlement agreements to pay the mothers not to bother him for anything except child support and college."

"So, the guy's horny and has the money to do right by the women. Big deal!"

"Did you know he had several nervous breakdowns?" he asked, knowing it wasn't public knowledge.

"Are you serious?"

"Yeah. And that's not all. But, I really shouldn't say anything. It might damage his reputation."

"I can't believe you told me what you already have."

"I trust you. After what you confessed to me what you did, I trust you."

Big mistake.

"You mean about the information I found?"

"Found? We both know that's not quite how you got it!"

"I'm surprised you didn't call the police on me! You seemed so straight-laced the last time we talked about this."

Grady smiled. "I guess I was surprised...I've never met a woman like you before."

"I hope that's a good thing?"

He didn't answer the question. "I've got to get to my office after dinner. Do you want to come again?"

Rene wasn't sure. This would be the third consecutive night.

"How long do you plan on working?"

"Pretty late. I need to consult with a couple of different clients by phone, and I need to review a private placement offering for a new limited partnership. It's in a field I've never dealt with...so, to really understand it, I need to go through a sample document with a fine toothed comb," he said, meaning he somehow got a document that another lawyer had drafted.

"Hmm…I don't know. I didn't realize you'd be working so much if I stayed in town."

"Come on! I have to work at night if you're going to drag me to farms during the day!"

Grady tried to keep it lighthearted, but he needed her to be reasonable.

"We entertain your clients at lunch or happy hour…"

She really enjoyed spending time with him and his celebrity clients, but she wasn't going to admit it. Of course, he already knew she loved his new Malibu beachfront condo.

Grady had a suggestion.

"How about doing your own business stuff here instead of when you get back to Scottsdale."

"I don't do any business that requires an office!" she admitted, not feeling very professional.

"Never?"

"Well, occasionally I'll type a thank you letter if I've sold someone a horse, but usually I send my clients a thank you card and a gift, like a crystal of an Arabian horse or a framed print."

"That's it?"

"No! Don't harass me…"

"Can't you think of anything you could work on? Or, how about just writing some friend a long overdue letter."

The more they talked, the more he wanted her to join him at the office again.

"Sure. I'll think of something. Let's change clothes first. I don't want to sit around with this tight dress and high heels on."

He's the one who asked her to dress like that.

Grady paid the dinner check with his American Express card and jotted down the name of the client he would bill for the expense.

They went back to his place. Rene went upstairs, washed off most of her makeup except mascara, and threw on her size six black jeans and a loose fitting silk blouse. When she came down and found Grady smoking a joint, she insisted to drive; he didn't hesitate to agree.

It was becoming a ritual at his office - as soon as he made sure no one else was in the office working late, they made love on his sofa. The first three nights it was exciting, but tonight Rene just wanted to get it over with fast. She wondered if he did this with everyone he had dated more than a few times.

Once they were dressed again, he showed her how to use one of his word processors in case she wanted to type a letter. Initially, she was complimented that he trusted her. She knew that no one should. It didn't seem right that he willingly gave her access to client information. The files in his office weren't locked up, and he directly told her about private matters concerning his clients using their names. He divulged things that she could never know otherwise.

Grady boasted about common legal practices the general public wasn't aware of. He confessed that most legal documents were 'boiler plate' prepared on a word processor. For instance, he said, he charged his first client $20,000 for the legal documents for a stallion syndication. He developed and provided documents customized for that client. Everything is now on the word processor. Each subsequent client gets charged $20,000 for their stallion syndication documents. In reality, the word processor document is changed to reflect the few items that are customized to that client:

the name of the stallion, sire, dam, birth date, number of breedings per year, sales price of the share, general partner's name and address, etc. Also included were the SEC filing forms. Simple things. Things that one of his legal secretaries does, and it takes perhaps two hours of her time, including the time for printing out the 80 page document. He reviews her work for an hour, if that. Grady still gets $20,000. He even bragged about it to her. He told her that a lot of his work was that way. Limited partnership agreements, contracts for record deals, film production contracts, and all sorts of things. Once he had the information he needed, he'd churn it out. He made it sound so simple, claiming all he was required to do was keep up with the laws in each specific field. It sounded unethical to her, but if it was illegal or unethical, she couldn't imagine his doing such a thing.

Don't lawyers take some sort of oath?

She overheard Grady talking to a client on the telephone about the potential terms of a recording contract. Bored, she turned up the music at one of the secretary stations so that he would close his office door. Able to tell when he hung up the phone because the light at the telephone console would go off, she decided to snoop around. He made it too easy.

When she felt sure he wouldn't know what she was doing, she went through his files of people in the Arabian business she knew or heard of. If she found a file of interest to her, she simply made copies of the documents and slipped them into her purse.

Rene found a file for a great stallion named Commando. The stallion was owned and bred by the Jablome family, a well respected family with a reputation for being good breeders and honest business people. Commando had won championships in every class he entered, and as a result, he was later syndicated for $10 million dollars. Commando became a leading sire of show champions.

Rene was surprised Grady represented the family that owned the stallion, because their son, Haywood, was a lawyer with a thriving equine law practice in Kentucky.

This file may be interesting.

At first, she didn't see the connection. After reading the Commando file for the third consecutive time, she put the pieces together. Haywood had prepared legal documents for the Commando syndication, and submitted the syndicate offering for approval to the Securities and Exchange Commission. Apparently, the SEC denied approval, based on the inadequacies of the legal documents. The formal letter of denial from the SEC was addressed to Mr. and Mrs. Jablome.

It appeared that Haywood's parents went to Grady with the documents and denial letter. There was a syndicate document with yellow highlighting throughout and accompanying notes in the margins. Grady apparently remedied the errors and inadequacies, which were substantial. Also in the file was a letter from Grady to Mr. and Mrs. Jablome explaining he actually had to rework the entire syndication. The letter assured them that he would not disclose what their son had done, which he considered malpractice. Also in the file was an approval letter from the SEC.

No information about mortality insurance and a veterinary examination, she noticed.

Now, this is getting interesting!

Rene could have a good time with Grady while it lasted. The sex was great and she was sure able to learn a lot about people in the business and about equine law.

That night, they left his office at about 10:30, arriving at his condo at eleven. The living room overlooked the ocean and a long wooden pier. When she was out on the balcony, he approached her holding a hand held mirror with four lines of cocaine.

She was flabbergasted - a sneer uncontrollably swept her face. Never having personally been exposed to drug use, she always thought of users as being bums, burn outs, hippies or rock stars. Of course, she heard that people from all walks of life used coke, but had never actually met anyone who admitted it to her.

"I know it's none of my business, but..." Grady put his hand out, as if to tell her to stop talking.

"Come on, let me finish..."

"You've already admitted that whatever you were going to say is none of your business, so don't bother!"

"I'm saying it anyway, or I'm leaving right now."

Grady took her seriously now.

"I don't like the idea of you being stoned."

"You drinking alcohol. What's the difference?"

"It's different and you know it. Alcohol is socially acceptable, it's legal, and I'm not drunk."

"Well, I'm not working, and I'm not driving, and there's no one here to bust me. What's your problem?"

"It's just the idea. And... I'm worried about you."

"You don't know me well enough to be worried..."

"Come on! We've been seeing each other for..."

"Listen, this is how I cope. Just leave it alone. I don't have a problem I can't deal with. I know what I'm doing."

"Well, the drugs bother me. A lot."

"We're not married... you can leave whenever you want."

"I'd like to help you. Do you want to talk about her? About what happened?"

"No. Not with you. That's why I have a shrink. Look, just forget it, okay."

Rene decided to drop the subject for the time being, not having any idea how to handle the situation. It wasn't as if they were in love and contemplating a future together, yet, she ached for him and whatever his pain was that made him want to escape it whenever he could.

She assertively told him she'd stick to her wine, thanks. They stayed up all night long. Grady continued to drink wine, smoke pot and do lines. It made him very anxious to talk.

"At your office I saw that the Jablomes are clients of yours. I've bought quite a few Commando bred mares for clients. Do you own a share in Commando?" Rene asked.

Grady laughed hysterically, but to Rene, it was an odd laugh. Not the kind of laughter she ever heard from him before.

"What's so funny?"

He was so stoned, he explained.

"You know, whatever I tell you is confidential. You can't tell anyone. Not even your closest friend."

"I assumed that, yes."

"Commando is not the horse you think he is."

"I think he's a great horse!"

He took another hit from the joint. "You don't understand. Think about the words I'm using...Commando is not the horse you think he is!"

"You're stoned. I'm going to sleep," she said as she started to stand up, ready to go upstairs.

He took her by the hand, clearly wanting her to stay with him. "Do you promise you can keep a secret?"

"Sure."

"I mean a really big secret! You really have to promise."

She was uncomfortable about how stoned he sounded.

"Yes. I can keep any sized secret."

"Do you know Haywood?"

"No. Not personally at least."

"Well, you know the Jablomes owned a mare with a nothing pedigree, and that eventually, they bred the mare, and the resulting foal was Commando. He was stunning. After a few years of professional conditioning, training and showing him, he became National Champion Stallion. He was four years old at the time and had one small foal crop."

Rene was anxiously waiting to hear something she didn't know.

"A few prominent stallions were being syndicated. It was a concept new to Arabians. Mr. Jablome convinced his wife that they should syndicate Commando because he had just won National Champion. Of course, they discussed it with Haywood because he could do all of the legal work for them."

Now, maybe he'll get to the interesting part.

She changed positions so that she could massage his neck and shoulders, hoping he would relax more and let his guard down even further.

"Haywood drew up the legal documents and they hired someone else to do the marketing materials. His parents and their trainer began promoting the syndicate at some major horse shows on the West Coast. The shares were selling quickly and easily. They were all so excited!"

He stopped and lit up another joint before he elaborated. Now, instead of the laughter the conversation started out with, he seemed distressed.

The suspense was excruciating.

"They received the down payments from all of the people who contracted to buying shares…a total of $500,000. Of course, they paid out all of that money for marketing costs and commissions. Installment payments were to be made over a ten year time span, giving the buyers a great tax advantage since they could depreciate the cost of the share 100% over a seven-year period. They knew that after the first year of the syndication, they would collect their profits from the subsequent payments."

"I'm glad it worked out for them."

"The Jablomes live on a mini-ranch with a few stalls," Grady's facial expression looked pained as he continued. "Four months after the syndicate shares were all sold, out of the blue, in his stall at home, Commando had congestive heart failure and died."

His breathing accelerated and his eyes got red. He snorted another line of coke.

"What do you mean? Commando's not dead! You're stoned!"

"It broke their hearts. The whole family loved that horse. Haywood told me everything. Trust me. Just listen. I can't believe I'm even telling you. "

Rene was confused, not knowing what to think. "It must have been horrible," she said, wondering if he was telling the truth or not.

"Haywood's parents were in shock when they found him. They went to the barn to give him his night hay and he was already stiff. His legs were sticking straight out as if he were standing up - and his eyes were wide open."

"My heart aches just imagining it."

She started to cry.

"Haywood said he could hear his mom in hysterics in the background when his dad called him to tell him what happened. She was there for Commando's birth and had always been the driving force in his career."

"I heard how dedicated she is to him. I thought it was marketing hype."

Rene felt guilty for her assumption.

"Once it sunk into Haywood's head what his dad said, he panicked."

"Panicked?"

He took a couple more hits from his joint as he weighed his words.

"Yeah. He panicked! As the acting attorney for the syndicate, he collected money from each shareholder to purchase mortality insurance, but ended up needing the money to cover his own payroll, business bills he couldn't pay on time, and major personal expenses. He intended to obtain the mortality insurance as soon as he was paid by clients who owed him substantial sums."

"So Mr. and Mrs. Jablome didn't know the shareholders weren't insured?"

"No. That's where the rest of the nightmare starts. The other thing Haywood didn't tell them was he never submitted the syndicate documents for SEC approval before they started selling the shares. It was on his 'to do' list. Selling the shares without SEC approval is illegal."

"They must have been furious when they found everything out!"

By now, the way he was telling the story, it sounded as if it were the truth.

"You haven't heard the worst of it. You better not tell anybody what I'm telling you."

"I won't tell."

It was the last thing on her mind. She just wanted to hear the whole story.

"Like I said, once it sunk in, Haywood panicked. So, he called his dad right back and he instructed him not to tell anyone about Commando - not even other family members, until he could take care of a few things. I'm sure his dad was confused by his reaction, but didn't know what to think. Haywood told him he would be right over to help bury Commando in the rear of their property. Mr. Jablome said he wouldn't call anyone."

"That's good."

What else could she say?

"It took him over an hour to get to their place. They have ten acres of horse property. Haywood dug a grave with their backhoe. Father and son maneuvered the lifeless body into the grave and covered it with dirt. He spent the night at their house and the next morning called into his office sick, informing them not to expect him for the next several days."

"What did they say?"

"Nothing. He's the boss."

"That's true."

"A couple of months before all this, he had heard about a horse that looked identical to Commando. It wasn't unusual that one horse could look like the spitting image of another, so when a friend told him that some small time backyard breeder owned a horse that looked like Commando, he filed it in the back of his mind to go see him sometime."

"Did he go?"

What does this have to do with anything?

"Not before Commando died. He went the day after he died."

Now I'm totally confused.

"He said he called the owners of the look alike and told them he thought it would be fun to own a horse that looked so much like Commando, and they agreed. It took a half day of driving to get to their farm. Sure enough, this horse was his clone. Haywood offered $20,000 for the horse.

"They jumped at the offer and even loaned him their truck and horse trailer. The horse was loaded up and he drove straight through, back to his parent's ranch, arriving in the middle of the night. His mom and dad woke up when they saw the lights and heard the truck. Haywood unloaded the horse and put him in Commando's stall. Once the horse was calm, eating and drinking, Haywood confessed everything to his parents."

"I can't believe it! What did they say?"

"Naturally, they were heartbroken and disappointed in him. Apologies didn't mean anything at such a stressful time. He begged them to carry on as if the stallion was actually Commando.

"The Jablomes were appalled. They refused, until he explained his dilemma: he'd certainly be disbarred from practicing law, would surely be sued by the shareholders, and could even end up in prison. His parents had to agree with his plan. What else could they do? He's their son. They couldn't let one mistake ruin everything he worked for and destroy his entire life.

"Commando was dead and there was nothing that they could do about it. He only had eight foals on the ground, so people couldn't really claim that this stallion didn't produce the same quality they had seen. Breeding to a young stallion is very risky and all of the shareholders knew it. The Jablomes reluctantly went along with their son's plea."

"He's lucky they love him so much. That's as unconditional as it gets. My parents would have disowned me," Rene said seriously.

"Two days later, after he rested from the ordeal of getting this look-alike horse from one farm to the other, Haywood started to drive the trailer back to the owners. When he reached an area of the coast with a really steep cliff at a view area turn-off, he backed up their truck and trailer to the cliff. He opened the driver's door and kind of hung outside of it and released the emergency brake, then jumped away as quick as he could. The truck and trailer rolled backward down 300 feet into the ocean."

Rene didn't know when she would stop being totally amazed.

"You're serious? This whole story is really unbelievable."

"Why would I make it up?"

"You're stoned! You probably want to see how gullible I am!"

"I am telling the truth! Anyway, Haywood flagged down someone on the highway. He had tears in his eyes, and told the driver that his new horse had been in the trailer, which was not retrievable. The driver told him he would call the police from the first phone he could locate and send the police to the site.

"When the police arrived, he introduced himself, making sure they knew he was an attorney. He told them that he purchased the horse, but when he got him to his parent's ranch, the horse just wouldn't settle in. Haywood said he was taking the horse back to the original owners to care for him in the environment the horse was used to. He explained that he was planning on paying them for board and training and would visit the horse as much as possible.

"The police didn't even consider questioning the story. They drove him to the police station to file a report, notify his insurance company, and call for a ride. Eventually, his dad picked him up at a restaurant near the station."

Rene couldn't believe his dad had gone so far to protect him.

"I can't believe it!"

"Anyway, after they got back to their house, Haywood called the people who he bought the horse from and told them the whole horrible fabricated story. They believed him. No one ever talked about the other stallion that looked identical to Commando again."

"I can't believe it! The stallion, the new Commando, ended up being one of the leading producers of show horses!"

"Why would you even know any of this?" she asked in an accusing tone.

"Because a week after all of this happened, the entire family came to me for legal advice, and they hired me to take over the legal matters of the syndicate," he said, sounding completely straight now.

"Wow! This is incredible. I guess everything worked out for the syndicate members and for the Jablomes though. That's good, at least."

"Haywood never was able to come up with the insurance money. His parents spent their own money to insure all of the member's shares and their own for that year. 3% of ten million! They had to dig into their life savings."

"Well, they did make a hell of a lot of money from the horse! I heard they sold the promissory notes to Prosperity Savings Bank in Ohio," she said, wanting him to know she knew a little inside information on her own.

"They did. They cashed out as soon as they could. I set it up. I recommended they sell the notes for a 30% discount and not take a chance of buyers defaulting on their contracts, or even having to deal with collection issues."

"I thought Prosperity Savings Bank only discounts 20%," she said.

"Normally, that's what they do, but they needed to add in a small commission to me, and because it was a ten year note instead of the normal three to five year note, they wanted to discount it more."

"Even though they were getting 12% interest from the syndicate shareholders?"

"Sure. Who knows...the market could collapse anytime... the bank would lose a ton of money. If they had too much invested in horse loans, it could put them out of business."

"The market's not going to drop out! It's going up 30% a year," she said, as if he had said something outlandish.

"You know how conservative banks can be. If it weren't for Craig Zillman being an Arabian fanatic, his bank wouldn't even be dealing in the horse industry at all. Most banks won't touch anything having to do with horses. They think it's too risky, even with mortality insurance."

"I know. I've had clients try to borrow money to buy horses and they couldn't use the horses as the collateral no matter how good their credit or how good of a relationship they had with their bank."

"Craig went through hell convincing his board of directors to loan on Arabians and to buy discounted promissory notes."

"I wonder how he finally convinced them," she said as she reached for some pretzels.

"He bought a farm with his own money and credit, and told the board of directors that if there were defaults, they could repossess the horses. The backup plan was to have his farm take care of the horses, breed them, and resell them so the bank wouldn't lose any money."

"Seriously?"

"Sure. It's a good plan. He's always got someone wanting to give him horses for free..."

She interrupted. "Why would anyone give him free horses?"

"As an incentive for him to approve buying promissory notes from them. Anyone who syndicates a stallion, even for only $5 million, if they can cash out for $4 million by selling the note to Prosperity, they have it made. People are always offering him really good horses for free, as a gift, for him to approve buying their notes. So, they have a stallion they don't have much cash into, they syndicate it for $5 million, payout 20% in commissions, and maybe $50,000 for legal expenses and marketing costs, then discount the note to Prosperity, and they still have at least $2 million left in profit. It's good business!"

"I never really thought about the details," she said.

"Stick with me. You've got a lot to learn."

"No kidding! Is that what the Scottsdale farms that hold the auctions do? I know Prosperity buys a lot of their notes at their auctions."

"Yes. Craig's gotten a couple of dozen really quality horses for himself that way."

"I can't believe banking regulations would permit that."

"Grow up!"

"What?"

"The banking regulators don't know...and his board of directors doesn't know! It's done on the side. Are you naïve or what?"

"How can he do that?"

"It's just how things work. Just business."

"So he has this herd of horses that he didn't pay for, and all he has to do is pay for stud fees and he sells the horses for the same kind of prices everyone else gets?"

Grady laughed so hard his stomach hurt. "Use your brain! He doesn't pay for stud fees. The big stallion owners give him free breedings so they can borrow money to buy horses."

"Shit! No wonder I can't get anywhere in this business. I don't know the ins and outs of the big timers. Even now that I know, I don't have a way to work with Craig like this."

"It's about time you're seeing the light."

"I wish I could see the light at the end of the tunnel," she said as her voice trailed off.

She thought she was disillusioned before. How much more was there to discover? Grady was coming in handy.

The next thing they knew, the sun was rising. Grady showered and dressed for the office; Rene went out to the beach and slept the day away. When he returned home in the late afternoon he didn't act as if he confided anything. She wondered if he remembered what he had told her about Commando. She didn't make any references to his disclosure about his clients.

That night after dinner, she flew back home to do some serious thinking. She had bought Commando daughters for Jared and several of her other clients.

Chapter Nine

A few weeks later... September 28, 1983
Santa Barbara, California

The band played just loud enough to make it festive, but not so loud that the bartenders couldn't hear the drink orders being placed by roaming cocktail waitresses and by the potential buyers at the portable bars.

To everyone's surprise, the sales pavilion was designed and built specifically for this auction. It housed an elevated stage, banquet tables and chairs close to the stage, an auditorium style seating area set behind the tables and chairs, a commercial style bar, reception area, kitchen, offices and an elaborate sales barn. The public areas were decorated in the theme of Broadway and Manhattan, NY.

Rumors were circulating about the stage scenery alone costing over $200,000 to build. Everyone said that Dominick Castinitas insisted on the theme, even though he only had a handful of horses in the auction. He paid over half the cost to decorate it the way he wanted it.

The full color auction catalog, printed on the highest quality paper, had three coats of varnish and a metallic colored cover with an embossed farm logo. Inside, there were twenty color photos of Freedom, Aston and other reference sires - and a full page color photo of each of the 32 horses being sold. Adjacent to each horse, another full page of information, including a five generation pedigree and production record. Most people took at least one catalog. The catalog, a work of art itself, was a valuable reference tool during the auction. For many people, it would be a collector's item.

Grady and Rene planned to attend the auction together, but at the last minute he canceled, claiming he had an important recording contract proposal to work on. She wondered if he simply decided he didn't want to be seen dating her.

Rene made her entrance decked out in a stunning designer black sequence ensemble. The floor length dress had the back cut to a low V down to her thin waist; the side was slit up the left to her mid-thigh. Her flat stomach and firm breasts were perfect for the dress. In Santa Barbara, an hour before she arrived, she had her hair professionally pinned and a professional make-up artist worked miracles. Her coordinated shoes and handbag finished the look that she was after.

All of the women were impeccably dressed, but Rene didn't feel secure about fitting in with the elite crowd. At least her appearance fit in – it was her bank account and line of credit which didn't belong there.

"Do you have an invitation?" one of the ring men working the auction asked Rene when she approached the banquet table area.

She handed him the engraved invitation, acting as if he should recognize her name.

"Yes. Thanks."

The tuxedo-clad man consulted his seating chart. People with invitations had reserved seats in preferred locations.

"Please follow me."

The ring man led Rene to a table that was an insult - it was the third row back and too far to the side. There was no way she would tolerate this. She fumed through each delicate bite of chocolate covered strawberries from the platter in the center of the table. No one else was being seated yet, so she ate, and ate, and ate. The next thing she knew, there were stems, and only a couple of strawberries left on the platter. What else could she do but finish those off? When she was sure no one was looking, she slid the empty platter under the table where no one would see it, thanks to the long white linen table cloth.

As more people were being seated, she knew the ring man would never remember where he sat her. Nonchalantly, she moved to a second row center table and seated herself where she would face center stage. Now, her back wouldn't be turned toward the stage and people wouldn't have a side view of her. She hated her profile.

Admiring Hearts-A-Fire, Lot #1 in the catalog, Rene daydreamed about owning a horse of her stature. Her sire, Bardon, was a Polish National Champion Stallion, and her dam was a Coment daughter. Hearts-A-Fire descended from bloodlines that commanded more money than all other Polish mares in the breed.

Determination set in beyond anything she believed she was capable of - with what she had on Ivy Farms, she just may be able to acquire a Bardon daughter for herself. Sitting at the table, her mind wandered, lost in her own world, calculating a plan.

Ultimately, the deceit by Ivy Farms would eventually seriously damage the legitimate people who were in fact buying the syndicate shares, buying the breedings, buying the get of the stallions, and buying mares in foal to the stallions. The value of the horses was a result not only of the quality of individual and pedigree, but from supply and demand.

When the truth surfaced, it would disgrace the entire Arabian horse industry. Misrepresenting the demand of their stallions was an unforgivable sin in Rene's eyes. And, of course, the other issues involved in their criminal activity were reprehensible. It wouldn't take long for their legitimate clients to be negatively affected. No wonder the industry had a questionable reputation - things like this forced honest people out of the horse business.

In Rene's eyes, she had every right to be the judge and jury in this situation. She didn't exactly know how, when or where, but she was unwavering in her quest to make them pay.

As instructed by the farm, noticing that her glass was almost empty, the cocktail waitress brought Rene a fresh vodka and tonic. Two tables away, Rene spotted John McKenzie, one of the people she was confident would be bidding on Hearts-A-Fire. He was collecting some of the best Pure Polish horses in the world, paying top dollar for them. John and Rene had spent time together on numerous occasions at functions such as this, and had casually spoken on the phone a few times.

Rene approached John at his table, holding out her hand to avoid being kissed on the cheek. She sensed it wasn't sincere, but he greeted her with warmth and introduced her to the other people at his table.

After the pleasantries, she leaned close toward him.

"I'm sure you must be interested in Hearts-A-Fire, but in all good conscience, I must tell you that I heard through the grapevine that the reason she's being sold is because she has a history of colic," Rene conspiratorially said in a barely audible voice. "I checked her auction health records, and there is no record that she ever did, but I feel obliged to inform you of what I heard. I'd only hope you would do the same for me in a similar situation."

"Thanks. I'll certainly give that information serious consideration. I appreciate your coming to me," John quietly responded.

She excused herself the moment the announcer appeared on stage and the music abruptly stopped. Settling back in her own seat, she glanced over toward John and saw him whispering to the gentleman next to him, who in turn disappeared into the crowd of people returning to sit at their respective tables.

Hopefully his quick departure had something to do with the false rumor she had just started. If Hearts-A-Fire sold for much under $1 million (the average price paid for Bardon daughters at public auction), chances were, most, if not all, of the bidders on her had become concerned about the rumor. She would soon find out.

The announcer, dressed in a black silk tux was very handsome, as was everyone else that worked for the Specialty Auction Company, including the spotters who took the bids from the audience.

Dominick Castinitas was introduced - he gracefully walked on stage and received a standing ovation.

"Hello! I'm pleased to see a full house! I'm disappointed you didn't pay for your seats as you would at one of my Broadway productions…but, that's the business!"

The crowd laughed.

"As you all know, this production is put on by Chandler and Leslie Ivy, owners of this magnificent farm. I thank them for allowing me to greet you tonight. I'm proud to be the breeder of Freedom, and I have to admit, I often regret that I sold him when he was just a few months old! I'm proud to offer several of my own horses at their auction this evening.

"I wanted to personally tell those of you who don't already know about my dedication to the Polish Arabian and the great breeding directors of Poland. The bloodlines from Poland are the very foundation of this establishment and my own farm, Castinitas/St. Claire. From my heart, I want you to understand the combination of great joy and enormous regret at selling the horses that we have selected to offer in this very special auction. Thank you for coming…and thank you for your support of this historic event."

Somehow, Dominick smiled as tears glistened in his deep set eyes.

In a flash, he disappeared from the stage in a cloud of special effects smoke. The live ten piece band started up again after the audience applauded with enthusiasm and respect.

Rene's mind wandered off briefly. She visualized herself as one of the affluent women at the auction with a handsome husband at her side directing her to buy whatever horses her heart desired, reminding her that money was no object.

Bursting out from a cloud of smoke, Freedom, with his high-stepping trot and animated action, appeared on the stage, ridden English by Chandler Ivy. The stallion, pumped-up by the loud up-beat music, smoke machines, strobes and colored lights, was well aware of his importance. The scene was nothing short of spectacular.

Next, Leslie Ivy ran onto the stage leading the sleek silver-gray stallion, Aston, who paraded across the stage wearing a twenty-four carat gold halter. The crowd roared and clapped. The two stallions gave their full attention to the audience. It was as if they were on the stage daily with all of the ambiance and as if this were an everyday response from masses of people to whom they were exposed. The stallions were not at all stressed by any of the hoopla.

In order to mentally prepare the crowd to spend freely, traditionally, auctions always began with the best horse, which presumably brings the most money. Putting the best horse first also encourages the crowd to arrive early for the start of the auction. Even people that weren't buyers always stayed until the end.

Tonight's auction began with Hearts-A-Fire. The smooth talking auctioneer attempted an opening bid for $500,000, but no one responded. Henry Copper, the color man, glorified the attributes of the mare and her pedigree. To everyone's surprise and disappointment, except Rene's, the bidding started at $200,000. Taking much longer than it should have, the gavel fell on Lot #1.

"Sold! $750,000. Thank you, buyer number 54!" the auctioneer called out.

No one stood in the crowd. My rumor worked. She was a no sale!

As is customary in reputable auctions, for the remainder of the evening, when each subsequent horse was sold, the buyer's name was announced. Then, at their seat, someone handed them a bottle of champagne and preliminary paperwork to sign as their photograph was being taken.

Rene surmised that the auctioneer was instructed not to allow slow bidding or small increments for any of the horses.

The thirty-one other mares averaged $125,000 each, not factoring in the supposed selling price of Hearts-A-Fire for $750,000.

Immediately after the auction was over, Rene stepped outside the rear exit for some privacy. Hearts-A-Fire was being loaded into a two-horse trailer and hauled off. Now, she was sure the mare wasn't really sold, unless the buyer paid green cash dollars, which was doubtful. A seller never releases a horse from their possession until payment has cleared the bank. But still, why was she leaving the property so soon?

When the crowd thinned out some, about an hour later, Rene approached Leslie Ivy.

"Leslie, I need to speak with you first thing in the morning," she informed him in an assertive voice.

"I'm not taking any appointments for at least four or five days. I'm exhausted," he said, looking toward the clients still lingering around the horses.

Without giving her a chance to respond, he turned on his heels and walked off to speak with one of the new buyers.

Infuriated that Leslie had declined her, she ordered another vodka and tonic at the bar. As if watching a play, she stood near a wall, loathing the excited new owners, studying their demeanor, and listening to their polite, shallow and one-dimensional conversations. Observing them impassioned her. She couldn't control her jealousy. Rage slowly radiated through her.

Why couldn't she have that much money?

Somehow, someday, she would be rich, but *she* would appreciate it. So many of these people didn't have a clue that they purchased some of the world's finest Polish Arabians. That's what made her most resentful.

Jacque Jardine, aka J.J., a close friend and colleague of Rene's from Brazil, stood near the doorway to the pavilion and spoke to Luke until Leslie summoned him to show a new buyer their horse.

J.J. spotted Rene, then approached her cautiously because she seemed almost trance-like. Normally, he would have come up to her and given her a long hug.

"Hi Rene! I didn't see you earlier. Are you with a client?"

Startled, she lost her footing in the fresh cedar shavings that covered the dirt floor.

J.J. braced her by the arm. "Sorry... I didn't mean to catch you off guard!"

After regaining her composure and repositioning her high heels in the cedar shavings, her eyes brightened and she gave him an affectionate hug. It was as if he had rescued her.

"I'm sorry, I was thinking about something. I'm tired, but I'm fine."

She didn't want to let go of the embrace.

J.J. brokered Arabian horses overseas. His business brought him to the U.S. twice a year to purchase horses for his clients who imported them to Brazil and Europe. J.J. and Rene had no feelings of competition with each other, making it a comfortable relationship. They understood the value of clients, of protecting them, of how difficult it could often be to acquire new clients, and even more difficult to have the clients deal with them exclusively.

Last year, on a beautiful beach in Monte Carlo, Rene and J.J. talked from sunset to sunrise while they were at a World Horse Organization of Arabians conference. Although they spent at least some time at all of the events that they ran into each other, Monte Carlo generated a bond between them that created a special intimacy and fond memories.

While in Monte Carlo, they were both experiencing a frustrating lull in obtaining new clients and in selling their current clients' horses. The support they shared helped them through a difficult period. Neither of them actually needed the money - it was more a matter of feeling a great sense of accomplishment when they were selling or a feeling of failure when they weren't selling. When sales weren't being made, it felt as if they were being rejected, both personally and professionally.

"So, are you here with a client?" J.J. repeated.

"No. Unfortunately, I don't have anyone who wants to buy right now. Even if I did, they'll only pay me a 5% commission. I would have discouraged all of my clients that were interested in coming. I'd convinced them that I could buy them horses for a better value. I certainly couldn't tell them that I wouldn't make enough money from their purchase, so please don't buy!" she said with a sly grin on her face.

"Chandler offered me 10%, and I know he's offered a lot of the top trainers 20% commission."

"Look at this crowd. It looks like they're doing a lot of work getting new people in the business. I think it's great, so long as they would quit taking the people I get interested," she answered.

"Right before the auction I heard the Bardon daughter has a history of colic. Did you hear about it?"

When he asked her this, J.J.'s eyes said he knew she started the rumor. She told him her dream was to have a Bardon daughter.

"Do you know who bought her? It was strange they only announced a number."

She acted as if she didn't notice what his eyes were saying.

He shook his head.

"I don't think anyone bought her! The Ivys probably made the last bid. The bidding was low and slow. She was just a draw for the auction anyway. You know how these auctions put in a certain horse to draw the crowds, then something happens to the horse, or some crazy story. They get their crowd and don't end up parting with the horse. Same old story," Rene said, disillusioned.

During an uncomfortable silence J.J. looked out the tall double doors of the arena and spotted Luke walking to the valet and then to the parking lot.

"Would you like another drink?" he asked, wanting to keep her occupied.

"Vodka and tonic, tall. Thanks."

Tired of being on her feet with high heels in the deep shavings, she found a park bench nearby in a setting that she assumed was intended to look like Central Park. She admired Dominick's creativity in making the huge area appear to be another world. The impeccable quality made the atmosphere more unique and enjoyable than the usual auctions, which were flamboyant and glitzy, but not creative. While she waited for her friend and her drink, she wondered if she could meet Dominick without having to introduce herself - she didn't want to resort to that.

At least J.J. was here. He usually only came for the February Scottsdale show and auctions and for the U.S. Nationals. She hoped he could spend more time with her. At this moment, it punctuated how lonely she felt.

J.J. returned with the drinks. He uncharacteristically sat closer than necessary for a friendly conversation, his body facing her. In one way it was menacing and in another way his closeness was comforting and felt protective.

In a smooth movement he casually put an arm around her shoulder.

"Is there anything you want to talk about?"

She hesitated to answer. Her body immediately tensed up and her hands became clammy. Unsure of her desire to talk about what really was on her mind, she chose to decide later.

"Can we meet for brunch tomorrow? I'm so exhausted right now."

"Then you shouldn't be having another drink. I'll get us coffee."

Before she had a chance to tell him she wanted cream, he took her drink from her hand without asking, then went directly to the coffee and dessert table.

Glad that he didn't push her to talk about it, she relaxed. Most of the tension drained from her body. She wished she could lie down on a comfortable sofa with a big pillow to cuddle.

When he returned carrying two coffees with cream, he sat next to her at a distance that he could gently rub her neck with one hand. They didn't utter a sound. The quiet said more than any words could. At that rare moment, Rene felt lucky. She considered the possibility that the world wasn't as bad as she usually thought it was. Being comforted by her friend was exactly what she needed.

When their coffee cups were empty he suggested a late night snack. Waiting for the valet attendants, they agreed to meet at Anderson's Split Pea Restaurant. J.J. tipped the attendant fifty dollars for bringing her Ferrari, which she had driven from Scottsdale. Hopefully, the right people had seen her in it.

As she went to sit in the driver's seat, she stumbled. The valet commented that perhaps she had had too much to drink in order to drive safely. She insisted she was fine and explained that her hotel was only 15 miles away. Once in the driver's seat, she noticed that someone, presumably the valet, had looked at the papers on the passenger seat. There was nothing of any significance: only the hotel receipt, farm brochures and sales lists from other farms in the area. She didn't comment.

J.J. bent down to the open driver's window and gently kissed her on the cheek. With a brotherly demeanor, he told her to drive safely.

She drove with the windows open and her hair flying in the wind while *"Lying Eyes"* by the Eagles played on her Bose stereo. Even exhausted, she couldn't clear her mind about how Leslie treated her. To stay alert driving, she hypothesized as to how she would get revenge against him personally. Out of the blue she realized she had driven at least ten miles past the road she needed to turn at. By the time she turned around and made it to the restaurant, she was drowsy. Inside, she didn't find J.J..

He must have left when I didn't show up.

It felt like a long journey, but she finally made it back to the Sheraton in Solvang. Before getting out of the car, she took off her shoes, knowing for certain she would sprain an ankle if she walked on them any longer. She'd rather ruin her silk stockings and have dirty feet than to sprain an ankle. The valet at the hotel was obviously accustomed to seeing women in dress clothes and barefoot… he simply looked at her feet and grinned.

She walked through the lobby to the elevator, not noticing that someone trying to conceal a two-way radio was watching her.

Chapter Ten

In room 220, the two-way radio sounded.

"She's on her way up."

"Can you stall her? I haven't looked under the mattress or in the chair cushions."

"Damn! She's already in the elevator."

"I need a few minutes!"

"You can't! Get out of there."

Rene exited the elevator and began searching her purse for her room key while walking down the long hallway.

Luke closed the suitcase he was rifling through.

Unable to find her key, she called the front desk from the house phone next to the ice and vending machines.

Luke hurried out the door and spotted Rene at the end of the hallway. He hoped she wouldn't see him when his back was turned. At a brisk pace, he walked to the emergency stairwell, took the steps two at a time to get to the ground level, and returned to the hotel lobby to meet his accomplice.

Someone promptly let her into her room. She tipped the man $20 and told him she would deal with getting a replacement key the next day. At that late hour, she was too exhausted to recall the fact she had put the key on the passenger seat of her car rather than in her small evening bag.

A message light flashed on the telephone. The front desk told her that J.J. had called and said he would meet her for brunch at 11:00.

They hid the two-way radios under a towel in the back seat of the pearl white BMW and sped away from the Sheraton.

In the quiet of the car, Luke's accomplice fidgeted during the short drive to Anderson's Split Pea Restaurant. Without waiting for a hostess, they sat themselves in a green tufted vinyl booth at the rear of the establishment. Their waiter came over with a pot of coffee to leave on the table, greeted them and told them about the specials being offered.

"We'll each have a Denver omelet, dry toast, crispy hash browns and A-1 steak sauce," Luke said.

After the waiter had left, they drank their coffee in silence.

Luke lowered his voice. "Just because I didn't find anything in her room doesn't mean a thing. It could be anywhere. It's been a month. Besides, why would she bring it with her when she travels?"

"Who knows who could've taken it. You don't know for certain that it was her. The building's rarely ever locked. You said that you didn't look for the file for days after you last remember seeing it," he said.

"I've always said we should lock up when no one's there."

"Maybe a secretary accidentally threw the file away. You may never know if it was swiped or if it's just innocently gone."

He was trying to ease Luke's tension.

"All I know is, if Leslie finds out that the only printed copy of the file is missing, he's going to kill me. He'll be furious. I can't believe I spilled coffee on the floppy disks and ruined them. He'll freak out when I tell him."

"What do you think will happen if he finds out?"

Luke took a few sips of coffee. "He'll throw me out on my ass before I can do anything to try to prevent it," he said as perspiration formed above his upper lip and around his collar.

"Couldn't you go back to work for Dominick?" he asked, wondering if anything close to a complete and honest answer would be forthcoming.

Disgusted with himself, Luke answered with a helpless tone of voice. "No, he would never hire me again. I wanted him to keep Freedom when he was a colt. When he sold him to the Ivys, I made this huge ordeal...I said that I'd go wherever Freedom went. Said I didn't need him or his money anymore!" ^^

"How'd you get the job at the Ivy's?" he asked.

"Leslie and Chandler's father offered me the title of 'partner' in his Arabian horse business so I would feel I had roots and security. Old man Ivy is who really owns the farm, at least back when I came on board. He didn't want me to leave for another venture. He knew the boys couldn't do everything by themselves, especially all of the training. In reality, the partnership was a matter of my not being an employee or a hired trainer, for the purposes of farm image and my ego."

"I can see that."

"The partnership agreement says that I get 15% of all net profits, calculated and paid annually, a house to live in, and a regular trainer's salary, to be paid monthly. The old man committed to having sufficient operating capital available to operate the business to its full potential. At the time, I couldn't pass it up."

"Most people couldn't!" he agreed.

"It was a great opportunity, but the agreement didn't address what would happen if there were a conflict. About a year ago, I showed an attorney the agreement. He said it might was well be toilet paper. That's all it's worth. I've got no protection or security, and really, don't even have any substantial rights and have absolutely no equity."

"I never heard about the father before. Why haven't you ever mentioned him?"

"He's not really in the picture. I don't even know if he owns the business anymore."

"Did the old man come to the farm much?"

"The first year I was there, the old man actually lived there, and would go to Chicago when he absolutely had to for business. Then, eventually, they got divorced…Chandler and Leslie say he was abusive to Marsha."

"Sounds like a long story…"

"Yeah. But I can tell you from what I know first hand, the old man sure favored Chandler… half the time he was around the boys, he'd ignore Leslie or he'd be putting him down…humiliating him in front of anyone around."

"Sounds like he was a jerk."

"Yeah. If the old man wasn't arguing with Leslie it was because they weren't talking. There was never anything in between, never a front put on for the family or anyone else. I never heard them say a decent word to each other. And, of course, Chandler and their mom, Marsha, would try to stay out of it, but it was tough on all of them."

"Is that why Leslie's such an ass sometimes?"

"Probably. Can you blame him though? I can't imagine how he grew up…"

Chapter Eleven

Four hours of restless sleep tormented Luke's exhausted body and mind. He woke up startled, in a sweat, overwhelmed by panic. The tension in his neck and shoulders was so intense his temples throbbed. The light of the full moon lit the room enough to outline the furnishings. Laying in bed, mesmerized by the ceiling fan revolving, he decided to do something more productive.

The flooring of his entire house was a Spanish octagon red brick tile. He loved the floor because it cooled his bare feet, helping him invigorate his body at dawn. He liked getting up and going before the farm was operational. The peace and serenity were part of what he cherished about his life. Since moving to Santa Barbara, usually, he was relaxed enough to pay attention to the horses nickering in the pasture closest to his house. At sunrise, the foals always whinnied in excitement from instigating a chasing game with their siblings and their mothers.

In his spacious sunlit kitchen he brewed a pot of hazelnut coffee. The aroma triggered his memory. He drifted back to before he worked for Dominick, back when he lived in Connecticut in a modest studio apartment above the barn where he worked. Once he was working for Dominick in California, it didn't take long for him to grow accustomed to his professionally decorated Spanish style three bedroom home, gourmet coffee, an expense account, ideal training and breeding facilities, plenty of labor, and countless other benefits and amenities. The Ivys gave him almost as nice a house and the same perks. His fear of losing his lifestyle over the missing file ate at him.

This morning, his mind searched for the possibilities as to who had The Freedom Alliance file. If he knew for certain that Rene stole the file, he wouldn't hesitate to confront her. On the other hand, if she hadn't stolen it and he confronted her, she was sure to realize there was something to be astonishingly suspicious of. He knew she would always hold the accusation against him. Knowing her, she would spread a story in the industry about how offended she was and that there must be something unusually confidential in the file to be accusing someone of stealing it. Undoubtedly, the story would get blown out of proportion each time it was told. Rumors in this business were created and spread like wildfire.

Being one of the leading Arabian trainers and showmen in the country didn't make Luke any friends, other than with his own clients. Amateur competitors didn't get too friendly with him, which was understandable, but Luke couldn't imagine that any amateur competitor would actually be an enemy. Their coolness to him was based more on a jealousy over his having so much talent, and the fact that he was more likely to win than they were. Amateurs quickly learned about the politics of showing. He couldn't imagine an amateur being so revengeful as to steal a file.

Luke was brilliant to have amassed a financial cushion from working for Dominick. He skimmed 10% to 20% of numerous sales by claiming that an agent was involved in the sale. In private treaty transactions, he was authorized to pay a 10% to 20% commission to an agent if he really wanted to sell the horse and didn't have any other immediate prospects.

Luke created Lee Thorn, a fictitious person, along with a bank account in the same name. When he could get away with it, he would have a commission paid to Lee Thorn, deposit the check, and then have access to the funds. He rarely made cash withdrawals from the account, but he did have a checking account and a gold credit card issued in the name of Lee Thorn. He used Lee Thorn's credit card whenever he was absolutely sure the merchant would not know him. No one would ever find out.

Dominick wasn't around enough to know Lee Thorn didn't exist. It was easy for Luke to justify his deception - Dominick was so wealthy he wouldn't even miss the difference in money. On the other hand, to Luke, it was a considerable amount of profit he felt he deserved and was entitled to.

Now he was desperate to conceal the fact that the file was missing for a few more weeks. By that time, his cut from The Freedom Alliance's member transactions would be distributed. Three million dollars was a ton of money to a horse trainer. If he could reclaim the file before any harm was done, he was likely to make $3 million a year, or more if things went as planned. That was, if the authorities and Chandler never caught on.

The coffee was ready. He poured the steaming brew into a cup emblazoned with his photo, his name, and "1983 Trainer of the Year" written in gold.

On this crisp, clear, beautiful morning he sat on his pool deck staring at his reflection in the water. Nervous about Dominick finding out the purpose of the syndicate, he wished Dominick had sold his shares when Leslie tried to buy them.

Everyone whose name was in the file had been to the farm for the secret meeting the day before he discovered the file was missing. That day, they documented their transactions and the members received their funds. Any of the members could have stolen the file, but why would they? The members were assured that the files used an alias for each of them, so they shouldn't have felt threatened by written records. All of the syndicate members seemed to appreciate the precautions being taken. ^^

On this first Sunday that he had off from work in months, Luke decided to spend some quiet time alone and enjoy brunch at the Sheraton in Solvang.

Chapter Twelve

J.J. woke up in his hotel room so exhausted that he had forgotten where he was. He couldn't think clearly for the first few minutes. Then, he remembered his plans to meet Rene. He was looking forward to seeing her, but he laid in bed wishing they were meeting for dinner rather than brunch.

Jet lag attacked his body. The flight from Brazil yesterday was 23 hours including layover time in the airports, then a three-hour drive from LAX to the farm. It didn't help that he drank alcohol and was up past midnight. As he stretched out in bed totally depleted of all energy, he was certain he was getting too old for this lifestyle.

In the brief moment before turning on the light, he realized he didn't even recall what the room looked like. It wasn't funny. When the room was illuminated, he looked around and admired the authentic Scandinavian furniture and décor. ^^

He propped himself up in bed, too exhausted to reach over and turn the radio/alarm clock toward him to see what time it was. The jet set lifestyle of flying all over the world to look at horses for sale and attend events such as major horse shows, auctions, seminars and open houses caught up with him. At least he'd soon be able to stop living like this.

The phone rang louder than his ears could tolerate. He jumped and grabbed the receiver to avoid hearing another ring.

"Hello."

"Hi! It's me. I've been having coffee and waiting for forty-five minutes. Are you okay?"

In his sleepy voice, he said, "Sorry. I didn't arrange a wake up call. I just woke up."

"Oh."

He hesitated, trying to moisten his dry mouth with his own saliva.

"I'm dazed. Do you want to wait for me to shower and dress or do you want to just meet for dinner?"

She was anxious to be with him, so she hesitated to answer.

"Do you want to rest longer or do you want to come? Whatever you want is fine with me as long as we can spend some time together. I forgot how much I missed talking to you until last night."

"I don't know. Whatever you want."

"Just get your rest. We'll get together tonight."

Rene informed the hostess she wouldn't be joined by anyone after all, and requested a table out on the veranda. The moment she walked through the beveled glass French doors leading outside, she was awestruck by the inspiring beauty of the rolling hills. The aromatic scent of the brilliant multi-colored hanging flowers permeated the fresh clean air. The smoked glass tabletop was accented with bright colors from a fresh flower arrangement.

Rene understood J.J.'s exhaustion and was sympathetic, but felt let down, in a way, because she really wanted to talk to him. Trying to look on the bright side, she resolved that it was better for her to have a few hours alone to decide if she should tell him anything about what she had discovered.

Savoring her coffee, she heard a voice she recognized. She couldn't place who it was until she turned around to look.

It was Dominick Castinitas talking to his waitress. He was alone. She turned back to the direction she had been sitting, which positioned her to be at an angle of shoulder to shoulder, facing opposite directions, although with plenty of room between them. She contemplated introducing herself to him, but decided it would be prudent to wait and see if he were joined by anyone.

The wine steward approached Dominick's table, uncorked the bottle and poured a small amount in the wineglass for his approval.

Dominick turned and casually spoke to Rene.

"Excuse me, I'm sure that I won't be drinking this entire bottle of wine. May I offer you a glass?"

Pleasantly startled, she accepted without hesitation. Noticing that her manicure still looked fresh, she handed him her wineglass from the place setting.

"Thank you," she said, sounding appreciative but not impressed with who he was.

She mingled with wealthy and famous people enough to understand they didn't want to be treated any differently than anyone else. Consequently, she never asked for their autograph or commented about their music or movies or whatever made them famous or wealthy. Because she was at ease around them, they seemed comfortable around her.

"You look familiar," Dominick said, initiating a conversation with her.

"Probably from the Ivy Farms preview, then at the auction last night."

"Wonderful! Did you enjoy yourself?"

"Of course! Who wouldn't?" she answered in a cheerful tone.

"I didn't. I'm glad it's over. People don't realize how much work auctions are."

"Excuse me, but I can't imagine that you did any work! Don't you just show up and then take the money later?" she boldly said with a playful tone, not caring if he was offended.

"Actually, I do a lot of the work. Would you like to join me? I'll tell you about it and you can feel sorry for me."

"I'd be delighted. Thanks. But I doubt if you'll get any sympathy from me," she said as she gracefully moved to his table.

"You're refreshing. Most strangers don't talk to me that way."

Dominick was relaxed as he spoke.

"Do you mind if we get some food before I try to earn your pity? I haven't eaten since breakfast yesterday. I was so nervous about the auction I couldn't eat a bite. Now I'm starved."

"Why were you nervous? You only had five or six horses consigned."

"Well, you know, I bred Freedom, and I'm not completely secure that the public likes him as much as I do. And of course, I'm always worried about the prices I'll get for my horses at the auction, and I really worry about if they are going to go to good homes... homes where they'll be cared for the way I care for them."

"Don't worry about people loving Freedom, he's great!"

"I have my reasons. Anyway, I'm glad it's over."

There was a short line at the plates for the buffet. While waiting for the few people in front of him, a middle-aged woman came up and asked Dominick for his autograph. He signed it with a warm smile on his face. Rene presumed he wished he hadn't been disturbed.

"That woman must not recognize me, or she would have asked for my autograph too. I'm glad though...don't you get tired of always signing your name in public...I do!" she said in only a half-kidding way.

Dominick didn't seem to know what to think. He wondered if she was teasing or if she really was famous and he didn't recognize her. He was amused she intentionally said it in a way that piqued his curiosity. In the little amount of time he had spent with her, he decided they could possibly become friends.

Dominick didn't have many friends. His career and his horses kept him so busy there was never enough time for a social life. People he met who weren't in the entertainment business made him feel uncomfortable being a celebrity. People in the entertainment business kissed up to him, felt threatened by him, or ignored him. Rene was refreshing.

After filling their plates and being seated, Dominick realized that although the woman he was with knew his name, he didn't know hers.

"I'm embarrassed, but I don't recall your name."

"Rene Killian. I was wondering if you would get around to asking me. Usually, I introduce myself of course, but I thought it would be interesting to see how long it would take for you to realize you didn't know my name."

He waved his index finger in the air. "Ahh! I should have recognized you after all then. I've seen you in magazine interviews in *Arabian Horse International* and *The Arabian Horse Tribune* about Polish Arabians, and I believe that Luke recently mentioned your name a couple of times," Dominick said as if a light bulb lit in his brain. At the same time, he wondered if people really asked for her autograph. Probably not.

"Luke mentioned my name? Do you recall in what context? I can't imagine why he would bring me into a conversation with you," she said as her entire demeanor changed.

"I don't remember off hand."

He couldn't help but to be curious as to why she became disturbed.

"Is this wine from here in the valley?" she asked, now back to her relaxed manner.

"It's from the Greeley Vineyards. Not the best I've had, but when I'm here, I drink the local wines. They're a fraction of the price of what I'm used to drinking. My accountant tells me to economize. This is the best I can do!"

"I'm sure the price difference of wines really matters to you!" she said as her eyes sparkled. The idea of Dominick thinking about the price of something made him seem more down to earth.

"Do you always speak your mind so candidly?"

"Want an honest answer?"

While he refilled their wineglasses, he nodded his head, unable to disguise a very slight snicker.

"I usually don't bother."

Dominick sipped his wine and marveled at her honesty. He didn't respond verbally, hoping she would elaborate.

The waiter refilled their water goblets.

"I'm glad you offered me the wine. To be honest, I had hoped to meet you at Ivy Farms."

He was amused, chalking up her attitude to youth and innocence. Most people were nervous or afraid to talk to him. It made his world lonely sometimes. That's why he was absorbed in his work and his horses. Everyone probably assumed he thought he was too good, too talented, too famous, or too wealthy to be friends with them. This obviously didn't even enter Rene's mind.

"I'm flattered. You ought to come to the farm and visit."

Based upon what he had read about her in the magazine articles, he recognized she also was an expert on Polish Arabians and the marketing aspects of the business. They had something important in common.

Rene finished the wine in her glass.

"I'm sure you don't really have the time, but thanks."

"Actually, it would be nice to have a friend there. I'm not friendly with anyone at the farm."

Rene raised her brows, which said enough.

"I don't mean that to sound stuck up. It's just that if I get friendly with the female help, rumors start that we're having an affair, or the female actually hopes to have one with me. The men at the ranch are all Mexicans. Need I say more?"

"What about Wilson? Surely you're friends with him."

"No. Not really. We're nothing alike. He's very quiet and intense. I don't think we've ever spoken about anything that wasn't related to my horses or farm finances in some way or another."

She nodded her head.

"He doesn't have much personality."

As soon as his words left his mouth, he realized he was out of line. He hoped that she would keep his admission in confidence.

"I thought it was just me he was indifferent with! I guess with someone like him, you just have to respect his talent as a horsemen."

It was as if an ice-cold glass of water spilled on her head. A wave of recollection engulfed her - the information she obtained about The Freedom Alliance - he was part of the syndicate.

"May I excuse myself? I need to use the powder room."

Not really. What she needed was time to think. It hit her like running into a brick wall - she had all of this information she planned to use against the farm, and, more or less, The Freedom Alliance. Now she realized, if she used the information, it could actually damage Dominick and the few legitimate members. He seemed so nice - she couldn't imagine doing anything that could hurt him.

Now what?

She needed more time to think this out. Besides, Dominick could be personally involved. *Could he be the one with all of the contacts and who is orchestrating everything?* He shouldn't get absolution just because she enjoyed his company and was a nice man. Her final decision was to do or say nothing until she had more time to think. After collecting herself enough to go back to the table, she freshened up and returned to Dominick.

"Sorry I took so long."

"No problem. Would you care for a cappuccino?"

"I've had enough caffeine for now, thanks."

She noticed he paid the check while she had excused herself.

"I really should get going. Do you want to walk me to my car? I must have left my room key in it last night. I need to look for it."

"Sure," he said. As they walked out of the restaurant to the parking lot, he spontaneously asked, "Would you like to come to the farm and walk the mare and foal pastures with me? I'd like to hear your honest opinions about the horses and my breeding program."

Looking at her diamond studded Rolex watch, she saw it was already 1:30 in the afternoon; she was meeting J.J. at 5:00 and knew she'd need a nap in between.

"How about tomorrow? I'm meeting a friend from Brazil later."

"Sure. We'll make a day of it. Bring your swimsuit and we'll relax at the pool, too. I'll have my chef make us a picnic to eat at the lake. We can go for a ride at the back of the property and enjoy the peace and quiet…if you have the entire day and if that's acceptable to you," he said enthusiastically.

"Sounds great. Are you sure you have enough time? Don't feel as if you need to entertain me."

"Actually, you'd be entertaining me. I have plenty of time. I've taken off for a month between productions to see the horses. What time do you want to come?"

In the parking lot they agreed on a time to meet and he described how to get to his house and around back to the pool. That way, he could relax with coffee if she were running late. He didn't want her to be pressed into a tight schedule.

Dominick was surprised to see that she drove a new Ferrari.

"The payments must be expensive on this! I don't even have a car that costs this much!" he said astonished.

"I paid cash, actually. The interest almost doubles the amount of the car. I had some great sales one month and decided to treat myself," she answered modestly.

"Quite a businesswoman."

"You certainly could afford a Ferrari if you wanted one. You just aren't shallow and superficial like I am. Personally, I'd rather have your horses than my car!" she said with complete honesty.

"Why didn't you buy one last night then?"

"Because I only buy for clients, and I only buy when I can make good commissions."

"This is a conversation we'll have plenty of time for tomorrow."

As he stepped out of his car, Luke spotted Dominick and Rene in the Sheraton parking lot.

Why were they meeting?

He abruptly slid back into his own car and scooted down in the seat so that they wouldn't see him if they turned in his direction. His stomach churned as he practically lost control of his bowels.

Had Rene told Dominick that she had the syndicate file?

Chapter Thirteen

Rene drove away content. She was able to meet Dominick, and she was going to spend the evening with her friend. On the other hand, she was frustrated about how she would use her information, or if she would even use it, now that she met Dominick. There was so much to consider. If she didn't do something, how would she get Jared to leave her alone and get out of her life? Even if she didn't walk away from the business, she needed to come up with the money for him or the nightmare of her career would escalate.

Her first priority would be to decipher what the stolen information even meant. Grady was so upset about what she had done he wouldn't even look at it; he said he wished she hadn't told him about it.

When she returned to her hotel room, her message light was lit. J.J. had called to confirm their meeting at the restaurant for 5:00 p.m. She was amused.

\ \ \ \ \ \ \ \ \ \ \ \

J.J. was waiting at the bar when she arrived. He already had a drink, which, when Rene took a sip, surprisingly turned out to be club soda. They hugged and kissed each other on the cheek. For the first time, she noticed how large and powerful his hands were. It startled her. He was a black belt in Karate and worked out on a regular basis. He could kill someone.

"It's still beautiful outside. Should we change tables? I love sitting in the fresh air."

"Me too. Our waitress looks busy, let's just take your drink and go out. She'll see us."

The deck was on the third floor of the building, offering a view of the quaint Scandinavian town of Solvang. The traffic wasn't enough to cause any fumes, although the main road through town was a mere twenty feet from where they were seated.

He ordered two vodka and tonics, tall and weak, so they could drink and talk all night. The waitress served them complimentary pot stickers and Chinese noodles. Rene always thought it was strange that when people looked rich they were given so many things 'on the house,' but when people seemed average or poor, their small budgets had to cover everything or they had to do without. It didn't seem right.

"So, how's your love life?" she asked.

"No one serious. How about you?"

"It's not really serious, but I'm seeing Grady Reed."

He raised his eyebrows. "Isn't he married?"

"His wife died."

"Really? How?"

"I don't actually know. He doesn't talk about it, and I just ignore all the rumors in the business. He seems to be doing pretty well dealing with the loss, except he started smoking pot and doing coke when he's not working."

"I thought you hated drugs!" he said.

"I do. I don't do it with him. But under the circumstances of his losing his wife so recently, I just can't hold it against him."

"Doesn't he live here in California?"

"He lives in Malibu, and his office is in Beverly Hills. I don't mind commuting for a while...he promised that when the weather gets decent he'll come to Scottsdale."

He was surprised she would date an attorney. She always swore she hated the profession.

"Do you see the relationship going anywhere?"

"I don't know. I'm dealing with so many other things. Who knows!"

At about six-thirty they ordered their food. By the time they were halfway through the meal, J.J. told his story: his parents were killed in a car accident three months ago. There was a sizable estate to be shared with his sister, who was still in college studying to get her MBA. Aside from the emotional trauma of suddenly losing both of his parents, he told her there were financial problems he had to deal with.

The will did not provide for estate taxes to be paid out of the estate because there weren't any liquid assets. His parents had cashed out their life insurance policies the previous year to build an atrium, indoor pool, hot tub and exercise room at their home. They planned on replacing the life insurance policies, but never got around to it.

Being single, J.J. didn't bank much money, spending lavishly on travel, entertainment, clothing, his luxury condo and his sports car. Consequently, he personally didn't have nearly enough money saved to pay the estate taxes. His sister didn't have any money; she was still a student and her parents supported her.

If the taxes couldn't be paid from a source outside of the estate, either the family business or the family home would have to be sold to pay the government. Both the business and the real estate had been in the family for five generations. The estate was nestled on 175 acres of prime real estate in an otherwise overly crowded area of expensive custom homes. His parents planned for his sister to eventually take over as CEO of the family business.

Now, J.J. said, he was trying to make the most difficult decision of his life. Sell the business or the real estate. He needed $850,000 or he and his sister would lose something that his parents and four generations before them had worked for with their hearts and souls. If he sold the business, his sister would lose the future she looked forward to for her entire life. On top of her depression about losing her parents, she was now stressed that all of her years of intensive studying would be wasted. He said at the rate her depression was escalating, J.J. was worried she may become suicidal if he couldn't raise the money, which so far, he couldn't.

After hearing about his problems, there was no way she was going to tell him about what was going on with her, at least not now. He had burdens far more serious than she had imagined when she first realized that he was troubled.

"So, enough about me. What was with you last night? You weren't yourself!"

"Don't worry about it. You've got enough on your mind."

"Not that I want you to have a serious problem, but if you already do, and you tell me about it, it'll take my mind off of my own problems for a change."

"My problems are insignificant compared to yours. Forget it."

He took her hands in his when he saw her slightly trembling.

"Tell me. Really. I want to know."

"You're sure?"

"I'm sure."

"Well, you know how easily top quality horses sell here in the U.S.?"

"Yes."

"A while back, I got a little too cocky and put myself in a bad position."

"What? What did you do?"

"The worst of my problem is with this guy Jared Rava - a client that led me to believe that if he could make a huge profit quickly, he would then get his clients into the business, buying from me. He led me to believe that he was a financial planner or investment broker or something like that. He said that he had client funds to invest if it could make a really good return."

"Okay."

"So, I told him that sometimes I can locate horses that are exceptional deals, and that if I had the cash available to buy on the spot, I could buy him one of these horses, and turn around and sell it for at least triple what we paid."

"And he took you up on it?"

"Yeah. We started with one horse that I paid $7,500 for. I sold the horse to him for $25,000 and then resold the horse to another client about a month later for $75,000…"

J.J. cut her off. "Don't tell me you sold the horse to another client of your own! Another new person to the business?"

"I didn't intend to! It just happened. The new buyer was an investor who always wanted to be a jockey, but he grew too tall. Anyway, he wanted to buy a few mares to be in it for the long haul. I mean years and years, and not even sell the first offspring. He said he would let the first group of mares have foals, let those foals grow up and breed, use them for breeding, then wait and sell the third or fourth generation."

"Yeah…"

"So, when Jared started putting pressure on me after only a month, and kept reminding me that if I make him a good profit quick I'll get lots of clients, I couldn't resist but take the easy way out and sell the jockey wannabe the horse for $75,000."

"And you got your 20% commission from the sale?"

"Right. I made $17,500 profit from marking-up the horse to Jared, then I made $15,000 from reselling the horse for him."

"So, you made thirty-two grand from just one client – just one horse - in about a month."

"Yeah. But, you know, it's not like it happens all of the time!"

"I know it doesn't. So, what's the problem?"

"The problem is, Jared says he wants me to prove it to him with two more horses before he'll feel comfortable advising his people to buy from me."

"So, what, you did it again?"

"Yes, but this time I bought one horse for $20,000 and sold it to him for $35,000 – and bought a second horse for $10,000 and sold it to him for $35,000. I told him I could get about $100,000 for each horse, but that it could take up to six months, because of the time of year."

"How does he think you make your money?"

"He knows I get a commission when I sell for him, but he never asked about how I make my money when I buy for him. I never volunteered anything. I never do, and no one asks."

"Nobody ever asks, don't worry about it!"

"I know. So, anyway, I'm on a date with this guy trying to impress me by flying me to San Diego. He takes me to some fancy regatta with a lot of rich people, including his family. So, at this regatta, everyone's drinking of course, and you know me, I'm always prospecting! I end up talking with this rich married couple about the Arab business. To make a long story short, they seem filthy rich and they say they'll buy a couple of horses for breeding. They think it will be fun. I did tell them about the investment aspects, the appreciation of 30% a year, and the tax deductions, the whole story, you know, and they say, oh, that sounds great…it would be fun to buy a couple of good horses."

"I'll bet they're saying all of this in front of some friends!"

"Yeah. But I didn't think about it at the time."

"So, they were just showing off to their friends?"

"Sort of. After only a couple of weeks of owning the horses, Jared is pressuring me to get them sold! And, of course, he keeps reminding me he has so many clients who will invest. I took the fast, easy way out and sold these people Jared's two horses I bought for resale.

"Are you kidding me?"

"No. These people insisted they couldn't care less about making a dime back and emphasized they just thought it would be fun."

"Okay. So, you sort of made a pyramid…"

She interrupted him.

"No! I didn't! The regatta people said they weren't trying to make money - it was just for fun. And the jockey wannabe had years to put into it, and he never said he expected some great value. He just said he wanted high quality horses and he asked how much it would cost him. That's not a pyramid!"

"What aren't you telling me? Get to the point!"

"Well, I make all this money for Jared and me pretty fast, and I get my ego built up. You know how it is."

"Go on. What are you trying to tell me?"

"Okay. So, Jared tells me he's got money from his clients to buy five horses for quick resale. I explained how those deals were rare and extremely difficult to find, and I don't know of any right now and I don't know how long it might be until I can find one horse like that, let alone five.

"He says, well, how about five horses that we can double our money on? So, I tell him I'll keep an eye out, but I don't know. The original idea was that it was just him expecting such a high profit, and his clients would be willing to wait for two years before they expected to sell and make a profit. Two years would be enough time to buy a mare that's in foal, for her to have the foal for me to sell, rebreed the mare, and have that foal to sell, then sell the mare when she's back in foal.

"Jared says, no, his clients don't want to wait after all. He says he sees good money can be made, and he'll just find someone else who will do for him what I did. Of course, I then tell him to wait, let me see what I can do."

"And?"

"And, within about a month or so, I buy five mares that we can sell for double, but, there's not all that much money in it for me, at least not compared to before, but you know me, I like the buying… and the sellers kissing up to me so that they can get their horses sold… you know, the whole thing…"

"I know... you're insecure, it makes you feel important... go on with the story."

"Well, on the purchase of the five horses, I make about $70,000 or so...not much, but not bad for doing something I really love, right?"

"Right."

"Well, as it turns out, Jared ends up calling Leslie Ivy, because me, the idiot, encouraged him to subscribe to Arabian magazines and learn all that he can. He likes the Ivy Farms advertisements, so he ends up meeting Leslie, and Leslie talks him into keeping the mares and breeding them to Aston. What can I do? Jared just dumps me, saying that he feels much more comfortable doing business with a prominent farm and actual trainers and people who own their own stallions. He says because it's his client's money, he needs to be more conservative and protect their investment, which means he really shouldn't do business with me anymore."

"That's a tough break, but like we've talked about before, it happens all the time. What's your big problem though?"

"I guess I got side tracked. Sorry. Well, of course, I don't want to speak negatively about other people in the industry, so I don't tell Jared about Leslie Ivy's reputation. Leslie ended up selling Jared or his clients some outrageously expensive horses they surely can't make a profit with unless they wait years and years.

"Then Jared realizes he got screwed - instead of going after Leslie, he's now pressuring me to resell the horses I sold him, and their Aston foals – and he's demanding a ridiculous profit! Like I'm supposed to make up for what Leslie did to him!"

"Just tell him no. Tell him that he's an Ivy client now, and not yours. Don't worry about it."

"I tried that. Jared demanded to see my purchase contracts for the horses I bought for him. When I refused, he had an attorney contact me and threaten to sue me. So, I gave them copies of my contracts."

"Whoa! I guess he was pissed at how much you made off of him?"

"Not just pissed, the lawyer is threatening to sue me, insisting that because I'm his bloodstock agent I have a duty to make a full disclosure of all of my profits."

"No one tells anyone what profits they make! That's crazy!"

"I know. But what can I do? Jared and his lawyer said that if I resell the horses, including the Aston foals, for the profits I projected plus $100,000, he won't pursue anything," she said, intentionally not telling him about the other threat.

"Holy shit!"

"I know! Of course, with this pressure, now I don't have any buyers, let alone enough to generate that kind of money for the jerk!"

"I thought I had it bad. Sounds like you've got quite a problem on your hands too," J.J. said as he took her hand.

"If they actually end up filing a lawsuit, it's going to destroy me. They'll depose all of my other clients."

"Sounds like you're worried about something more..."

"My problem is compounded. I got quite a few people started during the same time period, telling them to give me a chance to make them money by letting me buy them horses at a really great deal, then selling the horses for a good profit. The idea was for them to let me buy them two horses with the money from the sale, horses they would keep indefinitely."

"Why did you do that?"

"Apparently, I'm an idiot! I just wanted to get clients before the big farms did. I feel like I'm saving them. I keep thinking they'll stick with me if I make them profits and if I teach them about the horses."

"And…"

"I got too greedy, I guess. Now, I've got about twenty horses I need to sell for at least double what the clients paid, but I'm not finding enough buyers already in the business. I've sold about ten horses to new buyers who I didn't tell about the fast profit potential, and that's great, but I still need to sell twenty horses pretty quick, or these people are going to come after me."

"How many clients are you talking about?"

"Nine."

"Have they all threatened to come after you if you don't sell their horses?"

"None have threatened anything. I'm just getting the feeling it's going to happen. But one man, the one that owns six horses, his business is having financial problems and he really needs the money. I'm getting paranoid."

"You're probably overreacting."

"I don't think so. You know how you can just feel the tension, but nothing's said? That's how it is each time I talk to any of them."

"No one has actually threatened to sue you though, right?"

"Not directly. I don't have a written contract with anyone anyway. It's just my conscience, I guess."

"What do you mean, not directly?"

"One of the client's is married to an attorney who deals in business law. She's saying that if I can't sell her horse for the profits we talked about real soon, she'll have to discuss it with her husband."

"Oh. That's a nice way to threaten you. You know that, don't you?"

"Yes. And that's not even the worst of it. Jared claims he went to an attorney to cover his tracks - he said that if he has to take matters into his own hands, he will!"

His eyes widened.

"Do you think he means violence?"

"What else can I think? Hopefully he's all talk, but when he said it, even though it's vague, I got really scared. This guy looks like a gangster…"

"Really?"

"Well, no, not really, but in my mind I start conjuring up pictures of being buried in cement. You know me and my imagination…it sounds like he's threatening me with more than legal problems, doesn't it?"

"Yeah. I'd be really careful. What's Grady say?"

"I haven't told him," she admitted.

"Why? Isn't he your attorney…I assumed you started dating him from him being your lawyer."

"No. He's not my lawyer. I don't have one. And I haven't talked to Grady about it. I had planned to, but once I got to know him more, I didn't think it was a good idea."

"Why?"

"How should I put this? He's too loose mouthed. You won't believe the things he's told me about his clients - people that I even know."

"That's not good."

"No kidding! So, I'm not going to confide in him, let alone retain him as a lawyer."

"Right. But you better get someone in Arizona to represent you."

"I might need to, if things I have going now don't work out," she said.

"What do you have going?"

"I'll tell you later. I don't want to take a chance of being overheard here."

"This is getting interesting."

"Anyway, don't worry about it. Your problem is more urgent and on a much bigger scale than mine."

"I don't know about that, but I feel bad for you. I know you have good intentions when you deal with these people."

When they finished dinner, they went to a cozy and quiet coffeehouse to brainstorm as to how he could come up with $850,000. At two a.m. the owner had to tell them he was closing, so they decided to finish talking at her hotel room.

Without words or explanation, it was clear this was not an invitation to sex, it was merely Rene wanting to comfort her friend.

At the hotel, they sprawled on separate beds and talked, laughed and cried until dawn, with long periods of quiet contemplation.

Worried about what he would think of her, she still hadn't told him about the information she stole from Ivy Farms. She was absolutely determined to go up against them. Even if she couldn't disappear from the industry, she could at least get Jared off her back and could help J.J.. Now, she was definitely willing to go out on a limb. A very long limb.

Chapter Fourteen

The morning presented itself too quickly. When the bright sun radiated through the break in the curtains, it startled her awake. Before she wiped the sleep from her eyes, she was already thinking about how she needed to decipher what the other documents really meant. The more ammunition, the better. On her own, she couldn't come up with anything, but she knew something in the documents was not kosher or legal.

Doing stretching exercises on the floor, she weighed her risks. Her endorphins shot rampant through her body by the time she was well into her aerobic exercises. As her adrenaline rose, so did her confidence about at least getting J.J. the money he needed. By the time she was working on arm curls while jogging in place, she made her final decision.

"Wake up," she said softly as she shook him.

"Uh."

"Wake up. I need to talk to you."

"We talked most of the night. What more can we say?" he grumbled, half asleep.

"I'm taking a shower. Wake yourself up by the time I'm out," she demanded.

The long hot shower was invigorating. She was shampooing her hair when he knocked on the door.

"Do you want room service?" he yelled.

She thought for a moment. "Yeah. A fresh fruit plate, papaya juice, and coffee with cream. Just charge it to my room. Thanks," she yelled back.

A few minutes later she walked out of the bathroom with the thick white terry cloth robe provided by the hotel. It wasn't luxurious like the ones at the plush hotels she preferred, but it would do.

"I told them you'd pay double if the service was pronto!"

"You better not have! I love to spend money, but room service is already a rip off," she replied, hoping he had been joking. She knew she couldn't be certain until the bill was there for her to sign.

Knock. Knock.

That was too fast. He must have offered to pay double. She was aggravated and amused at the same time.

J.J. opened the door and directed the room service waiter to the table. The waiter tried to hand the guest check to him.

"She's paying. I'm her gigilo boyfriend. I don't have a dime."

"J.J.! You promised me you would be discreet about our arrangement. I'm not taking you shopping this week. You'll learn your lesson," she retorted as she signed the guest check.

There wasn't a double charge, but she wondered if he had in fact offered it. The waiter thanked them and told them to call if anything else was needed.

"You're great. I love how you roll with the punches!"

"What's great about me is that I'm going to save your ass," she announced confidently while towel drying her shiny hair.

He studied her facial expression. What would she do for him?

"I know I can do it. I just need to decide how to go about it."

"It won't involve weapons or poison, will it?" he asked, only half kidding.

"NO! What kind of person do you think I am?"

She acted insulted and began eating her breakfast.

"Are you finished?" she asked, referring to his breakfast.

"Yeah."

"Good. Get out of here! Come back tonight with a veggie pizza and a couple of decent bottles of wine."

"What's the rush? You have plans to rob a bank?"

"No! I need privacy to get dressed and put on makeup."

"For who?" he wondered out loud.

"I'm meeting Dominick Castinitas at ten. We're going on a ride," she told him, trying not to make much of it.

"Really?" he asked, as if he doubted her.

"What? You don't believe me?"

"Well, why would he go horseback riding with you? Are you sure you didn't dream this?"

"I'm sure the invitation wasn't a dream. And I am going!"

He paused. "Fine!"

It came out as if he was jealous, but she knew he hadn't meant it that way.

"If we were dating, I'd tell you where to go right now, but since I'd never date your kind, I won't bother! I have no idea how long we'll get to ride – the farm is 150 acres."

He became serious. "He's rumored to be happily married," he informed her as if she didn't already know.

"That's the beauty of it! I feel safe, like with you. Don't worry, I have no romantic notions."

"I hope not."

She owed her friend a further explanation since he was acting like a concerned big brother.

"We're going on a long ride and having a picnic, then we're going to walk his pastures and evaluate the weanlings and yearlings. We'll probably relax around his pool when we get too hot. I'm wearing a conservative one-piece suit. Kapish?"

She honestly hoped her explanation would satisfy him. It was the truth, and she really cared what he thought. She appreciated having someone around with whom she could be herself and honest with.

Well, fairly honest.

^^

"Do you mind if I read the newspaper on the balcony while you get dressed?" he suggested.

"That's fine, but I need to get ready."

It tore her apart to leave J.J. alone at a time like this. She contemplated whether she should take the liberty to invite him to join them. She didn't want to be selfish, but this was probably a once-in-a-lifetime opportunity.

While buying a newspaper in the front lobby, J.J. felt like he had just made a fool of himself. He didn't want Rene to think he was insecure or needy. What was worse, he didn't want her to think he doubted her. At his request, the concierge gave him a piece of paper and a pen.

He wrote:

Rene,

Do your thing and I'll see you tonight with pizza and wine. I hope you have a wonderful day.

Your Friend Forever, J.J.

The concierge agreed to personally deliver the note to her room immediately.

\` \` \` \` \` \` \` \` \` \` \`

Rene arrived at Dominick's house at 10:15 a.m. and found him at the pool reading.

"Good Morning! Are we still on?"

"Of course. Care for some coffee?" he offered.

"Please, with skim milk if you have it. What are you reading?" She was referring to a two-inch thick bound document on his lap.

"It's a manuscript I'm considering for a screenplay."

"Something you're going to direct?" she casually inquired, hoping she wasn't being too nosey.

"I haven't decided. The person who wrote it is an unknown. It's her first novel and she hasn't submitted it to a publishing house yet. She bought some horses from me, so she thought she'd have an 'in' to get me to read it first."

"Well, you're reading it! I guess she was right. Is it any good?" she was genuinely interested because she had always fantasized about trying her hand at writing a novel.

"The story itself is excellent, but it would go to a professional screenwriter to take the basis of the story and rewrite it."

"Do you prefer to ride English or Western?" Dominick asked.

"I like both. How about you?" she was actually surprised he knew how to ride. She really thought of him as a breeder.

"I ride both also. Let's do Western today. I haven't ridden in a while."

"Sounds good to me. I'm just anxious to ride on your farm."

"Are you a good rider?" Dominick inquired, wanting to match horse and rider.

She hesitated, not intending to sound as if she weren't confident, but she also didn't want to sound cocky.

"I prefer a spirited mount to a horse that doesn't want to work."

Her answer didn't really address his question, but he just let it go, then called the barn and designated two horses to be groomed, tacked up, and ready in thirty minutes.

Someone from outside the gate called into the pool area. "Mr. Castinitas! Your picnic is in the saddle pack on the golf cart."

"Gracias, Juana!"

Not that Rene knew his personality, but he didn't seem himself. The day before he was relaxed and easy going. Today, he appeared a little reserved, almost uptight and on edge. Hopefully he wasn't regretting her being there.

Dominick answered the cordless phone before the entire first ring, as if he had been expecting an urgent call. He motioned to Rene that he was taking the call in the house. She poured herself another cup of coffee and entertained herself by watching a group of young stud colts romping in the pasture closest to the house - they were playing so hard their hind legs brought up tufts of grass with each stride. Prancing with arrogance, their necks were arched and their tails curled over their backs. They snorted and whinnied loudly at each other. Rene wondered if Dominick could hear whoever was on the opposite end of the phone line.

He stayed on the phone for almost an hour, making her increasingly uncomfortable waiting. She contemplated suggesting they get together some other time and give him an easy out for the day.

"I'm sorry. I didn't expect to be on that long. Now, I'm ready to have a great day!"

His mood was completely changed, now sounding more like he had the day before. He secured the house, checking each of the doors, a quick glance at the window locks, and he set the electronic security system.

They made small talk about the weather as they rode to the barn in the golf cart.

"Good morning sir. It's good to see you," said Manuel, the groom who had saddled the horses. His work day started at 5:30 a.m., six days a week.

"Good to see you too. How's the new baby?"

In the employee lounge Dominick saw pictures of Manuel's wife in the hospital bed holding their newborn.

"Beautiful, but we never sleep anymore!"

"I remember. Thank you for preparing the horses," he said as he slipped the young father a portion of a stack of hundred dollar bills he hadn't counted.

"For your wife and kids."

"Gracias." ^^

They were having a wonderful time riding; the horses were responsive, the weather was perfect, and the nature was beautiful. It couldn't have been better.

During their ride and picnic, he told her about his background, about how he began his career as a director, about his wife Susanna who had MS, and about how he had met his trainer, Wilson St. Claire. He was very open and seemed completely candid. They talked about bloodlines and described famous horses, critiquing some and praising a few.

Dominick stood up, stretched his legs and back and twisted at his waist. He had gotten stiff while sitting and eating.

"This has been a great day. Just what I needed. Thanks," he told her.

"I'm in heaven. In Scottsdale, all of the riding is in the desert - if you see green, it's a cactus that you end up using as an obstacle in a nature-made obstacle course. It's so beautiful here!"

She made a conscious effort not to be too forward or sound patronizing. Hopefully he knew she wasn't interested in him romantically.

"Satire's a nice horse. He has a lot of potential. I like him. We've already bonded with each other."

"He obviously likes you too."

He made a quick decision.

"He's yours."

"Mine? What do you mean?"

"He's my gift to you for giving me such a great day."

"I don't need a gift. A great day's a great day. I'm having fun too, you know!"

He insisted. "Satire is yours. I'll pay for him to be hauled to Scottsdale and I'll pay for his board, vet and farrier bills as long as you own him."

Rene was flabbergasted. "I can't accept. Thanks though. I really do appreciate the thought behind it."

He smiled at her. "You're unbelievable. Everyone else I meet is looking for ways to take advantage of me, or at the very least, sell me something. You really do like my company just for who I am, don't you?" he said, touched by the thought.

"Of course I like you for who you are. As an individual. Not because you're Dominick Castinitas the director, or Dominick Castinitas, the wealthy man. Besides, I like that you're happily married and that I don't have to be concerned about anything leading to a sexual relationship."

"How about a compromise?" he continued before he could give her a chance to respond. "Satire is yours to use whenever you want. You can stay in one of the guesthouses whenever you want. I insist. As your new friend, I insist."

"How can I turn that down? Thanks. But please know, I had no intentions of getting anything out of you," she said. Her declaration was heartfelt. She was enjoying his company so much she had forgotten she hoped to sell him Jared's horses, or other client's horses.

They packed up the remains and supplies from the picnic and rode to the lake. The crystalline water glistened as ducks relaxed floating on the surface. They dismounted and loosened the saddle cinches, allowing the horses to rest and drink water from the lake. He took note that she was not only knowledgeable about riding, but also about the psychology of horse behavior and about Polish pedigrees and breeding. They talked about their trips to Poland and the stud farms and about her various trips around the world seeing Arabians.

At about 3 p.m. they arrived back at the barn. Dominick went to look for a groom to remove the tack from the horses and hose them down. Rene just did it herself while he was gone. When the groom returned with him, the horses had their tack off and she had just finished hosing the sweat off Satire. She had Baska standing in crossties in the adjoining rack. The groom insisted on taking over. Rene kissed and hugged Satire goodbye and told him she'd be back to see him…with carrots!

Dominick drove back to his house in the golf cart. They decided to go for a swim to freshen up. He went inside to shower and put on his suit while Rene did the same in the pool house. Although it wasn't actually lavish, she knew she'd be happy living in the pool house if it were at this fabulous ranch.

After five minutes in the pool, they realized they were too tired to swim. He suggested laying out and relaxing until the weather cooled down before they walked the pastures. She agreed. Between the long ride, the heat and the wine, she was sleepy.

"Mind if I lay out on a raft? Maybe you could read your manuscript."

"Fine. Make this a vacation."

Ever since he had become famous and wealthy, he had never met someone who was so immediately at ease with him. He needed a companion like her.

Rene fell asleep in the warm sun for a few hours, waking up startled with no concept of the time.

"What time is it?" she asked as she found a towel.

"I don't know, probably around six o'clock."

"I need to go. J.J. and I are getting together for dinner," she said while patting her cheeks with quick movements, trying to get her blood flowing faster.

"Sure. Can you come back tomorrow for us to walk the pastures?" he asked as they hurried back into the house.

"Can I call in the morning? I'm not sure. I want to, but I need to find out whether or not he's leaving for Brazil."

Dominick wrote down his private phone number, direct to the house. "I'll be here!"

Chapter Fifteen

The next day...

Dominick was sitting on the top rail of the fence looking out into the weanling pasture when she drove up beside him.

"What's the serious look all about?" Rene asked, before he had a chance to greet her.

He swung his legs back over the rails and planted his feet on the ground.

"Park your car. We need to talk."

She felt like she had been caught skipping school.

"Sure."

Dominick walked to her car, only a few feet away, and opened her door for her. She got out, feeling uncomfortable about being there. He was like ice.

"Lets take a walk," he suggested, using a soft voice.

"Fine."

After a couple minutes of silence, that to Rene felt like eternity, he finally spoke.

"I received a very odd phone call about a half hour ago."

"Oh," she said innocently.

"Yes. It was your friend, J.J."

"J.J.?"

"Yes. For some reason, he called to thank me for giving him the money to save his family's business."

Rene stopped dead in her tracks.

"He called you?"

"Yes. I think I deserve an explanation, and I deserve it now."

"I don't know what to say."

"Rene, look…I like you. You seem like a nice young woman. But if you thought you could befriend me and that I would give you $850,000 to solve your friends problem, you have…"

"I'm not asking you for anything! You're getting way ahead of yourself."

"I don't understand. I covered for you with J.J., but I have no intention…"

"First of all, what did he say to you? And what did you respond back with?"

"He introduced himself and apologized for bothering me and taking my time, but he said he felt compelled to thank me for agreeing to give him $850,000. He said he didn't know how he and his sister would manage without it."

"And what did you say?"

"I asked him what he meant! He said that he was your friend, and that you didn't know he was calling, but he just had to thank me for saving the family business."

Rene bit her lip, unsure how to respond.

"And then what?"

"I didn't know what on earth you told him, or why, so I just said that I was very busy, and that anything between you and him was none of my business. Then he told me he admired my modesty! Finally, I just told him that he would need to clarify some things with you. Frankly, I was so taken back, that I didn't know what to say."

"I can understand your position. I had no idea he would call you."

"I think I deserve an explanation."

"I guess you do, under the circumstances. Can we walk in the pasture while we talk?"

"Sure."

"Well, J.J. must have made the assumption I'm getting the money from you. I never told him that you were giving me, or giving him any money. At dinner last night I told him that within the next couple of weeks I'd get him the money he needed, and that he didn't need to be worried anymore. He must have just drawn a conclusion because you and I spent time together, and because you're obviously a man of great means."

"Okay. That sounds reasonable. But may I ask, how on earth do you intend to get $850,000 cash to give a friend?"

"You really want to know?"

"It's probably none of my business, but I can't help being curious now that I've ended up involved in this."

"You're going to be shocked, but I'll tell you everything - if you promise not to judge me."

Dominick stopped walking and faced her, looking her straight in the eye, trying to understand this relative stranger who entered his life out of nowhere.

"What is this about?"

"Lets go back to my car. I've got some paperwork in the trunk you'll want to look at. Otherwise, you'll never believe me."

Time seemed to stand still as she told her story and showed him the documents she still didn't fully understand.

Rene had his undivided attention.

"No one writes notes like this unless they have something important to hide."

"I have to agree. It's obvious they lied about the number of breedings, but you're right about doubting who all these inactive people are who supposedly invested in The Freedom Alliance and all those other horses. Something's not kosher," he admitted.

"No kidding! Whatever it is, I'm sure it's big."

"Looking back, about eight or nine months ago we decided to do the auction together, and then out of the blue, about three months ago, Leslie tried to get me to forget the whole thing and not be involved. It was really odd."

Rene became more suspicious.

"What did he say?"

"I don't remember exactly, but I was disgruntled about it, so when I was back in New York, I called Chandler to discuss it. Chandler said he didn't know a thing about Leslie not wanting me involved in the auction."

"Strange. He's obviously hiding something," she said, glad he was opening up to her.

"We need to figure out what all these peoples' names and horses' names and dollar amounts mean. Lets go in the house."

As he sorted out the paperwork, a thought came to mind.

"You know, I got so engrossed in all of this, we got sidetracked. What does this business with the Ivy's have to do with your promising money to your friend?"

She assumed he had already figured it out. Could she actually come out and say it aloud? She pondered the question before she answered.

"You don't see the correlation, do you? I have valuable information that can destroy them - they have access to money - I need money!"

"Wait a minute! You're not planning to blackmail them, are you?"

Dominick was appalled at the Ivys, shocked that Rene had stolen his mail, and stunned about this everyday looking woman being capable of blackmail.

"Of course not. I'm going to offer to sell them a horse."

His face fell blank.

"I'll let them know what I know, then I'll offer to sell them a horse."

"First off, let me go on the record as saying I think you're crazy, and in way over your head. Plus, to be honest, I wonder if Chandler or their mother even knows what Leslie is doing or saying or whatever."

"They obviously must know how many mares the stallions bred, and they must know what's in the magazine article. In fact, Luke and Rhonda made the statements to me about the numbers, not Leslie."

"You can't get yourself involved in blackmail!"

"Just forget I even said anything."

"Let's put our heads together and try to get to the bottom of what these papers mean," he suggested, still astonished by everything they were discussing.

"Good idea."

An hour later after scrutinizing every piece of paper, they had some speculations that seemed to make sense. Dominick called his savvy business partner from his film company and described to him what information they had and their suspicions. His partner confirmed their suspicions. He knew how these things were structured.

"All I know is, I'm going to sell them a colt of mine for three million dollars."

He studied her, then nodded.

"I wish you wouldn't handle it this way. I think you should go to the police instead."

"What good would that do J.J. or me? You don't have a clue what it's like to need a lot of money and have no practical way to make it. You've got so much money, you don't know what it's like for people like me," she said, hoping she didn't come off the wrong way.

"Why three million if your friend needs eight-fifty?"

Rene explained a little about Jared and the threats of his attorney.

"No one tells anyone how much profit they make! He doesn't have a case. That's bull. They'll never go through with it."

"Really? That's your opinion?"

"Sure. Have you talked to a lawyer?"

"No, I just assumed Jared's lawyer would be telling me the truth, that what I did was actionable."

"He's bullshitting you. He knows you're young and you'd back down easily. Haven't you even told Grady about this? You said your were getting pretty close to him."

"Actually, I don't think I trust him - for me to confide in him."

"Well, you probably shouldn't trust him as a boyfriend, but have him take a small retainer so he legally represents you as a lawyer. Then, he can advise you on a way to handle this legally, and he can't tell another soul a single word you discuss."

"That's the problem. He's told me confidential things about quite a few of his clients."

"Seriously?"

"Yes. Clients in the Arab business."

"Names and all?"

"Yeah."

"That guy's bad news then. Break it off with him. There are plenty of other men out there for a smart and good looking woman like you."

"I know, but I feel sorry for him after what happened with his wife. And, it's really interesting to find out so much confidential information about so many people in this business."

"Rene, you should have more respect for yourself."

"I should, shouldn't I?"

"Yes."

They munched on some pretzels, giving their frazzled minds a little break.

Dominick had a suggestion.

"Look, you don't have to worry about that Jared guy. Nothing will come of his lawyer threatening you. Why don't you let me give you the money for J.J.? Then, you can walk away from this whole ugly mess you fell into."

She drew in a deep breath.

"I don't want your money."

"I know you don't, but really, it's no big deal. I make more money than I'll ever spend."

She shook her head.

"No. I can't take your money, even if it's for J.J., but thanks."

"Come on. You can't go around blackmailing people! It's crazy."

"Don't consider it blackmailing then. I'm just going to intimidate them into buying the colt for three million."

"It is what it is, and you know it."

He didn't want to admit it, but he thought there was a certain mystique to the whole situation.

"Still, why so much? The more you ask for, the more likely it could turn dangerous. Maybe it's my imagination, but what if they threaten to harm you?"

She started looking worried, and he recognized the expression.

"What?" he said.

"Well, I don't want to sound melodramatic or like I keep changing my story, but..." she said, drawing out the last of the words.

"But what?"

She rolled her eyes, feeling faint just thinking about it.

"I don't know if he was serious or not, but Jared's got me scared already... he implied he may hurt me if I don't sell the horses for the prices he wants."

Dominick couldn't believe what he had gotten himself involved in. A few days ago he was just making idle conversation with a stranger at a restaurant, and now he was hearing her darkest secrets and problems."

"What did he do that's making you feel threatened?"

She swallowed hard and closed her eyes tight.

"He said he called his attorney to make it look as if he were handling the matter in a civilized way. He said that if I didn't take his lawyer's advice and sell his horses in time, he had other means to punish me," she told him. Tears formed in her eyes and her hands began trembling.

Dominick hoped that she was just telling a tall tale in order to gain his understanding or sympathy. He was starting to find her story unbelievable, as if she would say anything to get him to support her decision to blackmail the Ivys.

"Maybe you took whatever he said the wrong way," he suggested.

She reached into her purse. "Do you want to hear the tape from my message machine?"

He was taken back.

"Well, sure. I'm mean, it's not that I don't believe you, but I think maybe you misunderstood."

"I've listened to this a dozen times. I didn't misunderstand. It's really a matter of whether or not he's just trying to scare me, or if he really has the means and the intention to hurt me."

"Lets see if it works in my machine."

"Go ahead. I can tell you don't believe me. I brought the tape in case something happened to me. If someone found this tape, they would have proof of who hurt me or killed me."

The tape worked in his machine and sure enough, she didn't misunderstand. Jared was pretty stupid to leave a message like that. It would be clear evidence that he threatened her, if she could prove it was his voice. Under the circumstances, Dominick believed it was her client's voice.

"What's this guy do for a living?"

"He won't really say, but he told me he invests money for clients and friends. At first I thought he meant that he was a financial planner or something, but then the more I thought about the different kinds of wording he would use when the subject came up, it was obvious he was being very evasive about his relationships with these people. Like an idiot, I kept taking his money and buying horses for him, or them, or whatever. Sometimes I wonder if these other people really exist!"

So much for having a relaxing month at the farm, Dominick thought.

"I'll tell you, I don't really know you, but it seems like you've gotten a raw deal all the way around, Rene. Between this Jared character and Leslie Ivy stealing clients from you, and dating Grady - who you can't trust, and feeling like you need to help your friend J.J., I don't know how you can handle it all."

She looked sad and vulnerable now.

"I'm sorry to have told you any of this. I really never intended to. You won't believe this, but I'm really an upbeat and honest person. Shit happens!"

"I guess so!"

She laughed and cried at the same time, glad to have someone sensible to talk to, even though she wasn't going to follow his advice and not blackmail them.

"I have an idea! Maybe three million is too much for the colt, why don't I do this - if I needed to, I was actually going to use part of the money to buy back the horses I sold Jared, and pay all the expenses, just as he demanded…"

"I see where you're going – you'll tell them that for the three million they'll get the colt and Jared's horses…then you pay off Jared!"

"Yes. Then the Ivy's will feel like they're getting something more for their money, Jared will be out of my hair, and I'll have a good nest egg," she said as if it were all so reasonable.

Dominick still couldn't believe what he was hearing.

"If you insist on blackmailing them, this seems more reasonable at least. Still, I wish you wouldn't do this. You're too smart to get involved in a scheme like this. It could destroy your life if it backfires."

"My life's already destroyed. I'm sorry you even know any of this. I really had no intentions to burden you with anything. Sorry."

"I know you didn't. Like most of life, one thing leads to another and we don't choose most of what happens. It's a chain of events that you can't have complete control of. We can only choose how we react."

"Speaking of reacting, now that you know what's going on, are you going to stay in The Freedom Alliance?"

He hadn't even thought about it yet.

"No way. I'm going to need to consult with my lawyer and decide how to handle this. It's nothing I've prepared myself for."

"You weren't ever suspicious as to who the other syndicate members were? Or who was buying and selling the breedings?"

Dominick didn't reply. That was enough of an answer for her.

"So, do you think I should tell J.J. where I'm getting the money to give him?"

"No. Don't involve more people."

"I agree, but now he thinks you gave it, and you didn't give it. I can't imagine you want him to think you did."

"We'll have to give it some thought. Not that I want to take credit for generosity I didn't extend, but I also don't want you creating a story for him that might get out of hand. Let's think about it."

"Sure. You know, I think I'm just going to get out of this damn crooked business..."

He interrupted her. "Get out! I thought you loved the business."

"No. I don't. Not the more I learn about how things go on. You can't trust anything or anyone! I love the horses. I loved the money I could make by being involved with the horses. But to be honest, the more I know, the more I want out."

"What's happened so bad besides the Ivys?"

"You wouldn't want to take that much time to know! Between what I already knew and experienced first hand, and the confidential things I found out from Grady, and things I hear being an insider, I'm just sick and tired of it! And then, I get clients like this Jared."

"You're just stressed and disillusioned right now. You don't mean it."

"No, that's not it. I am stressed and disillusioned, but reality is reality. This business is a bunch of hype. It's the horses who are wonderful. Now, I'll have enough money to just go find the kind of work that I'll actually enjoy, and not have a guilty conscience about. I'll have enough money to stand my ground. To listen to my inner voice. To not have to worry about balancing business and ethics, all for the almighty dollar and for making an impression on other people."

"That's just how life is, Rene. Everyone does that to a certain extent."

"You don't understand. You're the privileged one who makes the money to blow on over priced horses. I'm the one who has to act like they are really worth these prices so people like you won't mind paying it."

"You've thought a lot about this, haven't you?"

"Yes. And probably a little too late. I just didn't know where to draw the line."

"Draw the line?"

"Yeah. I mean, I just play off of other people's hype and act as if I don't know it's an inflated market.

I play innocent, so I can live with myself and look in the mirror."

"Aren't you going overboard? You're saying that you can't look yourself in the mirror for charging people big bucks for horses, but you can blackmail someone? Think about what you're saying."

"I'm blackmailing the Ivys because they deserve it. J.J. needs the money for a good reason, and I need to get Jared off my back and get on with life."

"So, that's how you justify your actions?"

"You don't understand."

"I do. I just mean that you're going overboard about thinking you shouldn't sell high end horses. You're one of the few people out there protecting the innocent - you make sure they buy high quality, well bred animals. You educate people, try to get them involved. You show them that horses are to be admired, and loved and well cared for...they aren't just money machines."

"Yes. But I do make sure they know they can be money machines!"

"So, change your slant now so that you won't need to earn nearly as much money."

"I don't want to be involved with the people and the *'industry'* end of it anymore! I just want to enjoy a few horses of my own. I want to sleep at night without wondering how much I can mark-up a horse and still be fair. I want to sleep at night without calculating commissions. I want to go shopping for clothes and not think about if I would be dressing up to the standards of those that I'm trying to impress."

"Okay. You've obviously struggled with this for some time. I admire you – except the blackmail and your relationship with Grady!" he said, trying to get the conversation off on a lighter side.

"Gee, thanks!"

"Break it off with Grady. Find a nice guy like me. Not me, of course - just a guy like me!"

"Oh, so now you're the standard all others should be measured against!"

They both started laughing.

"Can we go riding? I really need to be on a horse right now," Rene asked, looking forward to riding Satire again.

"Sure. I'll call the barn."

Chapter Sixteen

The next morning...

"Ivy Farms. How can I help you?"

"Is Leslie available?" Rene inquired, assuming she would be leaving a message rather than actually speaking with him.

Without hesitation, the woman answered, "As a matter of fact, he's walking towards the office right now. Can you hold a minute?"

"Sure. Thank you."

She sat up straight in her hotel room chair, mentally preparing herself.

"May I ask who's calling?"

"Rene Killian."

"Here he is, he's just walking in the door," she said.

From her voice, she was on top of the world. Rene hoped it wasn't an act. Somebody deserved to be happy and at peace with their life.

Before she could reply, the woman handed the phone over to Leslie while telling him who was on the line.

His entire body instantly tensed up in anticipation. Just this morning, Luke confessed that The Freedom Alliance file was missing and he told him he suspected Rene as the likely thief. When Leslie asked him why he would suspect Rene, Luke told him that the day before the auction, the receptionist at CSC had called and left him a message when they were all out to lunch. The message said she had sent Rene Killian over to see Dominick's consignment horses and that she had suggested that Rene go after lunch time. Luke said Rene never showed up, but the next day he realized that the syndicate file was missing from his desk, along with a small notebook. Luke put two and two together through a process of elimination. Rene made it known publicly she was furious with Ivy Farms about their stealing her clients.

Leslie already knew his leather notebook and appointment book were missing, which upset him, although he didn't think anyone would be able to make heads or tails of the information. Luckily, he had already prepared organized documents and a file of the same information, which were now locked in his home safe. He put it in the safe to keep his brother Chandler and his mother from seeing anything that might make them suspicious about where so many new clients came from, virtually out of thin air.

"Rene. How are you?" he asked, not really caring.

"I'm fine. Is there another extension you'd prefer to use where you'd have privacy?" she said, hoping to throw him off guard by the strange question which didn't have a pretext.

Leslie mulled it over a second too long. His mouth went dry and he felt tongue tied as he formed his response. He turned his back to Brooke's desk and walked as far as the long phone cord would reach, as if he were just looking out the north east window to the smallest riding arena. This way, she wouldn't realize he didn't want her hearing his brief conversation.

"Actually, I can't talk right now. I have clients who just drove up and they're on a tight schedule going around the valley looking at horses. I'm sure you understand," he said, trying to sound convincing.

The uncontrollable twitch in his right eye started - his father claimed it always appeared when he wasn't telling the truth.

He's lying.

Her first glimmering thought was to call him on it – instead, she gathered her thoughts.

"I understand. Actually, I was just calling to set up a time when we can talk in person. Surely you have a minute to look at your schedule," she said.

The profound tension that swept over him caused three creases along the width of his forehead.

"This isn't a good week," he answered, speaking quietly, almost mumbling.

Swallowing a third of her iced tea, she was deciding how assertively she should demand that they meet. "This can't wait. I'm still in town and I need to speak with you in person right away."

He stiffened.

"Give me your number and I'll call you tomorrow."

"No. Tell me what time we can meet today or tomorrow," she demanded as she wrapped a chunk of her hair around her index finger.

"I told you, I'm too busy! I've got to go. Call me in the morning."

The phone disconnected before she had a chance to respond.

He won't get away with this!

His knees weakened and his neck and shoulders tightened so much he could barely turn his head. Feeling his face flush from anxiety, he hoped Brooke hadn't noticed. The office was air- conditioned to a comfortable temperature, but the abbreviated conversation made him so nervous he broke out in an uncontrollable sweat.

He walked to the training arena to checkup on an apprentice working with a mare that was slowly getting into condition after recovering from a tendon injury. As he looked for any signs of lameness, it gave him time to gather his thoughts.

How could his own father have gotten him into money laundering? He hated it. All he ever wanted to do his entire life was breed and train talented horses, and to have his father love him as much as his father loved Chandler.

After years of grueling work and dedication, the Ivys now owned one of the country's most elite operations. The fruition of the farm's success came only after Robert Ivy left the farm, thus his wife and sons, to return to his business in Chicago, that was failing as badly as his family unit had.

Everyone was glad to see him go - even Chandler, the favored son. Nobody could tolerate Robert's emotional or physical abuse of Marsha or Leslie any longer. Yet, even in spite of his hatred for his father, Leslie still longed for his father's approval–the same kind of approval and encouragement that Chandler, the eldest son, received.

Last year, when Robert approached Leslie pleading for help, Leslie assumed he would earn his father's love if he came through for him. Robert Ivy was having severe financial problems at his paper distribution company in Chicago. He convinced Leslie to get involved in the money laundering scheme to earn enough money to keep the company out of bankruptcy.

Of course, Robert never asked his first son, Chandler, to get involved. In fact, Chandler didn't even know what they were doing. Robert told Leslie that if he didn't cooperate, he would need to quickly liquidate everything he owned, including the farm and the horses. A fire sale would only bring a fraction of what anything was worth.

He told him that the only alternative was to engage in money laundering. The previous year, hoping it would be short term, his father borrowed money from the bank and mortgaged the farm and most of the horses. He claimed to be past due on the bank loan and that the bank was threatening to foreclose.

Leslie felt that he had to go along with the scheme or his father would abandon him and his family. The family would be penniless if he didn't help.

Robert paid both Luke and Leslie ten percent off the top, for being the front guys and taking the risk. Their roles were actually very easy. The problem was, it was all fraud and Leslie lived with a guilty conscience. Aside from the mental anguish, Leslie knew he could go to prison for a long time.

Back when he first reluctantly got involved, his father made it seem so simple and convinced him they couldn't get caught.

Here's how it worked: a client who needed money laundered would appear to buy a horse from the Ivys for $50,000.00 to $100,000.00. Each transaction had its own purchase contract for a horse. In reality, the same horse may actually be owned by several different people. Then, on paper, it would appear the mare had a foal. Next, on paper, it would appear the mare was bred to Freedom. The person would either pay the $12,000 stud fee for the Freedom breeding or would buy a syndicate share in Freedom for $100,000. Then, it would appear that both the mare and foal were sold for $200,000. If the person had bought a Freedom syndicate share, he would appear to have sold it for

$200,000. Sometimes clients appeared to be trading horses, buying low and selling high, quickly, and continually turning over their money.

It was a scheme no one would suspect in the booming Arabian horse business, with horses appreciating in value so quickly, with active buying and selling, involving so many newcomers with no equine experience. It was a foolproof plan - and now, Rene probably knows about it. Thank God, Leslie had the foresight not to record the real names of people, just in case. If the real names were disclosed, he surely would be permanently silenced.

Chapter Seventeen

Just after dark, Rene called Grady and told him not to drive up to Santa Barbara the next morning, and asked if he could delay his plans to come stay at the hotel with her for another day or two. He was swamped with work, so he eagerly agreed, although he had no clue why Rene wanted to spend so much time in Santa Barbara when she could have been in Malibu with him.

She threw on a pair of jeans and a sleeveless button down white oxford shirt and got in her car to take a drive. Before she knew it, without really planning to do so, she was at Ivy Farms.

The gate was wide open. She couldn't resist the temptation to just drive in, although she had no idea where Leslie Ivy's house was. No one thought anything of the headlights because farm help also lived on the property. As Rene slowly drove down the long winding driveway, she assumed the first house, which was the largest and most elegant of all the houses, must be Mrs. Ivy's. She decided to go to the next nice looking house and take her chances. If it wasn't Leslie's, they would tell her which one was.

As she stepped out of her car, dogs barked from inside the house. In a moment, the front entry light switched on and a woman's silhouette appeared at the front door. The dogs stood obediently at her side.

"Can I help you?"

Rene was out of the car by the time she heard the voice.

"Is this Leslie's house?"

"It is. We weren't expecting anyone. May I ask your name?"

"I'm sorry to bother you. He's not expecting me, but it's important."

The woman sized up the attractive visitor, hoping her husband wasn't having an affair with the woman who had unexpectedly arrived at their home after dark.

"I'll get him for you. What's your name?"

"Rene. Rene Killian."

"Come on in, he's downstairs in the game room," she said.

"I'll just stay outside. It's a beautiful night."

The woman didn't know what to think as she went inside and called for her husband.

"Rene Killian is in our front yard to see you!" she called down the stairs.

Leslie gasped. His wife didn't know anything about what was going on. How was he going to handle this? He raced up the stairs two at a time.

His wife was worried about him now - he wasn't himself with the kids this afternoon or at dinner, then he retreated to play darts by himself. Now, this.

"I'll be back inside as soon as I can. Kiss the kids goodnight for me," he told his wife as he walked past her.

Furious at Rene, he flung the door open.

His wife stormed after him and said, "I'm coming outside with you. Who is this woman?"

"Please, let me handle this," he said as he pushed past her.

She followed him out the door before he could close it. He stopped dead in his tracks, turned around and gently took her by the shoulders.

"Honey, I'll deal with this. We'll discuss it later."

"No. No we'll discuss it now. You're not meeting with this woman alone, at night, in front of our house with no explanation. Something is going on and you can't hide it anymore!" she said as quietly as she could.

"Sweetie, I promise, everything is fine. Just let me get rid of her."

"If everything is fine, you won't care if I come out with you!" her voice now a little louder than the whisper it was a moment ago.

Rene stood in the driveway, straining to hear them. She could only imagine.

"Please. Just trust me. Stay in the house," he said as he gently pushed her back inside the entry door just far enough so that he could close the door. He looked at her with a pleading she'd never seen before.

The door didn't reopen. He approached Rene with a vigor that startled her, and even scared her a little bit.

The blood drained from his face. All he could say was, "I told you we would talk in the morning."

"It's obvious you were just stalling, and I think you'll just keep stalling. You're lucky I didn't come when more people were around."

"What's your problem?"

"I need three million dollars, and I need it within a week."

"What on earth are you talking about?" he murmured, still acting as if he didn't know why she was there.

"I suggest you make arrangements to give me the money within seven days."

"Or what?"

"Do you really want to know?"

"Hell, I don't even know why you think I'd give you a dime, let alone three million bucks!"

"I have a list of reasons. Item number one, I have the original Breeding Report from the Registry..."

He didn't know it was even missing. Dominick's people were supposed to mail it in after he signed the document.

He stuttered, "I don't know what..."

"Number two, I have the syndicate file for ..."

"Okay! Okay! Hold on."

"What? You're worried I'm wired by the cops or something? I just want the money, and that's it."

"Where am I going to get that kind of money?"

"How about from your money laundering scheme... I really couldn't care less where the money comes from – I just better have it by next Wednesday!"

"What am I going to tell everyone? I can't have that kind of money just disappear!"

"You'll get all of Jared's horses that are already here on your property, and I have a two year old colt you're going to buy. You're going to buy the package from me for three million."

"Are you nuts?"

"No. But apparently you are, and I've got the evidence to prove it," she said as she swung open the door to her car.

She could see Leslie's wife peering out the window trying to analyze their body language.

"Keep your mouth shut about this! Write up a purchase contract and call me in a couple of days."

A sly grin extended across her face. "I'll be in touch!"

Chapter Eighteen

Three days later...

"Where do you see our relationship going?" she asked within five minutes of Grady arriving at her hotel room.

"Nowhere. How about you?"

"Well, I guess I feel the same. You don't talk personally about yourself, so I don't about me."

"I never led you to believe I wanted an emotional relationship."

"I know. In fact, given your recent..."

"Please, don't even start."

"Grady, don't I deserve to know a little bit about your feelings and what happened?"

"Deserve? That's hardly a word that I would think is appropriate."

"You're right. Deserve isn't the right word, but we've spent a lot of time together. You've told me so much about so many other people... things you shouldn't have told me... but then you never say a word about your wife."

"First of all, I trust you, that's why I told you things about my clients and other people..."

She interrupted him. "If you trust me for that, then why can't you trust me to share your pain about your wife."

"You don't want to know."

"Yes, I do."

"Then, if you want to know, it's out of morbid curiosity, not out of caring."

"I do care. Just because we're not *in love*, doesn't mean I don't care. What I care about is how whatever happened needs healing, not covered up by pot and coke. You need to talk about it with me, because talking to your shrink hasn't helped you."

"How do you know?"

"Because you're smoking and snorting!"

"I work my ass off. I deserve some relaxation."

"You didn't use drugs before Wanda died, did you?"

"No. Not really. I smoked a joint once in a while if I were at a party, but that's about it."

"So, stop using now. It's the only way you'll really be able to deal with whatever happened."

"Oh, I just love that term! *Whatever happened*."

"Well..."

"Just say it! Just say it...she's dead because of me! Everyone knows it's my fault. Just say it out loud."

"Actually, Grady, no one really knows what happened. That's why no one knows what to say. We just feel bad for you that you lost your wife."

"You want to know what happened? You really want to know?"

"Yes."

"You'll hate me."

"I can't imagine I would ever hate you."

He contemplated telling her as he cracked his knuckles. He stopped wandering around the hotel room and sat on the bed, his back against the headboard and his legs sprawled out in front of him. His face aged ten years in one minute. She sat cross legged, facing him, and put her hands on his knees and looked into his tortured face.

"Okay. I'll tell you. I insisted that we have a gun in the house for protection. Wanda didn't want it around, but I insisted. We didn't have a gun safe, since we didn't have kids. I had the gun for years. Wanda's best friend, Sara, came to visit her from Maryland, and she brought her son, a four year old. Wanda and Sara were in the master bathroom, giving each other facials and deep hair conditioners, like they did when they were in college. They were having a great time, reminiscing about their youth. Sara's son was watching cartoons on our bed, just relaxing, minding his own business. I guess he was being quiet, because Sara said she didn't hear a peep from him. In a split second, he stood at the bathroom doorway and he called out "Bang! Bang!" and giggled. A fraction of a second later, the bullet from my gun shot through Wanda's chest. She bled to death before the paramedics arrived. That's what happened. Are you satisfied?"

Rene cried, releasing all of the pent-up feelings she had about everything. She held Grady tight; at first he stiffened his body. Finally, he melted into her, sobbing so hard he could barely breath. They laid back onto the bed, on top of the comforter, and held each other and cried until the tears wouldn't come out anymore. Spent, they fell asleep in each other's arms.

When Rene awoke, Grady was gone. There was no note or any sign of the overnight bag he had brought with him.

Now she knew his pain. Now it was over. He didn't need to say another word. Hopefully, he'd be on the path of healing now that he was able to unburden himself to someone who cared in her own way.

Chapter Nineteen

Ten days later... Scottsdale Arizona

"Why on earth do you live here in the summer? Scottsdale is a hell pit in the summer!"

"I'm buying a small cabin in the mountains. A cabin with some land for my horses. I doubt if I'll even keep this place."

"You have plenty of money to buy a gorgeous cabin and decorate it however you want, even after giving me this Cashier's Check for $850,000!" J.J. said.

"I know! I'm so excited! I'm free! I'm out of this prison I created! Now I know what they mean when they say 'be careful what you wish for'!"

"I can't believe the timing of you making this huge sale!" J.J. said.

"Sometimes things just work out."

"Yep."

"I can't believe Jared isn't returning my calls. First he's threatening me if I don't sell his horses, then when I do it, he doesn't even return my call. What a piece of work!"

J.J. thought for a minute, then suggested, "Why don't you call his lawyer and tell him you can't reach Jared, but you've sold the horses as promised."

"Good idea. If I can't reach him soon, I'll do that. You should call your sister and let her know you've got the money! She'll be excited."

"Time difference. I can't call right now."

Rene walked barefoot on her driveway to get the local newspaper. In the middle of the paper, buried in the human interest section, there was an article about a group trying to raise money and get donations of well trained, bomb-proof horses for a local therapeutic riding program they were starting for handicapped and mentally disabled people .

She cut out the article with the contact information. She certainly had seed money to help them, and she was confident she knew enough people with horses that didn't work out for high level competition, but would probably be great for the program. She started forming a mental list of who she should call. The list was longer than she would have wanted it to be, but maybe it would come in handy after all.

The program may not be her life calling, but it was certainly something she could work on until something else struck her. Doing fundraising and finding horses for a program like this would let her sleep at night. All of her ambition and contacts wouldn't be wasted.

Later that afternoon, Rene drove J.J. to Sky Harbor International Airport.

"Just drop me off. There's no sense in your wasting time waiting for me to leave," he said.

"I don't mind. I've got nothing better to do."

"Really Rene, you've done so much already. Go home and get some rest, or go see your horses. You've barely been with them."

"Another couple of hours isn't going to make a difference. Besides, you're already going to have such a long flight all alone. No sense in your being alone in the airport too."

He bit his lip. "Okay. Just drop me off and I'll get my bags checked. I'll meet you at the ticket counter."

She smiled. "You didn't pack your Cashier's Check, did you? You've got it in your wallet, right?"

"Why?"

"If your bags get lost or stolen, it'll be a nightmare!"

"I've got it right here," he assured her as he patted his back pocket.

"Stop. This is where I need to check in. I'll meet you right here after you park."

When she stepped out into the heat to help him unload his bags from the trunk, she had a change of heart.

"Actually, just wait a short while for me. It's an oven out here! If I can't find a close parking space, I think I'll just head home back into air-conditioning, since you don't mind waiting alone."

"Fine. Just in case I don't see you, thanks so much. You don't know how this money is going to change my life!" he said as he hugged her.

"You already told me a dozen times! My life's going to change forever too!"

"I know. We're..."

A car horn blared behind Rene's car.

"I better pull out of here."

After he checked in at the ticketing counter, he found the bar he was looking for. The bartender took his order for a beer and served the foamy frosted mug and some nuts.

"You don't know how glad I am to see you!" a voice said from behind him.

They shook hands and each had an enormous smile on their faces.

"Let me drink this really quick. We've got to get out of here. Rene might be looking for me."

"Shit."

"I know. I feel like such an ass, but we better get out of here just in case."

"Yeah. Finish your beer," he said as he looked around.

They took the tram to the domestic flights terminal. Rene wouldn't think to look there.

"Our flight's on time," he said.

"Good," J.J. said.

"Have you ever been to Chicago?"

"No. Have you?"

"No. But we're just going to get my money from old man Ivy, then we can go anywhere we want. Anywhere!"

J.J. seemed excited and sad at the same time.

"It feels weird not to have ties anymore. I really loved my sister and my parents. I miss them."

"I know. But they're dead, and there's nothing you can do about it. They know you love them."

"I know."

"So, Rene fell for the whole story we concocted?"

"Every word. She'd have no way to know that my father didn't own his own business or a huge estate. We never talked about my family before, except that my uncle had Arabians. She's not a real family kind of person, so it never came up about my family. I'm sure of it."

"Good! We'll get my payoff, go to the Caymans, open bank accounts, and do whatever we want for the rest of our lives!"

"Sounds good to me."

They walked to the ticket counter together and checked in for their flight.

"Rene's such a sucker!" J.J. said with a smile on his face.

"No kidding!" Luke said.

Part Two

Three

Years

Later

Southern California

Chapter Twenty

"I've been leaving him messages for the past three days," Rene responded impatiently.

"I've given Mr. Reed your messages. There's nothing more I can do. His schedule is extremely hectic right now. I'm sure he'll return your call as soon as he can," she said diplomatically into her telephone headset while entering information on her computer to print a document.

Tension chiseled itself into Rene's face, causing wrinkles around her eyes--she became aggressive sounding.

"May I have your fax number?"

The woman told her the number.

"Tell him that if I don't hear from him immediately, I'm going to fax a detailed letter. Let him know it will be very personal and not at all laughable," she said hastily.

Completely frazzled, everything was out of perspective. Or was it?

All she wanted was a stiff drink, but she knew she couldn't revert back to her old ways. Now that she was married to Seth, she lived like a perfectly moral woman. Somehow, she would just have to find a way to cope. The more stressed out she became, the more every joint in her body ached.

Her husband Seth was out of town for another day, so at least she didn't need to be hiding everything from him. She needed her privacy - she had so much strategizing to do.

She flung her shoes off and collapsed onto the sofa in the den, her mind twirling like a twister. *Sleep. Maybe if I could just sleep*, she thought as she fell asleep on the sofa.

Waking up groggy, she let her eyes focus. She must have slept for a long time. There was a faint glow of light, barely illuminating the original commissioned oil painting of her Pure Polish stallion, Polsk, that hung over the river rock fireplace. Out the glass French doors which led to the deck, she could see birds on the railing with a beautiful amber sunset peeking through the trees in the background.

Rested and refreshed, things didn't seem so foreboding or as insurmountable. She poured herself a tall glass of cranberry juice and contemplated what she was going to do about dinner, given the fact she was alone. Mongolian Bar-B-Q sounded good, so she changed out of her wrinkled clothes into a casual knit pants suit.

As usual, she went for her purse and keys on the table just inside the garage door entrance. It dawned on her that she hadn't checked her answering machine. She could have slept through the phone ringing, she was so tired. Once in the office, she saw the message light on her business telephone line was illuminated. It could have been anyone. Nevertheless, her heart started beating rapidly.

At least Strathmore hadn't called again. Hopefully he was going to leave her alone. The first message was from her massage therapist, who wanted to know why she hadn't been in for her bimonthly sessions lately.

The second message was mysterious: "Please call me at 714-823-2221 before you attempt to call Grady again. It's important we speak as soon as possible," the woman's crackling voice said.

She dialed the local number.

"Hello."

"Hi. My name's Rene Grant. A woman left this number on my machine to call, but didn't leave a name."

"I'm sorry. It was me that called - Sandra Reed, Grady's mother."

Rene couldn't imagine what she wanted to talk to her about. Surely, Grady wasn't asking his mother to talk to her for him! An attorney with a guilty conscience?

"What can I do for you, Mrs. Reed?"

"Oh..."

Hesitation. She quickly turned serious. "Oh, yes. You haven't called Grady again, have you?"

"No, I haven't."

Relief.

"Good. Thank you."

"What's this about?" Rene asked gently.

"Can we meet somewhere convenient for the both of us?"

Rene's interest was piqued.

"When?"

"Tomorrow afternoon?" Sandra asked.

"I planned on riding most of the afternoon tomorrow."

"That's fine. How about if I come to your place?"

Rene thought for a moment.

"Sure."

"Good. How about around noon? I'll bring lunch."

"Sounds good. Something healthy though! If you've got a fax, I'll send over the directions with a map."

The anticipation of the meeting with Grady's mother kept her awake most of the night.

Seth took a redeye from Boston back to California and was surprised to find Rene sound asleep. She didn't stir when he undressed, showered and slipped into bed. He fell asleep by 9:30 a.m..

Rene woke at 10:00 a.m., cuddled up to her husband who was dead to the world. Trying to be as quiet as possible, she slipped out of bed, showered and dressed in her best riding clothes.

Jason was just leaving the barn when Rene strolled in. He was the only barn help she kept on the payroll.

"Hi! How's everything?" she inquired.

"Great. Everybody's been fed and turned out. The water tubs are full and the stalls are clean. After lunch, I'll put fresh shavings down, then groom."

Amazingly, Jason always looked neat and clean in his pressed button down shirt and Wrangler jeans. Rene felt guilty about all the hours he was working, but he didn't seem to mind.

"It's going to be a beautiful night. Take a break and leave the horses out tonight. It won't hurt the pastures for just this once. Skip the stalls and grooming, except the stallions. Maybe, just come back later in the afternoon for the stallions and night feed," she said nervously as she talked nonstop.

Generally, Rene was a perfectionist, but she'd at least let someone else get a word in.

"Are you sure?" Jason sounded relieved.

"You deserve it! Don't worry about it."

"Great. Who're you going to ride?"

"As many as possible, but I haven't decided who I'm going to start with."

She didn't mention that Sandra Reed was coming, which was the real reason she didn't want Jason around. Who knew what they'd be talking about or if there would be raised voices. No sense in having anyone else overhearing them.

Now, Rene and Seth had their own farm near Laguna Beach. When Dominick sold off all of his horses, Rene finally graciously accepted Satire as a birthday gift from him. Before Sandra arrived, Rene rode him for about thirty minutes up and down hills, traversing the lush green field in the expanse behind the training barn. She was working on building up his muscles and developing his coordination.

Now, there was a half hour to spare. She'd try to mount one of her three year old fillies for the first time. Normally, when she was alone, she wouldn't mount a horse that she'd never been on top of before, but this horse was coming along quite nicely. For the past month, she worked with the filly in the 50' diameter round pen with her wearing a saddle and bridle. The filly was learning everything possible from the ground. On cue, she walked, trotted, cantered, stopped, backed and moved away from pressure. The filly was a fast learner and was always content. Now she was ready for Rene to mount for the first time.

After saddling up, Rene longed her in the round pen for about two minutes to see if the filly felt like bucking. She was as well behaved as ever, so she went ahead to the next step. She put her left boot in the left stirrup and lifted her body up just enough for the filly to feel the weight. Calm. She did it five more times. Still calm. Next, she did the same thing, but also laid her stomach across the saddle so the filly could feel the new sensation. Still calm. Finally, she mounted her and slipped her right boot in the stirrup. The filly was a little scared from the unfamiliar feeling on her sides and from having a body taller than hers. Once she completely relaxed into the weight of the rider, she was asked to take a few steps. The filly refused to move after the first few steps because she was frightened of the feeling of trying to balance a rider. Rene kept asking her to move one step at a time and the filly initially refused each step. With patient urging, she eventually took one step at a time. It wasn't an unusual reaction. That was where the patience in horse training came in.

Out of nowhere, five deer catapulted across a 5 foot fence near them. The filly panicked, broke through the fence of the round pen and ran toward the barn. Rene lost control when the filly braced against the bit and raised her head high in the air. There was no stopping her.

If the filly had a couple of real rides under her belt, she would have learned to lower her head on cue, which would have promoted calmness. A lowered head would have allowed Rene to turn the horse's head to her side and move her hip around, which would have prevented her from running off. But in this situation, the scared filly was the one in control and running as fast as she could toward the barn - her place of safety. She knocked over a chair from the patio set outside of the barn, slid to a quick stop and reared up in the air.

Rene couldn't stay in the saddle. She fell off onto the pea gravel - the wind knocked out of her. The filly broke through two more fences to get back into the nearest pasture with her friends. The other horses came running to her, closely inspecting her saddle, pad and bridle by smelling and tasting. Surely, they congratulated her on her prompt escape from a rider. One of the horses started chewing on the $2,000 work saddle.

As she laid on the ground Sandra Reed walked briskly toward her.

Chapter Twenty-One

"Are you okay?" Sandra asked as she tried to wipe off all of the fire ants on Rene's neck, right arm and her exposed waist.

Rene could barely speak. Her skin burned and itched and there was nothing she could do to relieve it.

"I don't know," she groaned in agony. Her rib cage, front and back, ached with each word.

"Let me help you into the chair."

She saw flashing lights - feeling woozy, she could barely draw in a breath.

"Not yet," she managed to answer with extraordinary effort.

"I've got muscle relaxants with me. The trauma made your body tense up. That's part of your problem."

Sandra was shocked at how easily the lie rolled from her tongue. For two days she had tried to figure out a way to be able to give Rene the appetite suppressant. Until now, she still had no idea how she was going to accomplish her mission of giving her the phandrilis in a large enough dose to be toxic and kill her.

Rene didn't respond.

"Can you get the saddle and bridle off my horse? Please?"

Sandra hesitated, not feeling confident to enter a pasture of strange horses. Finally, she accommodated her request. She carefully placed the chewed-up saddle onto the patio chair and hung the bridle on a hook inside the barn.

Wasabi stuck his head out of his stall, which was at the end of the barn, closest to where the women were. He displayed his concern and curiosity by pawing at his stall door and tossing his head up in the air. A deafening whinny erupted from his enlarged flaring nostrils from time to time, as if to say, *"Hey! What's going on? Are you okay? Who's this stranger? I don't like her near you! By the way, where's my lunch?"*

Still unable to even sit up or to inhale without searing pain radiating through her ribs, she managed to ask another favor.

"Can you take my helmet off?" she begged through clenched teeth. The bright spots in front of her eyes were gone, but her head throbbed and her neck stiffened.

"Sure. Lucky you were wearing one," Sandra said.

The words came out with great effort, one by one, with pain in her voice.

"Will you give that horse a couple of pounds of grain? It's in the feed room in the middle of the barn aisle," she asked.

"Sure. But then we need to take care of you. Is there anyone else here that can help us?"

She couldn't shake her head so she forced a quiet *'no'* out of herself.

Sandra opened the feed door on the exterior of Wasabi's stall, then poured the bucket and closed the door. The stallion wasn't at all interested in eating. He just wanted to watch over his owner, and ideally get out of his stall to be with her. Rene had hoped that if he got his grain he would quit pawing on his door.

"Do you have water in your office?"

"Yeah," Rene whispered, wishing she didn't need to speak, but nodding would have been impossible.

Sandra found water, took it back to Rene, knelt down and put five capsules in Rene's mouth.

"This is a muscle relaxant. You'll feel better soon," she said as she gently put the water to her lips. Ironically, it didn't even cross her mind that she assisted Rene in the gentle manner she would a young grandchild.

Within moments of swallowing the phandrilis her heart was pounding and she hallucinated for the first time in her life. As she tried to regain control of her mind, she didn't see Sandra anymore.

Sandra could see Rene was experiencing an adverse reaction. It shocked her because she thought it would take at least an hour before Rene would feel anything at all. Panicked, Sandra jogged out to the front of the arena and barn to see if anyone else was around or if any cars were coming up the long gravel road leading to the farm.

Rene knew she couldn't make it to her barn office or the house, but the pain from her collision eased up enough for her to stand up halfway, wipe herself off and trudge into Wasabi's stall. She needed to be with him so he would stop pawing and hopefully eat his grain. Unable to remain upright, in the cleanest corner of the stall, she laid down in a fetal position and tightly held her chest as if it would slow down her rapid heart beat.

When Sandra returned to the barn, she was amazed to see Rene curled up on the floor in the stall. She latched the stall door hook from the outside, then briskly walked away with her own heart beating wildly. Hers was from guilt, fear and nerves. It felt like an out of body experience to her.

Rene's hallucinations increased in intensity until there was no hint of reality. Horses were flying. Then they were swimming deep under the crystalline aqua-marine waters in the Caribbean ocean with her. Not knowing where she was or what she was doing, or that she laid down in the stall, her world faded. Everything transformed into darkness and oblivion.

Chapter Twenty-Two

By the time she drove down the long winding gravel driveway to the road, the salt from Sandra's gushing tears stung her eyes so badly she could barely see to drive. Not believing what she had done, not believing what she was capable of, her heart ached as it never felt before. She always thought of herself as a person who couldn't hurt a fly. There was no turning back. How could she have done this? The guilt was unbearable.

Unable to go home and face her husband as if nothing had happened, she mindlessly drove the coastline trying to put herself back together, if it were even remotely possible. When she was near the Ritz Carlton in Laguna, she decided to check in.

"Do you have a room?" she gathered herself enough to ask the desk clerk.

"Yes. How many in your party?"

She didn't answer. She stood still, eyes glazed, nearly dysfunctional.

"How many in your party?"

"Just me. Put it on my card," she said as she fumbled with the wallet in her Coach purse. She handed him one of the Gold cards.

The clerk ran her card, got her room key and called for a bell captain.

She managed to get the words out before she broke out in tears again.

"I don't have any bags. Can you just have someone park my car?" she said, handing him the keys.

"Certainly. Are you all right?" he was genuinely concerned.

"I'll be fine. Where's my room?" she said, barely audible.

She washed the smeared make-up that streaked her face and put a cold wash cloth on her forehead. The room clock read 4:10. Dazed, she wondered where she had driven for so long. Her mind was blank. The only thing that she could think of was the devastating guilt of having murdered Rene... and of how starving she was. She managed to call room service. They said it would take up to an hour because the kitchen was between shifts. What else could she do but wait?

There was something else to do.

In the desk drawer she found hotel stationary and began writing. When she was almost finished writing the tear stained letter, she swallowed a handful of prescription sleeping pills she picked up from the pharmacy early that morning. Before she fell asleep, she managed to scribble a brief note of apology to Rene's family, with no explanation. She said she hoped that taking her own life was enough to show how sorry and horrible she felt for what she had done. She stuffed each letter in an envelope and sealed them, addressing one to her husband, and the other to Rene's family.

Not five minutes after she passed out on top of the bedspread, room service knocked on the door.

"Room service!"

No response.

The waiter called the front desk with his radio.

"There's no answer in Room 311. I must have written down the wrong room number. Can you find out where I'm supposed to be for a Mrs. Reed?"

The front desk clerk was immediately suspicious of something being wrong since he had seen her so despondent when checking in. Hotel security was quickly dispatched to the room.

"She's passed out on the bed. It looks like she took sleeping pills," the hotel security man said when he called the front desk clerk.

After an ambulance was summoned, the front desk manager looked up Mrs. Reed's home telephone number.

"Mr. Reed? Randal Reed?"

"Yes."

"I'm calling from the Ritz Carlton. Your wife is here and it seems that she has attempted suicide by taking sleeping pills."

"My wife's at South Coast Plaza, shopping," he responded without thinking.

The clerk gave him a physical description and explained that he had her credit card imprint and described her car.

"Given this, do you think we have your wife here?"

"Yes. You must," he said as his heart dropped out.

"Where would you like the ambulance to take her?"

Randal instructed him to send her to Newport General Hospital, the hospital closest to their home, and the first place that came to his mind.

"Would you please check to see if there's a note?" he asked, despite his shock and anguish.

"Yes sir. What would you like me to do with it if there is?" he replied sympathetically.

"Is there someone that could bring it to the hospital for me? Of course, I'll pay them for their time."

"Yes sir. I'm so very sorry about your wife. We can take care of the car situation when it's convenient for you. I hope she'll be okay."

\ \ \ \ \ \ \ \ \ \ \

The emergency room was prepared to pump her stomach. They knew what she had taken and approximately how long it was in her system, based upon when she checked into the room and her room service order. Ten minutes after Sandra was wheeled into the emergency room, a young man from the hotel had the nurse's station page Mr. Reed. Randal was surprised to be handed two envelopes. There was nothing he could do for his wife - he told the nurse he would be in the hospital chapel.

He read the note addressed to Rene Grant's family.

Sandra murdered someone?

Then he read the second letter, addressed to him:

My Dearest Love,

I'm so sorry to put you through this. I love you with all of my heart. That's why I did what I did. I couldn't live with myself now that I've taken Rene's life.

Sometimes in life, one thing leads to another and things spin out of control. Sometimes one finds that they are capable of something so despicable, so out of character, so horrible, that they just can't live with themselves any longer. That's what happened to me.

I love you. Sandy

He was devastated. He needed to get his son to the hospital and he needed to find out where Rene's body had been taken and what the coroner knew about her death.

"Law Offices. How can I direct your call?"

"Put my son on the line. This is an emergency."

There were a few seconds of piped in music.

"Dad? What's wrong?"

"It's your mother. Get down here, now!"

"Where are you?"

"Newport General. Off of Harbor Blvd."

"What happened?"

"She's alive, but I need you to get down here right now."

Click.

He didn't want to alarm his son to the extent that he might not drive safely, but he wanted him at the hospital, promptly.

"Coroner's."

"Hello. This is Reed over at Newport General. Can I talk to someone from intake?"

He didn't really know who he should talk to, but this would be a start.

"Sure. Please hold."

A voice that was definitely not accustomed to talking to the public came on the line.

"Yeah. Intake."

"Can you tell me if an autopsy has been started on a Rene Grant yet?"

"I'll check."

After being on hold for several more minutes, the brusque man returned.

"We don't have a Rene Grant here."

"How about Jane Doe that would have gotten to you in the past several hours?"

"Nope."

"You're absolutely sure?" he asked perplexed.

"Yep."

"Is there a superior of yours I could talk to?"

"Nope."

"Any other department?"

"Mister, I can read a list of names."

He hung up the phone without another word.

Randal assumed that the body had been discovered. In actuality, he didn't know if it had, let alone where she was murdered. His head was spinning. The ER staff was encouraging; the only thing he could do was to wait to ask his wife when she was conscious.

He went to the hospital florist to buy flowers, wanting them in her room when she woke. While he was looking at the arrangements, some of them had already been purchased and had cards attached. A sloppily written name caught his eye on a card. He looked closer.

"Excuse me, miss," he said, trying to get the attention of the florist who was fiddling with another arrangement.

"Can I help you?"

"Yes. I'd like an arrangement for me to take now, but could you read the card here?" he asked, gesturing toward the multicolored assortment of tropical flowers.

It was highly irregular for someone to ask, but the she didn't see any harm.

"It's for Rene Grant. I'm waiting for the room number before we send it up. Why?"

"Up to a room?" he stammered.

"Where else? We're in a hospital!"

Relief beyond all relief. On the other hand, as things got better, they were worse. Murder is worse than attempted murder, but now what was Sandra going to face?

With Rene dead, Sandra would live with the guilt, but might not have been caught. He didn't know the how, when or where of the act she committed. Alive, surely Rene knew Sandra had tried to murder her.

He abruptly left the floral shop forgetting the flowers he intended to purchase. All he knew was that he needed to call his firm. Although he retired, his partners were some of the best criminal attorneys on the west coast.

It was urgent that he understood the nature of Rene's condition. In only ten minutes, he was able to find out she was in a coma when she was brought in and hadn't come out of it! She had surface lacerations on her face and very minor abrasions and bruising on her back and on her right arm. They discovered some rock dust, traces of manure and three dead ants crushed into the surface lacerations on her back. It was assumed she had fallen from a horse that same day. The fall could not have caused an immediate coma though, because she was found in a stall with a horse. The type of minor injuries to her skin could not have come from the horse in the stall. She tested negative for illegal drugs and alcohol in her system. Her husband indicated that she was not being medicated for any reason.

Now, the only thing he could do was talk to Sandra. He expected her to be lucid anytime. His beeper went off. It was Grady, alerting him that he was at the hospital. They met in the lounge.

"Don't ask me why, but your mother tried to kill some woman, then out of guilt tried to kill herself. She checked into the Ritz Carlton, then took a bunch of sleeping pills..."

"Who found her?"

Randal explained what little he knew, and showed Grady the letters.

Grady couldn't get his mind around this. He couldn't even imagine his mother thinking of killing someone, let alone planning it and ultimately doing it. Or attempting to do it. His mother? She couldn't even raise her voice when she was angry. All she ever would do is leave the house abruptly or lock herself in the bedroom and not speak to them until the next meal. But murder?

"Paging Randal Reed. Please report to room 770," the hospital speaker announced.

"Come on. That's your mother's room. She's awake."

Sandra was sobbing when they arrived. She was laying there still thinking she had murdered Rene. When her husband and son walked into the room she turned her eyes away in shame.

"Could we please be alone?" Grady requested of the nurse.

"Of course," she mumbled as she promptly excused herself.

Randal looked at his wife through new eyes.

"Sweetheart. We love you. It's okay. Rene's not dead. She's in a coma, right here in this hospital. No one knows anything but the three of us," Randal said as he embraced her with tears in his eyes. He felt her pain in every way.

Randal held Sandra's left hand.

"Honey, who is this woman, Rene?"

She glanced at Grady. Neither of them spoke.

Randal broke the silence.

"So far, no one knows why she's in a coma and they can't find anything significant."

She nodded her head almost imperceptibly. Today didn't seem to be reality and she still hadn't quite grasped everything that was happening.

Sandra pulled the blanket up and fell asleep again for about forty-five minutes.

"Are you up to telling us what this is all about?" Randal asked gently.

She met his eyes, looking embarrassed and worried.

"When Grady and I planned to meet for lunch a couple of days ago, I arrived at his office early. He was running late, as usual. I was fumbling through his message slips and saw several from some woman named Rene Grant. At lunch, I brought this up with him - it didn't seem professional for him not to be returning someone's calls. At first he tried to avoid talking about it. I'm his mother. I know when my son is trying to hide something from me. By the end of lunch, I pressed him enough to tell me about her."

"Calm down honey, you're shaking."

She continued, trying to steady her voice.

"Grady said he had an affair with her a few months after Wanda died, when he had his drug and alcohol problem. He feels irresponsible now, but he said he let her read his files and he told her personal things about his clients."

Grady walked to the window, unable to face his father who was once one of the most well respected attorneys in California.

Sandra went on, acting as if she hadn't noticed her son's reaction.

"As if that weren't enough, he knew she had stolen confidential information from some farm that was laundering money, and he knew she planned to blackmail them. When they broke up, it was mutual - he thought he'd never hear from her again."

Randal glared at his son. "Go on."

"He said that recently, an FBI agent interrogated him about his relationship with her and any business dealings he may have had with her."

Finally, Grady took the burden off of his mother.

"I called her and demanded to know why I was being questioned. The FBI hadn't contacted her, so she didn't have a clue what I was talking about at first. We put our heads together, and based on the types of general questions the agent asked me, we pretty much came to the conclusion that they must know that she had blackmailed the Ivys. We assumed the Ivys were caught money laundering, but we didn't know.

"Anyway, she's demanding that I swear the horses Ivy Farms bought from her was a real sale - not blackmail. In reality, she concocted a phony horse transaction to cover up her blackmail scheme. She wants me to say she didn't know anything about their laundering money. The bitch is insisting I tell the FBI I drew up the sales contract for the horses, and that I knew for certain it was a real sale."

Randal bit his lip, not really knowing whether to believe his own son or not.

"What did you tell her?"

"I refused to lie for her. Then, she started leaving me messages. She might have been planning on blackmailing me! I didn't return her calls."

Sandra was up to talking again.

"If she were going to be spiteful and expose Grady, he'd be disbarred. His life is finally normal again. No more drugs. A nice wife and a baby on the way. I didn't know what else to do. I panicked."

"What on earth did you do, mom?"

"I tried to kill her by giving her five capsules of that herb that's been on the news, phandrilis. The bottle has a warning label on it about safe usage levels. It said to take one capsule per day with food. I knew Rene would have an empty stomach because I was bringing lunch for us. I don't know how I picked five..." her weakened voice trailed off.

Randal's eyes widened in amazement.

Chapter Twenty-Three

The next day...

"Is Dominick there?"

She didn't recognize his desperate voice.

"No, he's on location."

"Is there a way I can reach him right away? Rene's been hurt and might not make it," he pleaded.

Peri realized she was speaking to Rene's husband, Seth. They had met during a party on Dominick's yacht.

"I'll call him. What number can you be reached at?" Peri asked without any genuine concern. She didn't particularly like what she knew of Rene.

She repeated the phone number before hanging up.

Dominick was notorious about protecting his privacy - so, she didn't give out his phone number to anyone. Peri's stomach began to churn from aggravation. Seth acted as if she should know his voice - as if she was just some housewife who sat around taking her husband's personal phone calls. How dare Seth not show her the respect she deserved!

As the lead anchor on three different award winning network television news shows, she was successful in her own right. She was one of the highest paid television journalists in the nation. Hell, she was on the April cover of People Magazine: *"Peri Montrose's Rise To Fame and Fortune."* When the issue hit the newsstands, Dominick proudly displayed a copy on the entry table of their penthouse. She still hadn't removed it, even now, five months later.

Dominick answered on the second ring.

"Hi honey, how are you?"

"I'm fine. Rene's husband just called. Apparently she's been in a serious accident or something. He wants you to call him right away."

His neck and jaw tightened.

"What happened? What's wrong with her?"

"I don't know!"

"Did you give Seth my number?"

"No. Why do you think I'm calling you instead of Seth calling you directly? You said you didn't want anyone else to have it!"

"I'm sorry...love you," he said as if reading a script out loud for the first time.

How could Peri not care enough to make even the most basic of inquiries about such a serious situation?

"Love you, too," she said hesitantly.

As the words came out of her mouth, she wondered what had happened with them for her to be acting this way. She didn't know why she turned so cold. He hadn't done anything to make her angry or to hurt her. It was only natural that he would respond back to her the same as she had spoken with him. Maybe her OB/GYN was right - she was actually menopausal. Hormones can do crazy things. Perhaps her estrogen levels were causing her drastic mood swings lately. She'd have to get that checked out. Put it on her list of things to do. Again.

For a change, the day had been just fine until the phone call from Seth.

Her invigorating jog in Central Park was just what she needed - singing birds, a light breeze, and time away from the studio.

Hopefully, she'd be able to discipline herself to make a habit of jogging. Regardless of her good intentions, she never kept up an exercise routine for more than a few consecutive weeks.

Over the past month or so, she overheard several of her colleagues commenting on her attitude. They claimed she had become antagonistic when she wasn't in front of the camera.

When she asked a close friend her opinion, her friend suggested she might be stressed out and in need of time off. Unable to take time off of work now that she had three shows going, she made a commitment to herself to either jog or work out at the health club everyday. It would help her unwind, relieve stress and her get into better shape. One of her producers recently hinted at her needing a more youthful look. He hinted about a new hairstyle among other rude suggestions.

As she considered calling Dominick and apologizing for how she sounded, she concocted of mix of fresh blueberries, strawberries, a half of a ripe banana, mango juice, soymilk and crushed ice. The vibrant colors of the fruit clashed with the muted blue slab granite kitchen countertop she regretted selecting. It was beautiful, but she could never prepare food that looked appealing when sitting on the counter.

Without showering or changing clothes, she stretched out on the sofa, drank part of her healthy concoction, then laid back and closed her eyes, wishing she never had to leave the apartment again.

^^

Dominick's tired body melted into the buttery soft hunter green, Scandinavian leather furniture. He hoped to cushion the shock of whatever the devastating news about Rene was going to be.

"Seth? Dominick. What's going on?"

"You're not going to believe it. Yesterday we found Rene unconscious, locked in a stall with Wasabi. He was calm and relaxed, eating his hay. No one had seen her since about eleven in the morning, and Jason found her at 4:30 in the afternoon. We called an ambulance right away. She's in the hospital."

Rene had told Dominick about Wasabi. If he weren't handled properly on a daily basis, he would be almost uncontrollable. She and Seth had been the only ones to actually handle Wasabi for the past year because she feared the stallion could seriously hurt someone. Rene always complained about people being litigation happy. Still, she refused to geld him or sell him because he was impeccably bred and was an outstanding individual. Wisely, she didn't use him for breeding either. Dominick understood.

"What do they think is wrong?"

"She's in a coma. They don't know at this point."

\` \` \` \` \` \` \` \` \` \` \`

Ever since they had met three and a half years earlier, Rene and Dominick spoke on the phone at least every couple of months. He hadn't heard from her in quite some time, and he had been so busy, he hadn't called her either. What he didn't know was that she had in fact been trying to reach him, but Peri wasn't giving him the messages. She didn't particularly care for Rene or their friendship.

"What do you think could have happened?" Dominick sympathetically asked.

Seth played scenes over in his mind time after time.

"The ranch-hand who discovered her insisted that both the top and bottom Dutch doors of the stall had been latched closed. I can't imagine he's remembering it right. It doesn't make sense."

Dominick didn't respond as he pictured the description.

"She wouldn't have hooked the stall door from the inside. I know it's physically possible to do it, but why would she?"

Dominick wanted answers as much as Seth did.

"Does Wasabi try to open the stall himself to get out? Maybe that's why she would have hooked it."

"No. At least never when I've been with him. She never told me he tried it, and she would have thought to tell me, so I wouldn't have a problem."

"How could..."

"Sometimes people come and talk to her while she's in a stall with a horse. I know that at least a few times, out of habit of keeping stalls latched, I subconsciously latch the door while we're talking. Still, I think Jason has an active imagination and is wrong about the doors all being hooked."

"Even if they were hooked, what could have happened to her?"

"Wasabi didn't kick her or anything. I don't have a clue."

Seth sounded grateful to have Dominick to talk to.

"Have the police been called?"

"Huh?"

He paused and thought about Dominick's odd question.

"Why would I call the police?"

"I don't know. I'm sure you were right not to call them."

There was a long silence. Seth and Dominick didn't know each other that well.

Dominick broke the lamenting silence and said, "I'll catch a plane in the morning. What hospital is she in?"

After they hung up, Seth felt relieved Dominick was coming. The nurses told him that talking to Rene while she's in the coma may help her come out of it. He hoped that if his own voice didn't help, perhaps Dominick's would.

"Mr. Grant?"

"Yes," Seth answered.

His head shot up quickly, startled out of his dozing.

"I'm having an orderly bring in a rollaway bed. You must have been uncomfortable last night."

Dazed, he didn't respond.

"When the doctor checks in I can ask him to prescribe a sleeping pill for you. Do you think you'll need one?"

"That would be helpful. Thanks."

That was at the 9 p.m. check.

The bed was rolled in an hour later. The long wait concerned him. Was his wife was getting the best treatment available if they couldn't even get a bed and a sleeping pill to him promptly? Another hour and a half later the nurse finally brought in the sleeping pill.

Seth swallowed the pill without even asking what it was.

It didn't take long for the drowsiness to set in, making him reminiscent of when he and Rene met for the first time, in the winter of 1983, while on a scuba diving boat off the coast of Antigua. By coincidence, they were staying at the same exclusive beachfront resort.

At that time, he was considering making a career change, having burned out from the stress of being an investment banker. He thought he'd go to the island, unwind, and have time to reevaluate what he wanted to do with his future.

He chose Antigua because a college friend of his, in partnership with several Japanese investors, owned *The Paradise Club,* a five-star resort. His friend always assured him there was a complimentary suite overlooking the sea waiting for him whenever and as long as he wanted.

So, there he was, at the breathtaking first-class resort, where he met Rene, the woman who became the love of his life. She had never talked much about her past. Were there important things he was unaware of? Why had Dominick mentioned the police?

'The police?' Seth thought in his last conscious moment before he fell asleep.

Chapter Twenty-Four

Dominick slouched on the sofa in front of the fire contemplating what Seth had told him. If Seth really knew Rene - her devious side - then he, too, would have reason to suspect foul play.

She had secrets her husband, and people who thought they were her close friends, would never know about. She confided in Dominick, but no one else. After all, they had a history.

Dominick phoned a Chinese restaurant and ordered a delivery of War Won Ton Soup, Sesame Chicken, Moo Shu Pork and Kung Pao Shrimp. He knew he wouldn't eat it all, but he couldn't decide what he really wanted.

While he was waiting for the food, he packed a suitcase for the trip. Just thinking about going to California was making him melancholy, even though Rene was hospitalized four hours south of Santa Barbara. He loved Peri, but at times like this he wondered if he had given in to her pressure without seriously thinking about what was really important to him. He was sure he made the wrong decision in selling out. What would she have given up for him?

The Chinese food arrived. He turned on the television while he ate, having no idea what was on, but he wanted the movement of people on the screen so he wouldn't feel so alone. He visualized all of the things that could have happened to Rene. You can't be a film producer or director without being so imaginative.

` ` ` ` ` ` ` ` ` ` ` `

Dominick began his career directing plays, all of which became hits. Later, he expanded into the feature film industry and became one of the most successful movie producer/directors in the country.

He was married when he and Peri met - she interviewed him for a celebrity profile segment. When they met, she was an ambitious journalist established in major local markets and had a promising network career ahead of her. The network chose her to do the interview because of his involvement in the horse industry. Peri grew up in Kentucky, in horse country, having shown horses as child and throughout her college years. ^^

His first wife, Susanna, was very supportive of his equine endeavors, and shared his enthusiasm for horses, although she wasn't nearly as involved as Dominick. She would have liked to have been equally as active with horses, but over the years she seemed to continually have health problems.

By the time she was forty, Susanna was diagnosed with Multiple Sclerosis. She handled it admirably well, including realizing her husband needed and deserved a vital and active woman at his side. Susanna loved him so deeply that she insisted that as long as he would provide for her, he should try to meet a woman who could bring him joy and excite him, as she once had.

Peri and Dominick cultivated a platonic relationship, just as he had with Rene. Initially, Peri confided in him about the struggles she faced in advancing her career. He confided in her about his hopeless feelings regarding his wife's deteriorating physical state. They became dependant on each other for moral support, eventually speaking on the phone or seeing each other almost every day. Out of respect for his marriage, neither of them displayed any outward indications about their deeper attraction to each other.

As Peri and Dominick grew closer, he realized how much he was missing in life since his wife had become an invalid. Once he admitted to himself that he had fallen in love with Peri, he was torn apart. Susanna was such a compassionate woman and they had once had a fulfilling life together.

After discussing his emotional turmoil with Rene, she convinced him that he should be with Peri in an intimate relationship, but warned him that he should be honest with Susanna.

With a heavy heart, he finally found the right time and place to tell Susanna about Peri. The guilt was like the life force being drained from his body. Gracefully, Susanna encouraged him to act on his feelings for Peri and let the friendship grow into a romantic relationship if that was their destiny.

Several months later, on a brisk autumn evening while the sun was setting, Dominick and Susanna embraced on the sofa in the solarium. They were silent, peacefully watching the burnt orange sky transform into deep azure blue, then black. There was a stabbing pain in his heart when he gained the courage to tell her he and Peri had fallen in love. With a slight tremble, Susanna's hands reached for his aging face. Looking deep into his eyes, every wrinkle was a loving memory they shared. She longed for him as she cupped her hands over his gently sagging cheeks. Stinging tears of both sadness and relief welled in her eyes. She peacefully told him she was happy for him and he deserved to live a life with someone vital and with a future.

Susanna suggested a fast, easy divorce, only wanting assurance from him to provide for her financially because it was impossible for her to work. He vowed to provide for her in the same manner to which she was accustomed.

His heart was so full and so empty at the same time.

Life hadn't been the same since.

Last year, Peri finally convinced him to sell his sprawling Santa Barbara farm. She was independent, making plenty of money. It wasn't a matter of her being greedy. It was simply that her career was firmly established and successful. Finally relieved of at least some of the stress and pressure in building her career, she yearned for more quality time with her husband.

For them to be together enough for her liking, he couldn't continue going to his farm in California. In her opinion, he was away from her enough when filming movies. Also, as she repeatedly pointed out, the horse operation lost money, costing him anywhere from $40,000 to $60,000 a month. As a direct result of her assertiveness, his trips to the farm became less frequent.

A week after the farm hosted its 4th Annual Fundraiser for MS Research, Dominick discretely put the property on the market and began liquidating horses.

The farm sold eighty-nine horses, including foals. Regardless of Peri's displeasure, he was adamant about retaining five mares from CSC as a legacy to what he once treasured. Dominick had the mares shipped back to his East Coast farm to join the five that already lived there. Out of sentiment, he kept the first five Arabians he had purchased; one for each of his five grandchildren. The kids rode with the trainer almost every weekend.

Peri ideally wanted him to make a clean break from the horses. In his opinion, it was because she was flustered and bitter about the fact that when she was younger and showing horses, she was not a talented enough rider to compete at high levels of competition. She excelled at everything else she had ever done, and didn't want to be reminded about her limitations with equestrian endeavors. Unfortunately, she had no interest in pleasure riding or in breeding.

He hadn't been back to California since the ranch was sold. Apprehensive about what the breeding directors at the Polish stud farms thought of him selling out, he hoped they could find a way to understand the pressures of his marriage. He couldn't lose his wife over owning the farm and horses, which is precisely what Peri implied, had he not sold out.

His deep regrets in selling the herd of Arabians and the farm haunted him when he was alone with plenty of time to contemplate his life's decisions. Lately, he spent too much time reflecting over and regretting his decision to sellout. He tried to ignore the wedge that widened in his marriage because of how Peri so strongly influenced him. When he sold out, he had hoped to get over it and go on with life as she had it planned for them.

Lately, he tried to come to terms with the choice he would be faced with if he did what was right for his spirit. His wife or his passion for horses. Why couldn't she just understand and support what he wanted? He wasn't complete anymore. He lost himself when he relinquished the horses and the farm that meant everything to him. In his heart, he was sure that the horse breeding operation was his soul's desire.

Just a few months earlier, Dominick and Rene talked on the phone for nearly three hours about his differences with Peri. After he hung up, Peri was very quiet and slept in the guest room the next several nights. He couldn't help but wonder if she had been listening to his private conversation, but he didn't say anything.

Since then, Peri hadn't been acting like herself about anything. Their friends must have sensed her change also - the dinner invitations stopped coming.

Chapter Twenty-Five

The next day...
Newport Beach, California

"Hello."

"Hi, I'm at the airport. How are you?"

"I'm glad you called. I was just getting ready to go home and take a quick shower, then check on the horses. I'll wait until you get here."

"You don't need to wait. I should be there in about twenty minutes. Get some rest. Take your time. I'll sit with her," Dominick urged him with the ultimate declaration of finality.

"You're sure?" Seth responded with fatigue in his voice while fighting to keep his red, glassy eyes open.

"Yeah," Dominick insisted.

He really preferred to be alone with her anyway. Not that he didn't like Seth. It was more that he knew Rene in ways her own husband didn't know her. That made him uncomfortable - as if he were the one keeping the secrets from Seth.

Early in their marriage, Dominick suggested she be more open with Seth and confide in him if she really wanted a close relationship. Every time he brought it up, she rejected the idea. She was fearful that Seth wouldn't accept her if he knew the kinds of things she had been involved in. She didn't think he could give her the unconditional love she dreamed of having. What nice guy could if he knew everything she had done? *The deceptions. The manipulations. The threatening relationships.*

"It'll be a relief not to rush back. I'm about ready to collapse," Seth admitted, slurring his words, sounding as if he were about to fall asleep.

His whole body hurt from exhaustion - he was afraid to sleep in case she regained consciousness.

It took forty-five minutes for Dominick to arrange for his rental car and drive to the hospital. He stopped in the hospital's floral shop and bought two dozen long stemmed red roses with the thorns removed. As the elevator swiftly took him directly to the 5th floor, he admitted to himself that it was he would enjoy the beauty and sweet scent of the roses. He assumed she wouldn't be aware of their presence. He briefly wondered if there was even a remote possibility she would sense the presence of the flowers.

Walking down the hallway to room 515, his heart sunk hollow and his eyes glistened with a hint of tears. Wearily, he remembered how he religiously took Susanna red roses when she was hospitalized.

His heart pounded from conflicting emotions. His left brain was eager to be at her side - his right brain dreaded seeing her in the condition she was in. He couldn't fathom what it would be like to see her unable to communicate.

Cautiously, almost in slow motion, with unintentional hesitancy, he opened the door, afraid of what his reaction might be. At least she was in a private room, he thought. The illumination from the sun shining directly through her window forced his eyes to adjust before she came into clear focus. His first thought was that she looked angelic, wearing a sleeveless pastel green soft cotton gown which came down to her calves. The reality of the surroundings engulfed him. Pale beige hospital sheets had the easily identifiable look of overuse and too much fabric softener. Her head, turned slightly to the right, rested on a goose down pillow encased in cream color flannel. He assumed it was her favorite pillow and that Seth had brought it. She had a tiny bit of drool sneaking out of her mouth. There was an illusion of her peacefully napping.

Dominick stood by her side and gently touched her cheek with the back of his smooth hand and manicured fingers. In an instant, he snapped back to reality. The reason she was there hit him like the Titanic crashing into the fatal iceberg. Only he knew it was likely someone intentionally caused her comatose state.

He had the same feeling as when he dove too deep in the ocean and wasn't sure he would be able to make it back to the surface before he lost his breath. A moment of fear and panic.

Needing time to adjust and accept what had happened to Rene, he had to at least try to clear his mind of the painful memories of the countless days he spent in hospitals with Susanna for the last few years of her life. Just being in the room with the crimson red roses brought back the void in his life without her.

Dominick spent what felt like an eternity staring at Rene, as if staring hard enough and long enough and praying that she'd wake up would be the solution, if he could just do it right. In one way, he thought she looked peaceful and content. In another way, he thought she looked like she was battling the demons in her soul. Sometimes she even looked dead.

He sat beside her and took her hand into his as he gazed out of the window to the natural gardens below. Dominick knew she was alive, but he couldn't resist feeling for her pulse himself. He couldn't resist watching for her shallow breathing, confirming her chest was faintly rising and falling. At one point, he was unable to resist checking to see if he could feel the slight bit of warm air from her nostrils each time she exhaled.

In time, he stopped letting his imagination run rampant. He rubbed her hand between his, hoping the circulation would wake her.

The shift nurse came to check her vital signs.

"How many nurses are on the shift?" he asked.

"Twelve," she answered, wondering why he was asking.

He removed a credit card from his wallet and handed it to her.

"Call in the best delivery food you can for everybody on the shift."

She was grateful for his generosity. As she left the room she had a noticeable bounce in her step.

He appreciated the hard work and grueling hours hospital personnel endured. Until he did a film that involved a lot of time in a hospital, he had no idea the commitment involved and the strain on the staff. When Susanna was hospitalized so often, he gained more insight. He tried to show his appreciation whenever he could. At Susanna's hospital, he paid for the employees' lounge to be redecorated and bought new appliances, a new television, video player, stereo and gave a $2500 gift certificate at a local bookstore so they could stock the lounge with books and magazines of their choice.

Mesmerized, he sat watching Rene's chest rise and fall with every shallow breath. Minutes felt like hours. Not willing to suffer the silence anymore, he spoke slowly and calmly to her.

"Was this an accident?"

Long pause.

"What happened?"

A longer pause.

"Did someone do this to you?"

Bewildered, he wondered if it really helped to talk to someone in a coma.

Out of the blue, he thought he felt her hand give him an almost imperceptible light squeeze. His heart raced. He wondered if this happened to Seth. He didn't want to lose physical contact with her now. He massaged her hands and fingers, gently pulling each finger and flexing each wrist. Again, he felt a light squeeze from her. It definitely was not his imagination this time. Was she trying to tell him something? Or, was it just a physical reaction to his stimulus?

"Do you hurt?"

No reaction.

"Can you hear me?"

No reaction.

"Do you know I'm here?"

No reaction.

"I think you know I'm here."

No reaction.

"Did someone do this to you?"

No reaction.

Dominick gave up trying to solicit a reaction and considered calling in Dr. Lu, a Traditional Chinese Medicine practitioner. Maybe Dr. Lu could examine her, if Seth agreed. Everyone he knew who used Dr. Lu raved about his acupuncture and healing hands. For the first time he felt he could help and that, perhaps, there was hope. He convinced himself that Dr. Lu would be able to bring Rene out of her coma. They simply needed to go through the motions and everything would be just fine and back to normal for everyone. He was certain.

Chapter Twenty-Six

Dominick checked into the Ritz Carlton in Laguna Beach, his favorite Orange County beachfront resort. Because it was after nine in the evening, all of the suites were booked, so he took the last deluxe room overlooking the ocean. As he unpacked, he procrastinated calling Peri. He couldn't remember when he last called her just to hear her voice. Just to know how she was. Just to tell her he loved her.

Reluctantly, performing his duty, he dialed the penthouse.

Peri answered the phone on the second ring.

"Hello."

"Hi honey. It's me," he said, his voice sounding drained.

"I'm so glad you called. I miss you."

Yeah, sure, he thought.

"I miss you too," he replied.

I wish I missed you.

"Where are you?" she asked lightly.

"I just checked into the Laguna Ritz Carlton."

What do you care?

"Without me? You know that's one of my favorite places!" she said in a sentimental drawl, her old Southern accent peeping through.

"Just habit."

"How long are you staying?"

She actually seemed to care.

"I'm not sure, but I'll let you know as soon as I decide."

I can't believe she still hasn't asked about Rene.

"Guest what?"

"What?"

"I bought the most beautiful Channel suit this morning. I've already got shoes and a handbag that'll match perfect."

Who cares?

"That's great! Did the station pay for it?"

I guess I need to just keep making conversation.

"No. I didn't ask. I don't even want to deal with it," she said, temporarily reclaiming a lost vibrancy in her tone.

My good friend is in a coma and you can't think about anything other than a new designer suit...you've got closets full of them.

"I wouldn't have the nerve to ask them to reimburse you for what they pay you a year!" he said, trying his hardest to sound as if he were enjoying their conversation.

"That's how I feel!"

She's acting as if we're truly communicating about something important.

"Anything else going on?"

Still. Not a word about Rene! Cold hard selfish bitch of a wife. When did she stop being warm and compassionate?

"No. I just wish you were here with me. Can you come back for a few days? I miss you so much."

Was she sincere?

"I wish I could be with you too, but I can't."

Did I sound convincing?

"Danielle's on vacation. My temporary make-up artist is here. I've got to go now. I'll try calling you later. I love you, honey."

"Love you too."

I wish I still did.

He dialed another phone number.

"I need to postpone this project," Dominick said by way of apology to his production manager after contemplating the issue for hours.

"Are you serious?"

"I'm sorry. I don't have any idea how long it'll take to clear things up."

Dominick was just as concerned as Robert about the ramifications of stopping a production a month before the cast was scheduled to show up on location.

"Is it Peri? Is she okay?"

It was the only thing Robert could think of which would be serious enough to delay production indefinitely.

"No. She's fine. It's personal."

"Do you have any idea what this will cost us?"

Robert waited for an answer. None came.

"What if we lose our stars? They might have other commitments!"

Robert didn't know how to impress upon Dominick what he should already have thought of.

"I know. I know. We'll just have to shoot it as fast as possible once we start filming. That's the best I can do."

He second guessed himself, but he wasn't about to admit it.

"Dahmahniick..."

"Trust me. It'll work out. Just put everybody on stand by. Tell them it's my fault and that somehow we'll stay on schedule once we get going. I promise we won't go past the original quit date."

"It's your ass - not mine."

Robert felt as if he had run into a brick wall, but Dominick was the boss. He really couldn't do anything else.

When he hung up, he hoped to God he was doing the right thing. His stomach growled. The restaurant menu sounded great, but he decided to order room service.

Twenty minutes after he placed his order, the room service delivery person knocked.

"Thanks. Just put it over there."

"Yes sir," said the young man.

He hesitated.

"Aren't you that movie producer?"

"Yep."

"I've got a plot for you," he boasted.

"Is it short? I'm hungry and tired," Dominick said, wishing he didn't feel as if he had to be patronizing.

"Sure! Here it is: you feature three or four guests in a fancy resort hotel. They're all interesting, but one of them is a lady who tries to kill herself and leaves two suicide notes. That's the big mystery. Why did she do it? Does she live or die? You know, it's like, you just make a great story out of it!"

The kid was really *stoked*, as his generation says.

"I don't know... I don't write 'em. People just send my company screenplays and novels... and I decide if I want to buy them. Even then, there are usually lots of rewrites. Thanks though."

Dominick had no intention of using the idea.

"Sure. Can I get you anything else, Mr. Castinitas?"

"No. I'm fine."

After double checking the order under the warming lid, he signed the check and added twenty dollars to the regular tip.

The kid coolly strolled out the door and started down the hallway.

For no particular reason something inspired Dominick to find out how the kid got the idea he proposed.

The hall was deserted, so he yelled out, "Hey! Can I ask you something?"

The kid turned around and waited to hear the question.

"How did you get your idea for a story?"

The kid walked back toward him and explained.

"It really happened? Here?" Dominick said, thinking someone would go to a motel to try to kill themselves.

"Yeah. It happened two rooms down from here. I was freaked out!"

"It's like, you know. I just went to deliver her food. Then finding her just freaked me out. They don't train us how to deal with anything like that."

Dominick nodded with compassion.

The kid continued. "Then, the manager sends me to Newport General to give the husband her suicide letters."

"Uh."

"Well, I heard she didn't die. I'm glad the food was ready when it was!" the kid said, sounding genuinely relieved.

"No kidding. She sure is lucky!"

Now the kid was excited.

"Yeah. Plus, her husband is paying me and my friend a hundred bucks to drop-off her car at the hospital later. A hundred bucks for a half hour max of driving! Can you believe it?"

"I'm sure he just doesn't want to deal with it," Dominick reasoned.

The voice came from a few cars down in the underground parking garage. Dominick looked over and recognized the room service kid.

"Hi, Mr. Castinitas!"

"Oh, hi. I was just getting my organizer from my car."

"That's cool. I'm getting my dad one for his birthday."

Dominick was surprised the kid wasn't star struck.

"Your dad will love it."

"Hey - this is the Mercedes I'm taking to the hospital. I can't wait to drive it!"

Trying to patronize the kid, he looked toward the Mercedes. He stared at the rear of the car. The vanity plate said 'Reed2me.'

Chapter Twenty-Seven

"Mathew, it's Peri. Do you have a few minutes?"

It wasn't really a question. She would give him instructions whether it was convenient for him or not.

"I can barely understand you. Are you on that damn speaker phone again?"

"Yes. Everyone else can understand me when I'm on it. Just sit down with a notepad and write down this list of things I need for you to do while I'm gone."

Her impatient tone wasn't anything new.

"Where are you going?"

Peri neatly packed an overnight bag and a hanging bag as she spoke to Mathew.

"I'm leaving on the redeye to surprise my husband in California. I'll be back in a few days."

She no longer had to ask permission from her producers or anyone else.

"What about the Nancy Reagan interview?" he asked, hoping he wasn't stepping out of line.

"I'll work on the plane. I need you to look into a few things for me. Got a pen handy?"

Chapter Twenty-Eight

"I've got some good news gentlemen," Dr. Weinstein said as he opened Rene's chart.

"Somehow, even though there were tiny red bite marks on Rene's skin, it slipped through the cracks to do a blood serum analysis for insect or rodent bites."

"Go on," Seth said, finally feeling hopeful.

"As it turns out, Mrs. Grant was bitten by fire ants and had an unusually severe allergic reaction. That's what put her in the coma."

"Fire ants?" Dominick asked.

"Yes. I understand she fell off of a horse. Apparently, she landed where there were fire ants. A severe allergic reaction could have put her in a coma within five to twenty minutes."

"What made you do a blood serum test for it?" Dominick asked, impressed by the doctor.

"I thought of it because I grew up on a farm. We were always outdoors with our horses and farm animals. I was with my sister when she was bitten by fire ants as a teenager. She had a severe reaction - although not as severe as Mrs. Grant. When I couldn't find anything that explained the coma from all of the tests that we ran, and I couldn't imagine any other types of tests, I thought of the blood serum. The ER only checked for drug and alcohol poisoning."

"I'm glad you thought of it!" Seth said.

Dr. Weinstein had more good news.

"There's an anti-serum to counteract the reaction to the bites. She should come out of the coma in anywhere from twenty-four to forty-eight hours. I can't guarantee it, but I think she'll be fine. Keep talking to her. Personally, I believe patients in a coma know most everything going on around them."

He spoke to her as if she were awake.

"Hi Rene. I'm back," Dominick said quietly.

I'm trapped in my own body.

How do I get out?

I need out.

Why am I so confused?

The voices...Help me!

"You wouldn't believe what's happened. I don't even know where to start. Have I told you that things haven't been going too well with Peri and me lately? Well, it's been pretty bad actually... I guess she decided to surprise me and make an unannounced visit. She said she wants to try to make our marriage work. I told her I want a divorce and there was nothing to work on. We're just too different."

She lightly squeezed his hand. He was so into describing the events of the past few days he didn't even realize it.

"She was furious when I told her. She left the hotel and checked into that spa in La Costa."

With all of his heart, he wished Rene could talk to him. Comfort him. Help him confirm that his inevitable divorce was for the best. He sat contemplating his situation, tears streaming, and rubbing his temples. He leaned forward with his elbows balancing on his knees. Everything came pouring out.

A deep sigh.

"All I know is - I need out of this marriage."

He stood and paced as if he were solving a creative problem.

"This relationship's killing me."

He couldn't believe the words coming out of his own mouth. He had been so busy working lately he didn't realize things had deteriorated to this extent. His heart felt heavy for a moment and then the first hint of enthusiasm washed over him.

"I'm going to buy a big farm again. Get back in the horse business. I don't care if it's going to lose money or not. You know what I mean. You know. I know you do."

The relief of saying the words aloud was the first good feeling he had in months. He finally felt a tinge of relaxation as he lowered himself back down into the chair.

A few minutes of quiet brought him peace now that he decided what he had to do about his marriage and moving forward in his own life. He took Rene's hand in his and stroked it.

She lightly squeezed his hand again and made a sound that was barely audible. He thought he imagined it. He was so deep in his own thoughts, he assumed he imagined it.

Another soft movement of her hand…a slight turn of her head…a single tear.

Dominick was sure. Absolutely, positively sure! She was responding to what he was saying!

Let me out…

I'm gliding in air through a tunnel…

Let me out…

He didn't know if he should call the nurse or doctor. Rubbing his cheeks, he realized they hurt from smiling so big. His racing heart caused his adrenaline to race through his body.

"You hear me! I know it. I know it in my gut!"

A stronger squeeze and more tears. Her right leg moved several inches.

"Hold on, let me get the phone. I need to call your husband. He had to run home and meet with your vet. You've got a horse that showed up lame; Jason's sick and can't work."

As she heard the phone dialing she mumbled, "Not yet."

He looked at her, not totally sure he really heard her speak.

"Not yet," she softly said again as she tried to reach for his hand.

This time, he definitely heard her, and understood her words.

"Is there something you need to tell me without Seth here?"

He could tell she was trying to nod, but couldn't. She blinked her eyes as deliberately as she could.

"Fine. The important thing is the serum's worked. Just take your time. We'll wait to call Seth. Hopefully a nurse won't come in."

"Why didn't you call me back?"

He assumed she was confused.

"Call you back?"

"I left you about a dozen messages in the past month! I gave Peri my phone number each time, in case you didn't have it with you on location."

He stiffened.

"She didn't tell me. You know I would have called if I knew."

"Has the FBI contacted you?" she asked with no preamble.

"No. Why would they?"

"I thought they might have. They questioned Grady about me. He called me, and was absolutely furious..."

He cut her off. "Grady Reed?" he asked, although he knew to whom she was referring.

"Right."

"The FBI contacted Grady?"

"Right."

"What did they ask him?"

"If we had a business relationship mostly..."

He shook his head. Suddenly, it dawned on him. Before he could put his thoughts into words, Rene sat up in bed, almost vibrant.

"I remember something! Grady's mother, Sandra Reed came to my house. I mean, my barn. We made plans for her to come over..."

"You're friends with Grady's mother?"

"No. I've never even met her. She called and asked if we could talk. I had been trying to reach Grady and he wouldn't return my calls. So, when she called me I was curious, so I agreed. Before she was supposed to meet me at my barn, I went riding and was thrown off a horse. She helped me. That's the last thing I remember."

He doubted she was thinking coherently.

"You're sure she helped you?"

"I'm sure. She took the saddle and bridle off the horse. She gave Wasabi some grain to try to quiet him. She tried to help me - she brought me water. I don't recall anything else though."

"Do you remember how you got here?"

Rene was so preoccupied about the FBI issue she didn't think about the fact that she woke up in a hospital bed.

"To the hospital? No."

"I'm staying at the Ritz Carlton. The room service kid told me about a woman who attempted suicide at the Ritz, and happens to be here at Newport General - that's where we're at, by the way. Anyway, it's a long story, but the car she parked at the hotel has vanity plates that say 'Reed2me.' Isn't that strange?"

"Grady's plates said 'Reedmyrts' when I was dating him. I remember thinking they were stupid because he wasn't a criminal attorney."

"Something's not right."

Her head was almost clear now.

"Why don't you pick up the phone and ask for Sandra Reed's room and see what happens."

"Good idea," he said, then did what she suggested. "Sandra Reed's room, please," he told the operator.

"Hello," a deep voice said.

"Is Sandra Reed available?"

"Who is this?"

"Is this her room?"

"Yes. Who is this?"

Dominick hung up and nodded his head.

"This is strange. Let's call Seth - he's been with you most of the time, you know. He just left a little while ago to meet your vet. Jason is too sick to work - you have a lame horse he was worried about. Seth's been at your side almost day and night. I've relieved him a little, just so he could get some rest."

It didn't feel right waking up without her husband. Telling Dominick about the FBI could wait.

"Let's call him."

Chapter Twenty-Nine

As she dressed for dinner Rene relished the view of the pastures out the bay window of the third floor bedroom suite. She was glad to be back home with Seth, but she needed to update Dominick and get his advice. At the hospital there wasn't time for her to tell him about Strathmore and Bradborne. By the time Dr. Weinstein finished examining her, Seth had come to take her home.

Seth and Dominick were on the veranda when she went downstairs. Her husband basted food on the grill while Dominick set the table.

"This is a picture that I'd like to see more often!"

"I'll bet you would!" Seth said. He winked at her and motioned her to his side so he could embrace her.

"Aren't you a cute couple," Dominick said in a playfully obnoxious way. He poured three glasses of fresh squeezed grapefruit juice.

Rene gave a quizzical look. "No vodka? Aren't we celebrating that Seth's not a widower?"

"Celebrate? I was already deciding how to spend your life insurance proceeds on some sweet young model."

"Like you could get a model! I'm the best thing you could get, and you know it. Thank God you have money, or you wouldn't even have me!" she teased.

"You told me you didn't care about his money! You said you married him because he was hung like a horse," Dominick added.

"Oh yeah. I forgot. He's been traveling so much lately…"

"That's enough!" Seth jumped in before the conversation escalated. He was easily embarrassed by her, yet, it was part of her charm.

"It's Never Enough!" Rene said.

"You mean about sex or money?" Dominick asked.

"Both, for her," Seth admitted, yet he tried to sound as if he were kidding – but they all knew he was serious.

"Anyway, we don't need alcohol to celebrate," Dominick told her.

For the first time in days, Seth didn't look as if the weight of the world were on his shoulders.

"I can't believe I wasn't there when you woke up."

"Stop saying that, sweetie. You had to be with the vet. It's not like you just left me alone!"

"I know, but all those hours waiting, and the hour I leave…"

"So what! I'm fine, and everything's going to be fine."

That wasn't quite true, but Seth didn't know what had been going on. Neither did Dominick.

After dinner, Rene was desperate to get rid of Seth for awhile. There was one sure-fire way.

"I'm just absolutely craving some double fudge nut chunk ice cream!" she said as she licked her lips.

Seth popped out of his chair like a jack-in-the-box.

"I'll go get some. Do you want another flavor?" he asked Dominick.

"If I can have two scoops - I'll have mint chocolate chip too."

"Sure. Anything else while I'm out?"

"Carrots."

It needed no explanation. The carrots were for the horses.

"You know, if Peri didn't give you the messages that I called, what if she didn't give you a message about an FBI agent calling?"

He bit his lip and pondered what she had said.

"Would an agent leave a message saying they are an FBI agent, or using the word agent at all?"

"I don't know."

"Did they phone you?"

"No. They just showed up out of the blue and rang the doorbell. Of course, when I answered, they identified themselves and flashed their badges. One of the badges didn't even look real - it was so worn."

"What did they want to know?"

"The big guy, Strathmore, did all the talking, and the other one hardly said a word. He mostly just took notes on index cards. It was really weird."

"So, what did this Strathmore ask you about?"

Rene didn't need to give it a moment's thought. For weeks she had been replaying the whole scene over and over again in her mind, trying to recall if there was anything of significance she hadn't caught.

She sighed. "First, he just sort of warmed me up, made small talk, like I used to do when I would have a first meeting with someone I wanted to sell horses to."

It sounded pretty absurd.

"Like what kind of small talk? He tells you he's with the FBI and then he just acts like it's nothing and tries to make small talk?"

"I know. It was really awkward. I mean, making chit chat with the FBI in my own house!" Her fingers tingled, just thinking about it. "He starts asking me things, trying to act all casual, but asking how long I've lived in California... but he said something that made it like he knew I moved here from Scottsdale."

"How did you answer?"

"Well, I think I told him that right after Christmas in 1983 I moved in with Seth, but hadn't actually sold my house in Scottsdale. I think I told him that. I don't remember now. But, he knows I moved to California because Seth lived here and, because of his business, he couldn't move to Scottsdale."

"I'm sure that was an opening for him," he said.

"Yeah. I don't know when it turned from sounding like casual conversation to feeling like I was being interrogated, but I was really nervous."

"I'll bet. Who wouldn't be when they've done the kind of..."

She didn't want to hear what he had to say. She hated it when he started sounding as if he were her moral judge instead of a friend.

"Anyway, somehow, he gets me to tell him how Seth and I met, and got married and moved into his house. Then, of course, he wanted to know if Seth were into horses, and I tell him 'no' and then he asks why we have this farm..."

"What do you mean why?"

"That's what I thought! Why? What kind of a question is that? We have the farm because we want to live with the horses. Plus, I have to wonder what they already know about me. I mean, I can't imagine the FBI just goes around talking to people for fun."

"Rene, you know they must be aware …"

"Stop it! You have no idea what they know about. Neither do I."

"Okay. So what else did you tell him?"

"Well, I told him about how Seth and I bought the farm because I wanted to live with the horses, and Seth said I could breed a couple of mares… and of course, I told him about the therapeutic riding camps I hold a few times a year, and I told him about having the tours for people from the senior citizen centers..."

"What's that? You never told me."

"Oh. Well, I sent letters out to all the senior citizen centers and senior organizations offering to schedule a couple of hours for their people come visit the farm, so they have something different to do. I present five or six horses in the arena and tell them about Arabians, and Jason rides one through the different gaits. Then I let them go into the pasture with the retired and rescued horses. You know, they're all so old and arthritic just like the people, but they love the company and to be pet. They're so gentle. The gray hairs love it. Of course, I always get a few who want to tell me their stories about when they were young and had a horse or whatever - but that's fine. Then, we do a little lunch buffet."

"Sounds like a great idea. What do you charge them?"

"Nothing. Seth doesn't mind."

"That should have impressed Strathmore."

"I don't know if impress is really the word, but he was curious."

"Curious about what?"

"Where the money came from to do all this I guess."

"Didn't you tell him that Seth makes a good living as an investment banker?"

"Sure. I told him, but I don't know if he believes me."

"Anything else?"

"Well, he asked how I got into horses, and I sort of explained. I told them I got out of doing it for money when I got married, because I didn't need the money anymore."

"Then, they asked where the money went from the sale of my house in Scottsdale. I was pretty shocked they would ask me, and I think he could tell."

"How did you explain yourself out of that?"

"Well, I kind of minimized it. I said I had some legal fees to pay, and that I used part of the money to buy horses from clients."

"Shit! Did he drill you on it?"

"More or less. I mean, he had this way of asking, which, in a way, was really imposing, and in another way, was just like a new acquaintance trying to get to know you. One minute I felt like I should be asking for a lawyer, and the next minute I thought I should offer some pastries. It was so unnerving!"

"So how much detail did you go into?"

"Not a lot. I told him I had some clients who had expected me to sell their horses, and when I told them I was quitting the business, they seemed so disappointed so I offered to buy their horses from them. The way I worded it, it sounded reasonable."

"Yeah. It does. But it's good you told him you spent some of it on legal fees so that if they look at cancelled checks or something, there's an explanation as to why you paid that Scottsdale lawyer so much."

"I hope so!"

"You're probably right. Anyway, even if they question him, he's not going to tell him that he basically had you over a barrel because of Jared."

"I'm not worried about his handling himself."

"I'm sure it felt awful to have the FBI questioning you, and to know they questioned Grady, but what are you worried about? From what you've said, nothing was really asked about Ivy Farms. Or did they?"

"Not really. Other than casually asking if I bought and sold many horses in California when I lived in Scottsdale. I told him, sure, because they were less expensive than the high quality horses in Scottsdale, and I really couldn't compete for buyers in the Scottsdale market. Most everybody in Arizona with money for really good horses goes straight to the big farms. He said he understood my reasoning."

"But he didn't ask anything about the Ivys?"

"No. Not about any farm in particular, and he didn't ask me for any names of farms I've bought from or sold to. Or any clients, for that matter."

"I wonder what they wanted then... I just assumed they found out that you blackmailed the Ivys."

"Me, too. I don't get it. But, I'm really nervous. I haven't told Seth a thing. Thank God he's been traveling on business so much."

"You really ought to tell him, Rene. He loves you. Just tell him about your past, and assure him you haven't done anything wrong at all since you've met. He has a right to know."

"I can't. I just can't. I'm afraid I'll lose him."

"You won't! It's not like you killed someone! And it's not like you ripped anybody off."

"I sort of ripped Jared off…depending on how you look at it. You're the one who had to make a point of making me feel like a horrible crook over it! That's why I went to Antigua – to try to come to terms with what kind of person I had become. It was your idea for me to go there, and you know it!"

"It was a good idea. You had time to put your priorities back in order and get a sense of who you really were, and what you wanted in life. And, you met Seth. So don't tell me it wasn't a good idea!"

"I'm not saying that! I'm just telling you I feel like a crook in regard to Jared's investments and how I handled it. How can I admit that to Seth? How could he ever trust me? He makes a lot of money, and I have access to it all. Plus, just being his wife, I want him to trust me and be proud of me."

"I'm sure he's proud of you! You're a great wife, you're good to the horses, and your community involvement sounds impressive. You're not one of those country club wives who takes tennis lessons from a pro, or the golf lessons, or anything. You just love your horses."

"But what I do with the farm and the horses probably costs more than if we belonged to a country club and did the tennis and golf scene."

"I don't know. It depends on which club you belong to. That's not the point. Anyway, you put in over a million dollars of your money toward the farm…"

"That's long gone! It was just the down payment…"

"Rene, you're totally getting off the subject. The point is, you need to fess up to your husband. I can't believe the FBI is just going to let go of whatever they're working on. They came to you for a reason. And they went to Grady for a reason."

"But they didn't ask anything about Ivy Farms!"

"What are you so worried about then?"

"I know. I know you're right. But I just don't know what to do! You don't know what this feels like."

"I don't. But that's because I don't get involved in things I'd have to worry about."

"You never need to. You've got tons of money!"

"Don't start that shit again with me! I started out broke like you did. And the movie business is a hard and dirty business - so is Broadway! You think it was easy? I worked my ass off to get to where I am - to have 'tons of money,' as you say. Do you think I never had the opportunity to make money from something sleezy in my industry - the stories I could tell you! But I have my dignity. I know who I am – I always have and I always will. I stay clean and I can sleep at night and look myself in the mirror during the day!"

"Stop it! I know that! I'm sorry. I didn't mean it that way."

"Yes you did. You always say the same thing when you try to justify how you used to be…"

"Look - I agree with what you're saying about looking yourself in the mirror. That's why I wanted out of the business so much. I couldn't stand it, let alone what I got myself into by being stupid and greedy."

"Thank God you married someone with money…"

"I love Seth!"

"I know you do. But, if he didn't have money, who knows what you'd be doing still!"

"Shut up! I've got enough problems right now... wait... I think I heard Seth come in the kitchen door. Just stop talking about this. Okay?"

"Okay. It's your life. Your marriage."

They met in the kitchen at the center island counter. Rene put the ice cream scoop into a deep stainless steel bowl of hot water and she set out the sundae dishes, spoons and napkins.

Seth unpacked Rene's double fudge nut chunk, Dominick's mint chocolate chip, and his own favorite: chocolate chip cookie dough.

"And, as a special bonus - the newest flavor out – chocolate raspberry truffle!" Seth announced. Then he did a drum roll on the counter with his hands, although on granite, it didn't have the right effect. "For the grand finale – fresh whipped cream from the bakery!"

Dominick's eyes lit up! No wonder she was in love with him. Who needed alcohol to celebrate Seth not being a widower?

"I can't believe you! You're going to drink chocolate milk with this too?" Dominick asked Seth.

"Just a little. It's low fat..." he said as he patted his rock hard abs. "Tonight's ice cream feast is well deserved after all the stress we've been through."

Chapter Thirty

The next day...

Seth returned to the house on the ATV. He had spent the last two hours checking and repairing fencing in the back of the farm. It was the only place they didn't put in PVC fencing since it was hidden in the trees, and there was already older wood fencing in place. When they bought the property and did the upgrades she wanted, Rene didn't think they needed to replace fencing at ten dollars a linear foot, when it wasn't meant to hold in livestock. Instead, Seth always checked it and made minor repairs, not minding the extra exercise.

When he walked up the stone pathway, he was surprised that Rene and Dominick weren't on the terrace talking still. He checked the garden in the rear of the house. They weren't there either. The kitchen? No. Maybe they were playing pool in the game room? No. Finally, he used the intercom for the entire house.

"Rene," he said into the devise.

No answer. Maybe they went to the grocery store. Did he miss a note on the kitchen counter? He checked. No note. This wasn't like Rene, but she was with Dominick. They probably assumed he'd be out doing repairs longer. Maybe they ran a quick errand.

He decided to shave and take a shower. Certainly they would be back by the time he was dressed.

Seth hadn't thought to check outside the front entry of the house. They never used that entrance unless they were having a formal party, which was very seldom, like for a private fundraiser.

Helpless, Dominick stood to the side, out of the way; he watched in horror and tried to listen.

Special Agent Strathmore and Special Agent Bradborne flashed their FBI badges. The U.S. Marshal wore his badge on his belt buckle. He held his hand on his weapon in its holster as Strathmore showed Rene the warrant for her arrest and a second warrant to search the property and seize all financial records - personal and business.

The U.S. Marshal read Rene her rights as he handcuffed her wrists behind her back. Then he led her into the house.

She broke out in tears and said, "What's this about? I haven't done anything!"

"Rene. Shut up. Don't say anything. They have a warrant and you've been read your rights. Don't say another word," Dominick said, hoping to help somehow. Part of him wished Seth were there. The other part was glad he wasn't seeing his wife in cuffs. He couldn't believe he was in this situation.

In the house, the U.S. Marshal stood next to Rene, permitting her to sit on a bar stool in the kitchen. The agents searched the premises. They filled boxes with documents from Rene's office, which was on the walk-out basement level of the house.

Finally, Dominick heard Seth come out of their bedroom. Before anyone said anything, Dominick quickly walked to the stairs and stopped Seth in his tracks.

"Seth, try to stay calm. I've got something to tell you."

Chapter Thirty-One

Dominick and Seth went to the police station together. Two honest, hard working, successful businessmen were on their way to jail to bail out a woman they both loved in their own way. Who would have ever thought?

On the drive, Dominick decided he had to betray Rene's trust and tell Seth what had happened. There would be no keeping it from him, and in the long run, it would be easier on both Rene and Seth if she didn't have to tell him herself.

"So you're saying that my wife actually blackmailed someone?"

"I know. It seems impossible to believe, doesn't it? But believe me, she's a whole new woman since she met you. Even before she met you, she swore to me she wasn't going to do crooked things anymore. That's why she wanted the blackmail money - so she could walk away from the business," he explained.

"Why did she need three million dollars to walk away from the business? Wasn't she ever going to work again another day in her life?"

"Actually, she gave $850,000 of it to a friend of hers from Brazil. That's another long story. She can tell you about that sometime. She had a client, Jared Rava, who led her to believe he was just an investor looking for a good investment. She bought quite a few horses on his behalf, making each of them a quick profit – she was reselling the horses for high market value. That's a long story, too.

"The end result was, she planned on using almost a half a million of the blackmail money to buy back the horses from Jared – you see, he actually threatened her life if she didn't get him the return, including the profit, that she said he could make – the asshole actually threatened her life – I heard a tape recording of it myself.

"Anyway, to get him out of her life, she entered into a contract with Ivy Farms for them to buy his horses, and a colt she owned herself, for three million dollars. After she received the money, she kept leaving messages on Jared's answering machine telling him she sold his horses and that she had his money. First, for months, he's harassing her to get the horses sold. Then, when she does, she can't reach him.

"Finally, after about a month of not reaching him, she decided to call his attorney. The guy is scum. He told her to meet him at his office. So, of course, she did, and she had her checkbook with her, prepared to write Jared the check. The lawyer proceeds to tell her that Jared was in prison for tax evasion. Rene discovers that, all along, Jared had been in the Arabian business in San Luis Obispo, but he didn't make much money from his horses. I'll let Rene tell you the details, but he posed as an investor, who knew nothing, in order to get Rene to make him money to help support his business or pay his taxes or something… I don't know. But anyway, Jared is still in jail.

"So, his lawyer told Rene that instead of her paying Jared the $450,000 she was supposed to, she could just pay $150,000 to Jared's wife, who knew nothing about the scam. Jared's wife was grateful for that much money since the IRS seized everything they owned and she was practically penniless. The catch was the lawyer wanted $150,000 for himself in order to facilitate everything. Rene jumped at it - she could end up with another $150,000 for her nest egg that would allow her to get out of the Arab business."

Seth's head was spinning. He couldn't believe his wife was capable, morally, or by intelligence, of doing any of this.

"So," Seth said, "Rene's been arrested for blackmailing the Ivys?"

"I guess. I couldn't really hear the charges they said when they were cuffing her. I was too far away and the guy talked so fast."

The next day...

They sat with the criminal attorney that Seth paid a $100,000 retainer to.

"Seth, Rene, this is serious, as I'm sure you know. Right now, the charges are for conspiracy and for aiding and abetting in a money laundering scheme. Conspiracy carries the highest penalty when they know you're not the top person in the organization. Plus, they can always add more charges."

Rene couldn't hold back the tears.

"But can't I just tell them what I know of how the Ivys did it? I wasn't part of laundering the money! I just blackmailed them because I found out! Just tell them that... I can tell them all that I knew. And this lawyer I was dating at the time knew it. And Dominick knew it...in fact, he's the one who helped me figure out what all the stuff I stole from them really meant. He went through every paper with me. I'm sure he'll help me."

"Rene, then Dominick would incriminate himself in a crime and so would the lawyer you talked about. You don't want to bring other people into it. You caused it…keep it your own problem," Seth said.

"But they can prove that I didn't participate in the money laundering!"

Her attorney said, "We can't tell the prosecutor you blackmailed someone. They'll just add more charges. And even though you didn't do the actual laundering *per se*, you can be charged with the crime because, legally, you can't knowingly accept money derived from a criminal enterprise in return for property or anything of value. That, in itself, is considered money laundering. Not even bringing up blackmail, you sold the Ivys horses for inflated prices and you knew the money they paid you came from a criminal enterprise."

"Shit! I can't believe this! Seth, I'm so sorry. You must hate me. I'm so sorry."

He was speechless.

"Look - I'm going to set up a plea-bargain conference with the U.S. Attorney's office and see exactly what we're up against. Depending on which prosecutor they've assigned, I may be able to have an informal meeting to see what they've got on you before the conference. I promise you, I'm going to do my best. Trust me."

The next day…

"Well Rene, these charges are not even about what you thought. They don't know a thing about any wrongdoing at Ivy Farms."

Seth turned stone cold. What kind of woman did he marry? He ran a background check on her and hadn't found a criminal record, any pending litigation, no judgments against her, or any credit problems. He thought his investigation was enough to give him security about her character.

"What do you mean? I didn't do anything else like this!"

"It's this Jared Rava. Apparently he made his money by being an arms dealer. He spent the profits on his farm in San Luis Obispo, and of course on the horses he was never able to make any money from..."

She interrupted him. "I thought..."

"Just listen. He bought horses from you with money he made from selling weapons. From what I gather, putting the pieces together that I know, he put the big pressure on you to sell the horses you bought for him because the thug that was importing the weapons he sold was murdered. He didn't have another source from whom to get weapons, so his money dried up. There was never enough money from his horse operation, but for years it was supported from the illegal activities. The ATF couldn't get him on weapons charges, so they got him on tax evasion just to get him locked up. Now, they want to use you to prove he was laundering money."

"But I didn't know! How would I know?"

"The FBI probably knows you didn't have any knowledge, but they don't give a damn. All they care about is making a case against him."

"How can they do this?" Seth asked.

"Agent Strathmore is going to say that Rene knew it was dirty money and that she put together horse deals for him - buying horses then selling them for grossly inflated prices..."

"The first horses I sold for him weren't for grossly inflated prices! Even the package Ivy Farms bought wasn't actually inflated - the horses were priced like other horses in the very highest end of the market - that's all!"

"The government is going to contend the prices were inflated. They've even got the contracts that show how little you paid."

"But that's how the business is. That's how brokers and trainers work. We have opportunities to get really great deals from the people who don't believe there is really this other market of buyers out there – or they just don't know how to reach the buyers who pay the really high prices. The prices I bought for are what brokers and trainers pay all the time!"

"Can you get a handful of reputable people to testify to that?"

Rene felt beaten down.

"Probably not. I really doubt it. They wouldn't admit it publicly or in a court of law under oath. Whenever other people find out how little they pay, which so seldom ever gets out, the trainer, or a broker like me, would claim it was such a rare opportunity. Shit!"

"How do people not know? Don't the sellers let other people know how little they got for their horses?"

"No. It's an unspoken and unwritten confidentiality agreement. And the sellers are usually pretty embarrassed in a way. It's really strange. I can't explain the reasoning, but it's a common business practice that no one wants to talk about, let alone testify to."

"There you have it then."

"But I didn't know he was using money from weapon sales or anything illegal! This isn't fair!"

"I know it's not fair, but inflating prices on items which are bought and sold by dirty money is the oldest trick in the book for laundering money, and it is impossible to disprove. You've got a big problem."

"Why do they want to go after Rene? I don't understand this... and it was over three years ago!" Seth said.

"It's a food chain – investigations take on a life of their own. To the government, when they really want to pin someone, they'll do whatever they want to anyone who can help them, innocent or guilty. Unfortunately, it's the cost of justice."

"Why on earth should my wife be paying for the cost of justice?" Seth demanded to know.

"She's probably their last option. I don't know."

"But how can they even come close to tying me to this? Jared must have bought and sold lots of different things and done business with tons of people."

"You're right. That's probably why they're coming after you this late in the game. What it comes down to is that they are going to paint a picture of you and Jared dealing in significant amounts of money changing hands with no appraisals to substantiate the value of those horses. The forensic accountant for the FBI will develop a complicated flow chart - he'll claim it proves you received illegal sources of income. You can't win. You need to play their game and hope for the best."

"This is bullshit! What's the worst that can happen if she pleads not guilty and you defend her in court and lose?" Seth demanded to know.

"Forty years in prison."

Seth wanted time alone with Rene for them to discuss the issue. The criminal defense attorney left his office so they could talk.

"Seth, I'm so sorry I never told you about what I had done. I love you so much! I'm so sorry…"

"I know you love me, but that's not really at issue, is it?"

He was glad she had signed a prenuptial agreement - she agreed that if they divorced for any reason whatsoever, she would accept a $100,000 settlement and would not contest the agreement. The longer they were together, the more he learned about her character, especially with what was happening now.

He couldn't believe what his wife was involved in, intentional or not.

Chapter Thirty-Two

When Seth met Rene in Antigua, he had already been seriously contemplating leaving the investment banking business, but just hadn't bothered to make the change.

Now, he was able to give his wife the gift of a lifetime. This morning, the day after they met with the prosecuting attorney, Rene and Seth sat holding hands, off to a new adventure in their lives. They were airborne in a private jet heading for Costa Rica.

The November 10, 1922 Extradition Treaty between the United States and Costa Rica was a blessing - Rene would be free from the reach of the U.S. government. Fortunately, money laundering was not of the list of offenses that would permit the Department of Justice to extradite her and force her to stand trial.

Seth owned a beach house in Costa Rica that he never told Rene about. Until now, he wasn't ready to disclose the extent of his holdings. She only knew of his assets in California. First, he wanted to know how she would handle a privileged lifestyle without being aware of all of his assets. As it turned out, she treated money with respect by not being extravagant or wasteful, and she was charitable with her time even more than with their money. Her feelings about money were the same as his.

When he married her, he only knew her for a few months. At the time she had asked if they could buy a farm, she was willing to put every penny of her own money, which turned out to be just over a million dollars, into the property. In fact, she said she'd be perfectly happy with a place that cost a million dollars.

The problem was, in Orange County, California, where his business was, you couldn't buy a decent sized farm for that amount of money. He let her turn over all of her own money, meaning all of her independence, to utilize as the down payment on a far more expensive farm - but it had been at his urging to buy the particular property. She insisted she didn't need anything so elaborate. He thought it would be a good investment in the long run, considering how surrounding properties were being developed.

Over time, he could see she hadn't really married him for his money. As it turns out, in Costa Rica he owned a profitable plantation and several pieces of profitable commercial real estate, as well as a beautiful home on a prime beachfront location.

Rene was completely unaware that about six months earlier, for tax purposes, Seth had paid off the mortgage on their property. He transferred the property to third parties. Soon, a private children's home would be notified it was the owner of a wonderful farm full of loving, safe Arabian horses, and a home which would easily accommodate at least a dozen orphans and their caretakers. He set up a foundation and endowed it with sufficient funds to retain Jason and another farm hand, and to keep the horses fed and well cared for, for at least ten years.

Seth and Rene would be able to live quite comfortably for the rest of their lives.

Epilogue

The guide spoke as he drove Ryan and Shawna Sanders down the dirt road to their resort. "You will soon discover that Bora Bora is a picturesque island surrounded by barrier reefs and small offshore moot islets. In the center of the island, the majestic Mt. Otemanu rises 2,385 feet. If you look carefully, you can see the volcanic ash at the peak."

The couple did what everyone does. They tensed up and looked at each other with a hint of fear in their expressions. Shawna gripped Ryan's firm thigh and clenched her teeth.

The guide chuckled and continued.

"Don't worry... the mountain is an inactive volcano. Shallow lagoons of aqua marine waters stretch a mile or two from all points of the mainland to small islets. The waters are spotted with some of the world's most spectacular sailboats and catamarans. In the distance, in their handmade boats, fishermen do their daily work."

The Bora Bora Lagoon Resort was everything paradise could promise. Dozens of resorts claim to be the most luxurious in the world, but this won hands down as far as Ryan and Shawna Sanders were concerned. The resort is the only developed property on Motu Toopu. Inspired by Asian architecture, built on large cement piers, the garden bungalows are literally set over the water.

When they arrived at the resort, the first thing they did after unpacking their clothes and cosmetics was to shower and make love. When they finished, they showered again, and then dressed in resort wear.

By the light of sunset, they strolled a short way on the beach to the resort's Otemanu Restaurant which offers a creative hybrid of haute French and traditional Polynesian cuisine. They enjoyed the fresh seafood and locally grown vegetables that were glazed with sinful sauces.

Next, they walked next door to the Rotopa Bar for after-dinner drinks. At the bar, they relaxed with a view of the softly lit boats floating in the lagoons.

"We really needed a trip like this," Shawna said with obvious content.

"I know. We should have come last year, when we heard about it," Ryan said.

"I guess. But maybe we're enjoying it even more after the marriage counseling having enough time to do us good," Shawna reasoned aloud.

Ryan knew it was the right decision - they spent the last eight months in intense counseling. Now that they were doing so well again and had committed to staying married, he didn't really like to bring up the subject.

"I do love you, you know that in your heart…don't you?" Ryan asked.

In counseling, it came out that Shawna was insecure about people genuinely caring for her and loving her. She desperately needed to be reassured in order to feel good about a relationship. During her entire middle school and high school years, she was passed from foster home to foster home. No one wanted to adopt her, making her feel as if no one could love her enough to want her forever.

"I know. I just need to hear it. I love you, too. You're my whole world, Ryan."

"I believe you love me, but I'm not your whole world! Not that I want to be - one of the things I love about you is your independence and your successful career."

Shawna thought about her response before she spoke. It was one of the most important things she learned in counseling.

"Ryan, you're so much more important than any career. You are my world. I couldn't live without you," she said as she took his hand in hers.

Ryan tensed as he listened to her dramatic words. Whenever she got emotional she exaggerated her feelings. *I couldn't live without you... I couldn't live without you...* She was the strongest woman he knew. Shawna had to be a tower of strength and had to be resilient in order to succeed in her career. She's in a high stakes, competitive, and cut throat business. He wished she would do what their counselor said. Say only what you really feel. Don't exaggerate or minimize. It would be the only way they would honestly know how each other felt.

"Another round?" asked the ebony skinned bartender.

Ryan was glad the flow of their conversation was interrupted. Hopefully he would be able to change the subject. He didn't want to deal with talking about their feelings and wondering why Shawna was exaggerating the way she felt.

"Yes. I'd like one. How about you, honey?" Ryan said to the bartender and his wife.

"I'll wait a few minutes. This drink's beginning to hit me."

Two cups of French vanilla decaffeinated coffee later, the sandy beach was a little bit of a challenge to walk on after a very long day and several drinks at the bar. They took it slow, marveling in the beauty of the stars above the waves.

When they returned to their bungalow, they were pleased to see it illuminated since they didn't think to turn a light on before they left. The bed was turned down, pillows freshly fluffed and chocolate mints on each soft Egyptian cotton pillowcase. Enormous arrangements of fresh tropical flowers were placed in each room of the bungalow, including the bathroom and the porch.

The most exquisite touch was the bottle of chilled Champagne in a pewter ice stand next to the bed. Champagne glasses with *'Ryan and Shawna Sanders'* and *'Bora Bora Lagoon Resort'* etched into the leaded crystal were placed on the night stand.

Forgetting about their exhaustion, they made love and immediately fell into a deep sleep.

Shawna departed from the resort at sunrise to island-hop for a long day. She wanted to see the variety of views of the Pacific and to visit Moorea, 'The Island of Love.'

Ryan started out his day drinking coffee and relaxing in bed reading the manuscript Grace had given him. The Sino-Asian wooden design of the bedroom was too inviting to leave. The view from the bed overlooked the shimmering blue water on three sides. He relished the breeze and sea air from the open windows until late morning.

For breakfast, he ordered in and enjoyed a fresh exotic fruit platter with imported cheeses on the expansive porch immediately outside of the bedroom. Absorbed in the story, he continued reading while eating, only stopping once to use the lavish bathroom that was accented with thick panels of coconut wood. Wearing soft natural unbleached cotton boxer shorts, walking barefoot across the oily and rich wood of the yucca palm floors, gave him a heightened awareness of the culture change from New York City. Here, the bungalows were styled with peaked roofs thatched with pandamus leaves, and the air was cooled by the never-ending trade winds.

Not wanting to stop reading the story, which drew him into each page, he read the manuscript at the restaurant over lunch and then while on the white sand beach for the rest of the day and early evening. After reading the final page, not thinking about dinnertime as he passed the resort's restaurant, he walked with a quickened pace directly back to the bungalow.

Ryan asked the resort's telephone operator to connect him to Grace Ashley's direct line telephone number. There was no answer.

He left a message: "Grace. Hi. It's Ryan. I need to know exactly when the manuscript you gave me was submitted. The copy I have doesn't have the author's name or the agent's information. Give Sam the information as soon as you can. It's very important."

The next call he made was to his in-house attorney, Sam Goldman. Sam started working for Ryan right out of law school when Ryan was ready to produce his second Broadway show, and before he had produced a movie. The enterprising men built the profitable business together.

Sam became a partner within twenty-four hours of announcing his resignation from Soaring Productions. He planned to start his own company specializing in the feature film industry. Ryan was sensible enough to acknowledge that Sam's expertise was not solely legal matters, but also the business aspects of the company. Dominicks own talent and enjoyment came from the creativity he could express. He was spoiled from all the years of having an in-house legal counsel and relying heavily on Sam to take care of business matters. Ryan wasn't confident he could replace Sam with someone who knew enough or cared enough about the business. He couldn't take a chance. When the partnership was formed, they ran the business the same as they always had. The only difference was, rather than Sam being on salary, he was paid 25% of the company's net profit. Sam attempted to negotiate a 50/50 split, but Ryan used his poker face and claimed 25% was his final offer.

"I've got a problem. At least I think it's a problem."

Ryan wasn't experienced in this type of situation.

"I thought you were on vacation. What's going on?" Sam said, surprised to be hearing from Ryan.

"I am on vacation. Grace gave me a manuscript before I left and I brought it with me. Do you have time to talk now?"

"Sure. Go ahead."

Ryan's voice was as serious as Sam had ever heard it sound.

"Someone wrote a novel and sent it to our offices. I'm assuming they want us to buy it and turn into a movie. Grace didn't say specifically. Anyway, I don't want this printed as a novel or made into a movie or have it go public in any way whatsoever."

"Why?"

"Just tell me if there's a way we can prevent the writer from having it published or sold for any purpose."

"Do you mean like having a court order that prevents it?"

"I guess. I don't know."

"Does it use real names?"

"No. But a lot is based on me and Shawna. Our names are changed - but still, it really pisses me off."

"Is the story true... the part you think is based on you?"

"Not the story line, but the characters are definitely us."

"Well, what makes you think it's based on you then?"

"It's got a character who is a movie producer in the Arabian horse business, with a farm in Santa Barbara, and a farm back East. His wife is an important news journalist, his trainer..."

Sam cut him off. "I don't know. There are lots of farms in Santa Barbara, Ryan..."

This time Ryan interrupted him. "It's not just that. There's so much in it that's based on other people. And there are a lot of industry practices that shouldn't be disclosed. On top of that, the fabricated parts make the Arabian horse business look really bad."

"What's the difference? It's just an unpublished book, isn't it?"

"Well, you know... I don't want some big scandalous thing out there about the business. Or me."

Sam tried to reason with him. "But you said the things in it weren't really true and none of the names used are real. What's the difference?"

Ryan had expected Sam's support in this.

"I just hate the idea of bringing up problems in the Arabian horse industry... and making people wonder what's true and what isn't. And I hate the idea that I'm in it... even if my name's changed and most everything about it isn't true... it's still based on who I am!"

Ryan really needed Sam to understand.

"Hold on a second. Grace just walked in. It might be urgent. She never comes here without an appointment."

Sam put the phone on hold and listened to Grace for a few seconds, then returned to Ryan.

"I'm back. Grace said she's embarrassed and feels unprofessional, but she doesn't recall seeing any other paperwork about the manuscript. She called down to Mathew and he said he didn't remember giving her a manuscript directly."

"You're serious?"

"Yes. But, I wouldn't be concerned. Someone will follow-up to see if it's been read and what we think. They always do. Be patient," Sam tried to assure him, not comprehending how important this really was to Ryan.

"Let's hope you're right. Hopefully, they'll follow up soon. And hopefully, they haven't submitted it to anyone else."

"I think you're overreacting, but I'll do what I can."

"No Sam. We'll do everything we possibly can. I'm not overreacting. I don't want the book exposed in any way whatsoever. The Arabian industry doesn't need the bad publicity. And I don't either. This is serious whether you realize it or not."

"Alright. Let me give this some thought. Off the top of my head, I can't think of anything you can do about it other than buy the book and all present and future rights to it. How much do you think it'll cost?"

"Who knows. I'm assuming the writer didn't use her real name. She knows too much about the business - or a professional writer paid someone for information. Someone who knows the business. If it's a successful writer who's already making good money, who knows how much it will cost us."

How much it will cost us? Us? Sam didn't say anything, but if push came to shove, he wouldn't agree to have Soaring Enterprises pay for the rights to the book knowing they would never use it or sell it. This was a personal matter to Ryan. Sam's share of the partnership profits shouldn't be affected. They'd have to deal with that issue when they could talk in person.

"Give me until you get back to think on this and see if I can come up with anything other than buying it out."

"Is there anyone you can call? Someone with experience in this sort of problem?"

Sam thought Ryan was getting carried away.

"I can't think of anyone off the top of my head."

"Find out everything you can before I get back."

"I'll do what I can. I've got other pressing business matters too, Ryan."

"I know. I know. But this is important."

"Our business isn't?"

"Yes. It is. You know what I mean."

Shawna returned from her adventurous day with flattened windblown hair, smeared mascara on her face, and no hint of the lipstick she always wore. Practically dragging across the wood floor, she lugged three large bags. He didn't need to ask. The bags were obviously filled with things she bought at the various stops she made while island-hopping. A few items might be for their Manhattan apartment, but as usual, it was most likely gifts and souvenirs for people who worked for her at the television station. Her hair stylist. Her make-up artist. Her wardrobe people. Her assistant. And last, but not least, each of her three producers… one for each show.

"You look exhausted! How was your day?" he inquired as he eagerly stood up and gave her a big hug and a gentle kiss hello.

"I had a great time! I'm not really exhausted…it's more a combination of being just a little motion sick and being tired from sampling Polynesian cocktails for the last seven hours! I only took a sip or two of each one, but they kept putting different ones in front of me and I didn't want to be rude! They say *'Just taste. See if you like it.'* Everywhere we went… they say the exact same thing to the tourists!"

"Sounds fun. Tell me about it over dinner."

"What did you do all day? Sleep on the beach?"

"No sleeping. I couldn't put that manuscript down."

"How was it?"

"It depends on how you look at it."

"Huh?"

"It was a great story. Lots of imagination…"

She interrupted him, always reacting like a news journalist.

"What do you mean then, when you say 'it depends on how you look at it'?"

"Don't worry about it. Long story short, I'm not making it into a movie!"

"Why not? You said it was a great story."

"It is great. But it's complicated. I don't want to bore you with it."

"All right… but you did like the story?"

"Loved it."

"Great. I'm glad you enjoyed reading while I was out playing with the rich and famous."

"I just showered for dinner. Why don't I wait for you while you shower and change."

Ryan poured himself his first cocktail for the evening.

"I'll take you up on that," she said, then pecked him on the cheek and tried to hide the twinkle in her eye as she turned around toward the bedroom and master bath.

From the bedroom, she closed the windows so Ryan couldn't hear her. She dialed the phone. Once the international operator got the information she required, in only two rings, her best friend picked up the line.

"Hi! It's Shawna, reporting in from Bora Bora…aka paradise!"

"You sound happy!"

"I am!"

"Did he read it?"

"Yes! And he said he loved it!"

"I knew he would. I loved it!"

"I can't believe it…Ryan loved the first novel I've ever written…and he doesn't even know I wrote it!"

"You haven't told him yet?"

"No. I haven't told him. I'm just so thrilled that he loved it. He said it's a great story and has lots of imagination."

"When you tell him you wrote it, do you think he'll make a movie out of it?"

"No. He already said he'd never make it a movie. I couldn't press him for an explanation, given the circumstances."

"Why don't you keep your secret and let me circulate it around to some of the literary agents I'm friends with? Like I told you a million times, they owe me big favors. I'm sure we can get you published. If it gets picked up, printed and on the shelves, you could just take Ryan to the bookstore and let him see it there! He'll be blown away!"

Shawna grinned.

"What a great idea! Yeah. I want to do that. Will you help me?"

"Of course. That's what friends are for," Grace Ashley answered.

"Great! When I get back home I'll let Dan know! He'll be so excited. If it weren't for him giving me so many details about how the Arab industry works and the things about grooming and auctions, and what it's like being Ryan's trainer, I could never have written this book! In fact, I think I'll send him a big fat check for helping out!

"Good idea. Maybe you should give him credit in the book too."

"No. He insisted I don't tell Ryan where I learned so much. Dan said he just thought it was fun that I was writing the story."

"Well, I think it's fun, too! You know, if you don't get picked up by a publisher, you could always use a pseudonym and self-publish, and pay someone to be your front person to take the credit and do the marketing."

"If I need to, that's what I'll do."

About Trading Paper by Cali Canberra -

At the peak of the Arabian horse industry in the 1980's, rough and tumble produce industry mogul Johan Murphy can't make an installment payment on his Triple Crown winner, *Love Letter*, an Arabian mare, he acquired at a prestigious Scottsdale auction. His financial problem, coupled with his unscrupulous new lawyer, sets the stage for the demise of an entire industry. The legal entanglements catapult into motion a chain of events that effect the entire Arabian horse industry in a way in which it will never recover.

Cali Canberra takes us on a wild ride of intrigue, murder, manipulation, corruption and suspense, with an insider's eye toward the inner workings of an industry previously reserved for the rich and famous.

Fast paced excitement awaits the reader with every twist and turn of the intricate story told from the perspective of numerous characters whose varied lives and professions are intertwined with one common element, their love of Arabian horses.

Read
Trading Paper - Chapter 8
on the following pages!

Chapter 8

As the glass elevator that stood dead center in the atrium was easing down to ground level, Dolan spotted his niece in the lobby with the remnants of tears streaming down her face. It appeared that she was making an effort to compose herself, blotting off the smeared dark brown mascara that circled her eyes like war paint. Her eyes were glassy and her nose was red and irritated from crying and sniffling. There wasn't a trace of make-up left on her face to conceal her large pores and blackheads. She always prided herself for wearing her foundation and blush in such a way that anyone would think she was going au natural and had a beautiful complexion. Thank God for quality cosmetics and trained professionals to teach women how to apply them properly. If only she kept them in her purse to touch up with...

Marcie caught a glimpse of her uncle out of the corner of her eye as he hesitantly stepped away from the elevator doors that were closing behind him. She took a deep yoga-like breath in preparation for clearing her spinning head and returning to the business at hand. Even though Dolan was her uncle, she was embarrassed to be caught in such an emotional state and looking the way she knew she did. When their eyes met, she unconsciously looked down toward the tile floor as if in shame for a sin that the parish priest caught her at before confession.

"I didn't mean to get you so upset honey," he said apologetically. "You guys just need to understand what's really going on here. I'm sorry."

"I know. I appreciate it. Really, I do. I just needed a few minutes to myself," Marcie said through her sniffling.

"We really need to get started with the questions. It's been a half an hour," Dolan informed her as he led his distraught niece by the elbow toward the elevator. He was finding it increasingly difficult to act professional with the girl who taught him how to play with *Barbie* dolls and build forts in just about every room in his house.

Greg tried not to look shocked at his wife's skin when she returned to the office. He'd never seen it look that way before. In spite of all that they were going through, he wondered if she wore make-up *all* of the time. Could it be possible that she even wore foundation and blusher to bed and put it on fresh in the morning before he woke up? Most of the time she was out of bed before him, even if it was only to empty her bladder and then go back to sleep. Was she really touching up her complexion? If she was, seeing her as she looked right now, he could understand why she would do it. Starting the night of their first date, he always told her she was a natural beauty... the eighth wonder of the world; he now supposed she didn't want to disappoint him that it wasn't natural at all. At least no more natural than a halter horse being shown to a judge. It was amazing what a small amount of skillfully applied cosmetics and shaving could do for a woman and a horse.

Greg swallowed hard as he looked at his wife with new eyes. "Ready?"

Marcie's voice was so soft that everyone else in the room only knew what she said by reading her lips, *'Sure, I'm ready'*.

"There are several areas that we are going to need to cover so that we know what we are up against," Jessica informed them. "Know that everything you tell us is considered work product and is completely confidential. We legally can't tell anyone, not even a judge. So, everything you tell me must be 100% truthful, with no sidestepping or sugar coating, no matter what."

"Attorney and client privilege?" Greg asked.

"Absolutely," Jessica assured him.

Jessica weighed her words carefully before she said, "The first thing that I have to do is put myself in the shoes of Alec Douglas, the Plaintiff's counsel. What would I be looking for that could be damaging? I would make a list of questions and build on that."

The Bordeauxs nodded their heads in understanding, but didn't repeat the words that were going through their minds... *but we didn't do anything wrong!*

Jessica was certain she knew what they were thinking, so she continued without waiting for a verbal reply. "My next step is to have a complete understanding of how your business works, how the industry works, and if you operated within the norm, using acceptable and legal business practices." She sat silent and studied their expressions to see if they understood what she was getting at.

Greg and Marcie nodded in unison but remained silent.

Dolan interjected. "I don't know about Jessica, but I think it's really important that we find out how the horses that you deal with went up in value so dramatically." He looked at Marcie. "I remember back when your dad was importing fabulous horses from Poland. He was selling their offspring for only $5,000... and grateful for that price."

Greg's adrenaline pierced through his veins. "What's the difference how the prices went up. It's just the market, like real estate. A worthless piece of land one year and the next year..."

Jessica interrupted, serving as an intermediary before he got off track. "Don't get defensive. It won't help anything," she said with the patience an adult would need to calm a child whose temper was about to flare.

"I'm not getting defensive. I just don't have time to waste," Greg said. He hoped that his voice didn't portray his conscience.

"What Dolan has asked about is precisely at the heart of the issue. From the looks of things, if I were representing a client who paid $2.5 million for a horse, I would sure want to know what made the horse worth that much money. And given that Mr. Murphy bought the horse at a public auction, I would want to know who was bidding against him... legitimate people or shills," Jessica said frankly.

Marcie's expression didn't change since she didn't know how the business operated. Like a spectator, she sat with her perfect posture absorbing the interaction between the three other people in the room.

The color drained from Greg's face and he tried to hide the quiver of his lips. A barely perceptible twitch of his eye started. He bit down lightly on his bottom lip as he thought about his response.

"Where do I start?"

"From the beginning, and don't leave anything out," Jessica said, now relaxing some since Greg had accepted that he needed to tell them everything.

"It'll take a while."

Jessica selected a pen to take notes with. "That's what we are here for."

Greg looked out the window for a moment to gather his thoughts and decide where to begin. His brother always teased him about being a winded storyteller, so today he weighed his words carefully to avoid wasting more time than necessary.

"Well... my parents always loved horses and went to farms that had Arabians, here in the United States. Long stort short, they fell in love with Polish Arabians after an intense study of their genetics and physical characteristics. In the early 1940's they bought their first Arabians. Later, they bought a horse for each of us to train and ride. My brother and I lived and breathed horses, so it was a great family activity. We started showing and excelled in everything we entered.

"We all decided to try our hand at breeding, so we wanted our own stallion. The whole family went to Poland in 1963 and selected a stallion that we all agreed on. His name was Lodz. Naturally, the next step was to buy more land to have a big farm instead of a few acre set up. Lodz was a hit here in the U.S. We sold lots of breedings to him just through people seeing him in the show ring and from word of mouth... keep in mind that there weren't many Polish Arabians in the U.S. at the time," Greg explained.

"Then what?" Jessica asked.

"Well, we started buying more of our own mares and breeding to our stallion, producing more and more foals each year. Eventually, by the time that we had a lot of horses for sale, and so did our clients who bred to Lodz, we decided to hold an auction..."

Dolan was curious. "Was this the first auction ever held for Arabians?"

"No. There were others, and they did pretty good. That's where we got the idea."

"Do you remember what year that was?" Dolan interjected, pen in hand.

"Sure. 1971."

"How did it go?" Jessica asked as she was jotting notes.

"Pretty damn good. The top-selling mare went for about $50,000."

"Really?" Dolan paused for a moment, doing the math in his mind. "In 1971?" he clarified.

Greg raised his chin up a couple of inches and looked Dolan straight in the eye. "Yes," he said feeling insulted. Did Dolan think he was fabricating facts?

"What was the sale average though?" Dolan pressed for a more accurate picture of the times.

Greg answered curtly, even more insulted. "At *our* sale," he emphasized, as if his family were superior geniuses, "the Pure Polish mares averaged almost $30,000. The Polish-bred, meaning not 100% Polish blood, averaged about $10,000."

"Who was buying these horses?" Jessica asked.

Greg couldn't tell if she meant that only someone who was crazy would pay that much for a horse. He tried to remain calm on the exterior, but his gut started churning. She had no right to judge him or any of his clients. "Lots of people. Mostly people who already had horses. They just wanted better ones, once they saw the quality of what we were producing and importing from Poland."

"Then what?" Jessica said, now learning how arrogant that Greg was. She couldn't tell if Marcie shared his ego.

"Then, my family and I held at least one auction a year," he explained as if he were reviewing a history lesson. As an afterthought, he added, "The prices paid were higher each time. The value of our horses and our clients horses appreciated an average of 30% a year."

Marcie sat perfectly erect, looking at him admiringly.

Jessica nodded, waiting for a crown worthy of a King of his own country to appear on his head.

He decided to get off of the subject of money for a moment so that he wouldn't get more worked up about them judging him.

"Well, Marcie and I met at one of the shows. We were competing against each other... it was all friendly competition. The first day we met, we hit it off. Went on our first date about a week later. I knew I was in love then," Greg said, obviously recalling a very fond memory.

"I watched Greg showing in at least a dozen shows before we were ever introduced. I was in love with him before I even met him!" Marcie admitted in an adolescent-like manner as her eyes radiated. At least there was a little something she could add to the session now.

Jessica assumed that Marcie was attracted to Greg because of his talent with horses, and perhaps his resources. It certainly wasn't for his looks. Sure, he was in great shape, but his face and hair were unquestionably on the dorky side.

"After we dated for a while, Marcie and I decided to get married and start our own farm and marketing program. We didn't really have our own money though."

Jessica looked at him quizzically, but he explained himself before she needed to ask him to.

"Everything I did was really with farm money. I got compensated, but not really based on any kind of a salary or commission or formula. When I was old enough to need my independence, my parents built me a house on the farm, but at the opposite end of the farm as their house. I used credit cards and got cash whenever I needed or wanted something. Everything just came out of the farm bank accounts. Even though the horses and the farm evolved into a full-fledged business, it was run very casually as far as money and responsibilities went. Everyone made sure everything got done, and everyone had the money to live comfortably. We never really thought about money until Marcie and I decided to get married," Greg said.

"It was actually because of my father," Marcie clarified. "He asked us about whether I was going to need to get a job; where we were going to live, and all those kind of questions."

"That's when we decided that since we both loved the horses and you could make a decent living working with them, we'd start our own operation," Greg said.

"Was your family upset?" Jessica asked Greg.

"No. Not at all. I think they were almost relieved. When the family started everything when we were kids, it was just a hobby. The horses accidentally snowballed into a business."

Marcie expanded on the subject. "In fact, Greg's father suggested that he consult with his attorney and his tax advisor to see how he could help. It wound up that his parents gave us 150 of their 200 acres. They kept 50 acres for themselves... the land that surrounded their house, and the house Greg and his brother grew up in."

Not that it mattered for the case, but Jessica was curious about the family dynamics. She directed her question to Greg. "Wasn't your brother upset?"

Greg answered with complete honesty and it showed in his expression. "No. We discussed it at length. He didn't want his own business. All he cares about is being able to keep training and showing. It's his only passion and interest. Marcie and I decided to run our new farm as a real business, paying my brother a salary and bonuses, and giving him specific responsibilities... just as any business would," Greg said, not implying that he was doing his brother a favor.

Once again, with this line of questioning, Marcie could chime in. It made her more relaxed. "The land that his parents gave us was the land that had the barns, the pastures, and the riding arena," she explained as she pictured everything in her mind. "They were so generous, I don't know how we could have done any of this without them."

"Right!" Greg said, quite relieved to hear his wife volunteer the admission, especially without them being in a completely private situation.

"So, your parents are still in the business, right? Do they operate separately from you?"

"Actually, they're legally minority partners in the business and all of its assets, but they also personally own about fifteen to twenty horses at a time that they keep mostly on their fifty acres. My father does consulting on selection of horses to buy and breed. I handle all of the rest of the business aspects myself," Greg said.

Jessica didn't understand this attractive, talented woman's admiration of her husband. Marcie came from a family that would be considered wealthy by most people's standards. It seems that Greg has himself on a pedestal. Vintage Arabians is a horse farm, not IBM!

"I understand. Let's talk about how the prices got so high," she said diplomatically.

Greg knew better, but he hoped that Jessica wouldn't bring up the escalating prices again. He drank down the last of his bottled water as he composed his thoughts. Honesty and truth are two different things, he thought to himself.

"There were several other farms in Scottsdale at the time. All of us owned a lot of land because it was so undervalued when we bought it. From time to time, we'd end up talking at a show or some function, and it would get around to how expensive it was to add fencing and more barns to accommodate more horses, whether they were our own or our client's. None of us could even come close to breaking even financially... especially with the labor and feed costs to take good care of the animals," Greg said.

"Go ahead," Jessica said, trying to keep an open mind.

"So, one night, a group of us went out to dinner together after a local show and got talking about forming a consortium. The purpose was to turn this expensive hobby into something we could all turn a profit from. We discussed having about six or seven farm owners in the group. By the end of our long dinner and drinks, a couple of them didn't want anything to do with our plan, but five of us survived and formed the consortium," Greg said, intentionally omitting the details of the plans they schemed.

"What did the five of you do?" Jessica asked.

"A week later, we had a twelve hour long closed door meeting. No interruptions. We ordered in food and beverages and we stuck to business. We decided that it would be easy to take a leadership role and turn Polish Arabian horses into an actual industry. We just needed to devise a plan and follow it. We agreed to be friendly competitors, but we also all needed to work together to grow an industry from what was, at that time, a casual hobby. The horses were a hobby that we couldn't make a profit at.

"I still don't understand how you got people to pay such high prices for the horses," Dolan interjected, getting impatient. He could see that Greg was skirting around the details.

Greg took a deep breath before he continued. He needed to set the scene, or they would never understand how and why things happened as they did.

"I'll get to that in a second. First, we decided that it was fine to have just the everyday kind of person buying and showing the horses, but we needed to get more wealthy people involved...like the Thoroughbred business. We talked about how wealthy people wanted everything to be first class... their country clubs, cars, houses, boats, clothes, jewelry... everything. So it was obvious that they would want the farms they did business with to be first class also."

"Makes sense," Jessica admitted. Now that she had money, she didn't want to have her horse at a run of the mill looking barn.

"So, we needed to build fancy facilities and have fancy marketing materials. We would have to wine and dine our clients. That would cost us a lot of money," Greg reasoned.

"So, it was a catch 22?" Dolan asked.

"Not really. The other three gentlemen in the group were quite well off on their own. They just didn't want to pour even more money into their farms than they already were, if it wasn't going to make a profit,"

"I can see that," Jessica said, nodding in agreement while she sat back in her chair. There was nothing to really take notes on in this point of his explanation.

"So, anyway, we all agreed to build our farms as spectacular and prestigious as we could imagine and afford... and to have professional people do our marketing materials in a first class style and quality."

Jessica shot straight from the hip. "What about you? How did you and Marcie come up with the money?"

"A couple of ways. After I explained my business plan and our goals to Marcie's parents, they wanted to help us expand the business. When I told them that we needed to upgrade and add on to the farm to accommodate all of the potential business that was out there, they could see that it was necessary also. To help us out, they gave us a gift of $250,000 and three Pure Polish mares that were in foal.

"We spent some of the $250,000 on working with architects drawing up plans... and they made us a detailed model to display in my barn office. While the architects were working on our project, we bought and imported Lancelot, a Swedish National Champion Stallion. We paid an equine attorney to take care of the legal end of a stallion syndication... we offered the very first stallion syndication in the Arabian breed. We also spent, what at the time, was a lot of money, on marketing materials to market the stallion syndication."

For a change, Greg was just describing the facts without a hint of arrogance, Jessica thought. Maybe she jumped to an unwarranted conclusion earlier. She would reserve her judgment for later when she got to know him better.

Marcie's eyes showed that she shared her husband's pride of accomplishment as she listened to him continue. Jessica was surprised that she seemed to be listening to him as if Marcie were hearing the story for the first time herself. Was there a chance that she didn't know very much about how her own husband had built up their business? Jessica couldn't imagine herself being that uninvolved in the details of her and Turner's life. They shared almost everything.

Greg kept talking. "Each of the other people in the consortium bought one or two shares of the Lancelot syndication to help me get it rolling. Then, just by my reputation and Lancelot's show record and pedigree, along with people seeing my plans for the farm development, they were impressed with the syndication. All of the shares sold out within about six months. I guaranteed to buy any shares back at a ten percent discount if they later wanted out of the syndication and there wasn't an actual resale market developed yet," Greg boasted as he sat up tall and puffed his chest out just enough to display his self-confidence.

Here comes that arrogance again, Jessica thought.

"Sounds like good business," Dolan said, knowing that Jessica thought the same as he did about their client's attitude.

"How much money did you bring in from the syndication?" Jessica asked. She was taking notes once again. The details might be important later. There was no way to be certain at this point in the game.

"There were 75 shares at $75,000 each..." Greg started to explain as if he were totally numb to the incredible dollar amounts.

Jessica interrupted him. "I thought a syndication was when someone buys lifetime breeding rights to a stallion... when they get one breeding a year until the horse dies or becomes sterile."

"That is how it works," Greg said, confused by her statement.

"Why would people pay that much money?" Dolan asked.

"Because we did projections showing that each breeding would sell for $10,000 the first year, $20,000, the second, $30,000 the third. The projections didn't show any further appreciation past the third year."

"So what you're saying is, that according to your projections, in the first five years people would make back $120,000?" Jessica asked, adding the figures to her notes and double-checking that she wrote them correctly.

"Even better than that... we let people buy the shares on five year terms. That way, *every dollar* they invested was fully depreciated on their taxes for that year... including their mortality insurance and their pro-rata share of expenses, *and* even trips to Hawaii for syndicate share holder meetings," Greg said with a huge grin on his face. Somehow, he forgot about the circumstances that led him to his explanation.

Jessica wrote furiously. Dolan asked the next logical question. "So, did your projections pan out?"

Marcie had to chime in and answer. "Yes! In fact, in the fourth year, the breedings were selling for $35,000 each, *if* someone could even buy one. Lancelot was such an outstanding sire that most people used the breedings on their own mares. I think there were only about 20 breedings for sale the fourth year." Her eyes were sparkling now, with no trace of the tears that consumed her earlier, other than the fact that her make-up had disappeared.

Greg jumped in before Marcie could continue to recount the success of the syndication. "In the fifth year, several people sold their shares and got $300,000 a share. Keep in mind, they had already used four or five breedings... or sold some of them." He got excited, telling his success story. He couldn't sit still any longer. Standing up and trying to find somewhere to move around in the office, even he was impressed with his coup.

Jessica was sure that if her office was large enough, Greg would have been strutting around with his peacock feathers spread wide open in the '*look at me*' position.

"Why didn't you just syndicate Lodz, the stallion your parents bought?" Jessica asked without giving him the satisfaction of indicating that she was impressed with his accomplishment.

"A few reasons. One, his age. By this time, Lodz didn't have enough predictable fertile years ahead of him to justify a high dollar share price. Second, we picked Lancelot specifically to cross with the daughters of Lodz. Dad and I thought it would be an excellent cross...and it was..."

'Wow,' Jessica thought... *'he finally gave some credit to his father. It's about time.'*

Greg barely stopped to take a breath as he described how incredible everything was. "Keep in mind, there weren't all that many Polish Arabians in the U.S. at that time. We needed to infuse new blood so that people wouldn't inbreed too heavily. Another reason was because a new stallion spreads renewed excitement and hype. Half the business is about hype. Everyone already knew and respected Lodz and they were already able to breed their mares to him. Lodz wasn't exclusive or a novelty anymore. We needed high quality, hype and exclusivity to make the syndicate work."

"So that's where you got the money to do the overhaul on the farm?" Jessica asked.

"The first overhaul... not the later additions," Marcie said, feeling like she wanted to be part of the conversation again.

Dolan did a quick calculation in his head. "You brought in over five and a half million dollars from one stallion! And all your clients made a big profit. That's impressive."

Greg sat back down since there really was nowhere to pace. "That's one of the reasons why my clients became willing to pay a lot more money for quality horses every year. The more they profited, the more they would spend on buying more and breeding more."

"It sounds almost like people just followed along with what everyone else was doing... but who started paying the really high prices in the first place? What I still don't understand is, how you got enough people to do it in the first place, to establish what others considered the 'market value'?" Jessica said, tapping the point of her ink pen on the yellow pad.

"It was easy... the other people in the consortium bought the first four shares of the Lancelot syndication the day I had it ready..." Greg said.

Dolan interrupted. "So you made $300,000 the very first day? I should be in your business!"

Greg paused and rubbed his forehead. He had to phrase this answer properly. "No. Not really. They signed the contract to buy the shares, and I signed contracts to buy horses from them of equal value. We were just trading paper... none of us really spent any actual cash..."

Jessica wrote *'Trading Paper'* in extra large block letters, making the words bolder through doodling, as she spoke. "So, really, you traded syndicate shares for horses?"

"No. We didn't take the horses, except for one mare," Marcie answered for Greg before he got a chance to decide what he wanted to say.

Greg couldn't believe Marcie admitted it. If she hadn't volunteered the truth, things could have gone a lot smoother. He could imagine what Jessica and Dolan were thinking of them.

"I don't understand," Jessica said, confused.

"We just traded paper so that we could honestly say that these other successful business people and breeders were excited enough to buy shares. It implies that whoever you're trying to sell to should do what the experts are doing," Greg said, not meaning to let the guilt in his voice come through. He sounded like a little boy with his hand caught in the cookie jar.

Jessica and Dolan looked at each other with concern. From a legal point of view, these were really sham sales conducted to mislead potential investors. In legal terms, it was fraud and misrepresentation. The Bordeauxs were fortunate that everyone really ended up making a profit... no one would have reason to complain since everything worked out in the end. Still, it is against the law to conduct business this way.

"What about the actual sales of horses?" Jessica asked, afraid to hear the answer.

Confession time. "Well... sort of the same thing. Each of us in the consortium would allow the others to tell people that one of us bought one or more of their horses, for a specific price... a very high price. We'd call each other and make sure to get the stories straight in the event that a prospective buyer or current client asked. When the clients thought other people paid the high prices, they were willing to do it too. At least most people," Greg said.

Greg's own explanation hit him in the stomach like a medicine ball. Telling the process out loud made it sound bad. Really bad. He hadn't thought anything of it at the time... it was Marcie's idea, and he thought it was a good one. So did the others in the consortium. None of them felt guilty. They didn't think it hurt anyone... as long as enough real buyers followed along and it continued to snowball, that's what the real market would be. They just needed to start it somehow.

"We did it at our first really prestigious auction too... it created so much excitement," Marcie offered enthusiastically. She didn't grasp the full import of the deception from a legal and ethical perspective.

Greg cringed. This wasn't what they need to expose.

"What do you mean?" Dolan asked her, afraid to hear his niece's answer.

"Well, we had the others in the consortium bid up and buy several of the horses at the auction. In fact, they even had some relatives and close business associates bid up and buy also," she said proudly.

Greg couldn't believe Marcie was elaborating. In most ways, she was very smart. What was she thinking?

Jessica tried not to change her expression when she asked, "So, the people you were referring to didn't actually pay for the horses? They just appeared to be successful big spending bidders?"

"Yes. And it made everyone else bid high too! Our plan worked perfectly. After the first several auctions, we didn't need to do it very often anymore, because there were enough real buyers to actually sell the majority of the horses for really high prices," Marcie bragged.

Jessica couldn't make herself look at Dolan. It wasn't the time.

"So, what you're saying is that you never really got paid for the horses by the people in the consortium? Did you give them the horses for free in exchange for bidding?" Jessica asked.

Marcie was a motor mouth now and Greg couldn't think of how to stop her. "No! We just reciprocated, doing the same thing at their auctions. But we did move the horses to the farms of the successful bidders. If we didn't, that's when everything would have looked fishy. We're all within a few miles of each other and we knew the horses would be well cared for," Marcie said.

Greg's heart was beating hard, his blood pumping fast through his veins. Hearing the story told, he realized that they had done unethical things. Somehow, at the time, it didn't seem like any big deal. It was just a means to an end. But now, hearing it out of Marcie's mouth and in the presence of lawyers, it sounded like big trouble. He was astounded that Marcie didn't seem to grasp it.

"Marcie, don't you see that you were scamming people by doing all of that. It was all a set up. A con. An elaborate scheme to trick people into buying horses for more money than what the market would really bear..." Dolan finally said, hating to have to tell his own niece that she was in big trouble if anyone else found out.

Marcie defended them with a raised voice, as if that would make the lawyers comprehend everything. "You don't understand... no one got hurt! All the people who followed along made money. They love the horses. The social aspects of being in the business. They get the tax deductions. No one is harmed in any way!"

"You did it all by fraud and misrepresentation. That's wrong. Illegal. Actually, it's even criminal," Jessica said.

Marcie started crying because she couldn't get them to understand. She tried to think of another way to get them to comprehend.

"Why can't you see we did a good thing by creating an industry that made middle class people rich… and rich people richer! A strong industry creates lots of jobs too… trainers, assistants, grooms, farm help… it goes even further than that. The suppliers make more money… the tack stores, the feed stores, the farmers who produce the feed… it goes on and on. Because people were able to profit, we could produce more horses. Now, the entire industry has become a dynamic force in the entire U.S. economy!"

Jessica couldn't believe her ears.

"Marcie, if you guys did it all without coercion and deception, I would admire you. But you and your group are nothing more than a bunch of crooks!" Jessica said emotionally as she thought about her husband always saying that they overpaid for the horse they had purchased from Greg.

Marcie stormed out of the office, slamming the door behind her.

"I'm sorry for how she's being. I understand what you're saying. I'll get her to understand. She's upset because neither of us looked at it that way before… and neither did the others in our consortium," Greg said in an embarrassed quiet voice.

"Do you think that Johan Murphy found out how you conduct business?" Jessica asked.

"No. We all swore we'd never tell anyone, no matter how well the industry went. I trust that no one told," Greg said, confident in his answer.

"Do you need to get your wife?" Dolan asked, restraining himself from going to comfort his niece. Right now, he was her lawyer, not her uncle.

"No. She needs time alone to absorb all of this. I know her."

"Are you up to answering more questions?" Jessica asked, almost as if the emotional scene hadn't even occurred.

"Sure. Let's get this over with," Greg said, resigned to the fact that they had in fact done something wrong.

Jessica turned to a fresh page in her paper pad, prepared to take more notes. "What about the auction last year? Did you have all legitimate bidders?"

Greg got a sinking feeling in the pit of his stomach. "What do you mean?"

"Were there any shills?" Jessica said bluntly as she elevated her head and stuck out her chin slightly in an accusatory manner.

"No," Greg said, then hesitated about answering with complete honesty. "Not shills. But we did entice several clients to keep bidding up on horses that they really wanted."

"What do you mean?" Jessica asked.

Greg felt mortified to answer, but his demeanor didn't show it at all. "Well, I offered about fifteen of our best customers... ones that were very wealthy, and had already made a lot of money from doing business with us... I offered that for every time they bid an additional $50,000, I would give them services, such as training, showing, and breedings to our stallions, that equaled 20% of the final selling price of the horse, regardless of who bought the horse."

Her eyes widened and her eyebrows suddenly raised a half an inch. "And they agreed?"

"Yes. Because I told them only to do it on horses they'd really want to own... just in case their bid ended up being the final bid. They really did have to buy the horse if the bidding stopped with them. And it did, several times. They understood the conditions."

Dolan found the explanation hard to believe. "On horses that expensive, how could you compensate them fully... the 20% formula you talked about?"

Greg looked Dolan straight in the eye and never broke eye contact. He spoke as if he had been caught cheating at school and was now addressing the principal who had the authority to expel him. "Well, we worked it out, one way or another. Each of the clients knew I would. They trusted me. It just worked out so that I kept my word..."

Jessica interrupted him. "Specifically, *how* did you keep your word?"

He didn't have to think about his response. "Like with some, I gave them a free colt... one I couldn't sell easily and that they liked a lot. In fact, one of the colts went on to become a Reserve National Champion and is now worth at least $300,000. That's what they've been offered for him, at least. But they don't want to sell him."

Dolan and Jessica waited for more examples. When Greg didn't offer anything else, Dolan looked down at the rug, closed his eyes, and pinched the bridge of his nose at the inside of his inner eyes. The gesture told Greg that Dolan was getting tired and was about ready to lose his patience.

"With some of the bidders, I sold some of their horses for them and didn't charge my standard 20% commission... so, say on a $100,000 horse, I didn't deduct the $20,000 commission."

Dolan finally shot Greg a look that implied that he didn't think that Greg was helping his own case.

"Everyone's been totally and completely satisfied with how they've been treated. I swear!" Greg said, wanting very much to gain the approval of Jessica and Dolan.

"I don't believe you," Dolan said honestly. The skin over his face tightened. "Not that I wouldn't have worked with you anyway, but what was all the bullshit about you and Marcie insisting that you didn't do anything wrong?"

Greg's mouth was suddenly dry and parched. He took a sip of the water that Marcie had left from hours earlier. The pit of his stomach churned. "Until this conversation, it didn't seem like we had done anything wrong."

Dolan and Jessica each looked at him as if he were out of his mind. They didn't say anything. By this time, they were almost entertained to hear Greg continue to put his foot in his mouth.

"Everyone loves their horses. Thanks to me, they're happy and making money... or could make money if they wanted to. No one has complained or questioned us. Our customers are treated like royalty and they're satisfied."

Jessica shook her head in both disgust and amusement. "Well, not *everyone* is satisfied. Remember Johan Murphy?" Jessica said with a hint of sarcasm.

"I don't know what happened. I never even met him until after the auction," Greg said, not elaborating, yet not actually lying.

"Was anything special done that got people bidding on Love Letter... to such an outrageous price as $2.5 million?" Dolan asked.

He didn't answer right away. Jessica could read Greg's face. She could see that he was deciding whether to be one hundred percent honest.

A flash bulb lit in her mind. "That reminds me of a quote by Champ Clark: *'While the percentage of fools in this country is not so large, there are still enough to fatten the swindlers...'* she said.

Before she could continue, Dolan abruptly stood up, walked behind Jessica's desk, and put his hand firmly on her shoulder. "I've let everything else insulting that you've said go, but that was uncalled-for. I think you're being far too judgmental. You shouldn't be speaking to a client this way."

"Dolan, they're cons. They cheat people..."

"Stop it! You don't talk like this to a client! Behind closed doors is one thing, but not to their face or right in front of them! What's gotten into you?" Dolan was angry and embarrassed. "We're criminal attorneys. Most of our clients do things that are illegal and immoral. Do you need to end this session and compose yourself?"

Greg reminded them that he was in the room. "Both of you, stop this right now. I know what Jessica's problem is. She's hearing all of this and not thinking of *me* as her client. She's thinking of herself as *my client*. Now, she knows more of the ropes to the business. And, I'm sure in the back of her mind she can't wait to get home and tell her husband..."

Jessica was impressed with his insight. She hadn't thought about it that way consciously, but she was sure that he was right.

"I can't tell Turner anything. Attorney-client privilege. You know that," she said in a surprisingly calm manner. "But, you are absolutely right. I've got to forget I've done business with you. Forget that I'm your client in something that, in a way, is completely unrelated. To start, I think I need to move my horse to another operation."

"If you want to, go ahead. I don't need your business!"

With those few moments there was a sense of relief in the air and each of them knew they had to continue with the line inquiry that was started.

"Greg. You have to tell us the truth. The whole truth. That's what this case is going to revolve around. The guy is going to sue you and you know it. We have to know everything... and I mean absolutely everything," Jessica said with authority.

"Fine. But, Marcie doesn't know any of this. It's not that she wouldn't approve... it's more that she's sort of greedy... she would have been upset if I told her how much of the action I was giving away to get the publicity of the highest sale," Greg said.

The suspense was intriguing Jessica and Dolan. Then, Marcie walked back in.

"I'm sorry that I walked out like that. I get emotional and lose my temper sometimes. I'm ready to deal with things now...in the proper frame of mind..." Marcie said, now that her Valium had taken effect.

"Did you take your tranquilizer?" Greg asked.

"Yes," Marcie said, wishing that Jessica and her Uncle didn't know.

"She doesn't have a problem with drugs... she just keeps tranquilizers on hand to relax her before she competes in an important show..." Greg said, defending his wife's integrity.

"And before I ride horses that like to buck! I only take a half dose. Don't worry. It's just enough to take the edge off. Greg's dad prescribes it for me... and he knows why and he knows I don't take them very often," Marcie said, not wanting to worry her uncle.

"I understand. I do the same thing before I go in front of a judge or jury that I'm nervous about," Jessica assured her.

"Honey, I was just about to answer an important question when you walked in. It's an answer that you're not going to like," Greg said.

"What was the question?"

"Jessica asked if I did anything special that got people bidding on Love Letter... to get her to sell for two and a half million dollars."

"Did you?" Marcie asked him, obviously worried about what his answer would be.

"Yes," he said, feeling the rush from his head to his toes.

Trading Paper

by Cali Canberra

ISBN: 0-9705004-0-8

283 pages - Four color film laminated cover

$14.99 + $3.50 shipping and handling

Newchi Publishing
1110 Surrey Park Trail
Duluth, GA 30097
770-664-1611

Trading Paper and Never Enough!

Ordering & Payment Methods

Phone Orders: 770-664-1611 or Toll Free: 1-866-314-1952
Toll Free Fax: 1-866-314-1950

Mail this form to:
Newchi Publishing
11110 Surrey Park Trail, Duluth, GA 30097

__ Check/Money Order (in U.S. funds, drawn on U.S. bank)

__ Visa __ Mastercard __ Discover __ American Express

(Phone # must accompany credit card orders) _(________)____________________

Credit Card Number:____

Exp. Date: ________
Name on Credit Card:____
Shipping Address & Credit Card billing address:

____

____

Quantity: __ **Trading Paper** Quantity: __ **Never Enough!**

Quantity: ______ x $14.99 =	________
U.S. Shipping & Handling (1st book)	3.50
Additional books @ $1.50 ea.	________
U.S. additional addresses $3.50 ea.	________
GA residents add 7% sales tax	
C.O.D. orders add $6.00	________
Priority Mail - add $3.50	________

E-Mail: ______________________________ Total $ ________

Do you want to be informed when other Cali Canberra novels are available? ___Yes ___ No

Comments:

Cali Canberra novels are fictional...

**For true and accurate information
about
Arabian horses
and
ownership of Arabian horses,
contact:**

International Arabian Horse Association
10805 E. Bethany Drive - Aurora, Colorado 80014-2605
(303) 696-4500
www.iaha.com

Arabian Horse America
12000 Zuni Street - Westminster, Colorado 80234
1-877-551-2722
www.arabianhorseamerica.com

www.calicanberra.com
for extensive links to resources about Arabian horses